Golden Girl

Also by Sarah Zettel

Dust Girl

THE AMERICAN FAIRY TRILOGY
⤳ BOOK TWO ⤴

Golden Girl

SARAH ZETTEL

RANDOM HOUSE 🏠 NEW YORK

Text copyright © 2013 by Sarah Zettel
Jacket art copyright © 2013 by Juliana Kolesova

Visit us on the Web! randomhouse.com/teens

Educators and librarians, for a variety of teaching tools, visit us at RHTeachersLibrarians.com

Library of Congress Cataloging-in-Publication Data
Zettel, Sarah.
Golden girl / Sarah Zettel. — First edition.
pages cm. — (The American fairy trilogy ; book 2)
Summary: As a child of prophecy and daughter of the legitimate heir to the Seelie throne, fourteen-year-old Callie poses a huge threat to the warring fae factions who have attached themselves to the most powerful people in 1930s Hollywood.
ISBN 978-0-375-86939-6 (trade) — ISBN 978-0-375-96939-3 (lib. bdg.) — ISBN 978-0-375-98319-1 (ebook)
[1. Fairies—Fiction. 2. Magic—Fiction. 3. Racially mixed people—Fiction. 4. Hollywood (Los Angeles, Calif.)—History—20th century—Fiction.] I. Title.
PZ7.Z448Go 2013[Fic]—dc23 2013006238

Printed in the United States of America

10 9 8 7 6 5 4 3 2 1

First Edition

To the Makers of Movies, the hits and the flops, the found and the lost, in Hollywood and around the world. Thank you.

Sincerely,
A Grateful Fan

Contents

Golden Girl

1

Someone to Watch Over Me

Los Angeles, California, May 1, 1935

Once upon a time in Kansas, there was a normal girl called Callie. I thought she was me. I'd been told all my life she was me.

Turns out, all my life I'd been lied to. Turns out, I was about as far from a normal girl as you could get. I wasn't even human. Not all the way, anyhow. My father, Daniel LeRoux, who'd run out on my mother before I was born, wasn't just a piano player; he was a prince of the fairies. The Unseelie court fairies, to be specific. He hadn't run out on my mama for any of the usual reasons. He had gone to renounce the throne so they could get married.

But he never came back, and I grew up with just Mama in the Imperial Hotel in Slow Run, Kansas. Times were worse than bad because the rain had stopped and the dust had come to cover Kansas. I guess Mama decided all that

1

truth—my being half a fairy, or having magic in my bones, or waiting on my father to get back from telling his Unseelie parents he wasn't taking up the family business of being royalty—was kind of a lot to lay on a girl stuck out in the Dust Bowl. I didn't know for sure why she hadn't told me about Papa and the rest of it. By the time I found out, Mama had vanished too, in the middle of the biggest dust storm the world had ever seen. But it wasn't the dust that got her; it was the fairies. The bright, shining ones. The Seelies.

· Now I was out looking for Mama, and Papa, and the rest of the truth about myself. As you've probably figured, that was a tall order, and a long road. So far, it had taken me all the way to Los Angeles, California. I had no idea how far it was going to take me before I hit the end.

"Callie LeRoux, where are you going?"

I froze on the stairs and looked down at my landlady. Mrs. Constantine was big and broad, with black hair, sandy skin, a hook nose, raw hands, and the sharpest pair of ears known to man. She ran a boardinghouse for families and "respectable" single ladies, and puffed up when she got angry or proud. She was also blocking the stairway I had been trying to sneak down.

"Sorry, Mrs. Constantine," I said, trying not to squirm. "I've got to get to the streetcar. I'm going to see about a job today."

"A job?" My landlady squinted around to see if I had my suitcase with me. When she didn't see me with anything more than a pair of high-heeled shoes from the mission store and the blue suit I'd been up all night stitching on so it mostly fit, she gave way.

"Well, you'd better get going, then, and you can drop the letters in the box on your way."

"Yes, Mrs. Constantine." I picked up the envelopes on the table in the hall and tucked them into my battered blue handbag, which almost matched the suit. The white gloves I'd bleached to within an inch of their lives stretched tight over my country-girl fingers. I'd have to remember to keep the palms turned in so nobody could see how worn out they were. I settled my blue straw hat into place over my black hair. I might know I was half fairy, but I was also the daughter of a brown-skinned man. People in Los Angeles didn't take as much offense at that sort of thing as they did back in Kansas, but they weren't all that keen on it either. Most days it was easier to try to pass for white. I had what mama had called "good skin," meaning it was pale, and "good eyes," meaning they were a kind of stormy blue-gray. It was my hair that I had to be careful with. I'd washed it the night before with lye water and lemon juice, like Mama had taught me, but that hadn't made it any lighter or softer. So far, the French twist I'd spent half an hour before sunup wrestling into place was holding.

As I watched my reflection in the hall mirror, I tried to find a way to hold my face that didn't show the guilt so plainly. I wasn't going out about any job. I was going to try to sneak into the biggest movie studio in the country.

"Now, just one minute, Miss Callie."

I spun around on my crooked heel, and had to catch myself against the wall. Mrs. Constantine frowned again. She was coming up the hall carrying a white napkin bundle.

"You can't go for a job without something to eat." She pushed the bundle into my hand and then straightened my jacket shoulders. We both pretended she didn't notice I'd stuffed my brassiere with tissues to help cover up the fact I was still only fourteen. "Don't forget to drop off those letters. You want your people to know you're safe, don't you?"

"Yes, ma'am. Thank you." I scooted out the front door before she could say anything more about me or my family. I was glad for the hot biscuit she'd wrapped in that napkin, though, and the apricot jam.

When I stopped in front of the mailbox, I sorted through the letters and pulled out one to stuff back into my purse. I'd written that one with Mrs. Constantine standing over my shoulder. It was a happy letter, saying how I'd made it to the city just fine, and how Mama didn't need to worry about me because I'd found a clean, respectable boardinghouse and everybody was being so nice and friendly. I'd addressed it to the Imperial Hotel in Slow Run, Kansas, and borrowed a stamp. Mrs. Constantine beamed as she handed it over, sure she was doing her job helping to look out for me.

But there was nobody back at the Imperial, and there wouldn't be until I got my parents out of wherever the Seelie fairies had taken them. Problem was, I only had hints about where that might be. They weren't very good hints either. One of the biggest problems with fairies and magic people is that they don't talk in straight lines, even if they're on your side, which, believe me, they mostly aren't. I'd been told my folks were locked up in the golden mountains of the west, above the valley of smoke, in the house of St. Simon, where no saint has ever been.

You see what I mean? And that was from somebody who was actually trying to help.

Fortunately, there aren't too many places you can mean when you say "the golden mountains of the west." That's pretty much got to be California, so that was why we'd come out here. "We" is me and Jack Holland. Jack's my best friend. Without him I wouldn't have made it ten feet from my own door. On the other hand, without me he'd probably be on another chain gang somewhere, so I guess it mostly evens out.

Now, California's a big place. It's got a lot of hills and a lot of gold, but another thing I learned about fairies is that they like music and bright lights, pretty people and dancing, and all those other things that are beautiful about human beings. And where are the brightest lights, the best music, and the prettiest people in the whole world?

Hollywood, and the movie studios. Me and Jack both figured if there were fairies hanging around anywhere in California, that's where we'd pick up their trail. After that . . . well, like Jack said, we'd cross that bridge when we came to it.

See, fairies live in a world of their own. Maybe it's a

bunch of worlds; I'm not sure about that part yet. But they don't seem to like it there much, because they want to get into our world awful badly. To do this, they need a special kind of gate between their world and the human world. If I could find one of those gates, I could open it or close it. That was the extra-special magic I'd been born holding. That magic is so special, in fact, the fairies have a prophecy about me. They say: *See her now, daughter of three worlds. See her now, three roads to choose. Where she goes, where she stays, where she stands, there shall the gates be closed.*

I've got no idea what that means. Jack says that's normal for prophecies. He says that until they come true nobody knows what a prophecy's actually about. If you ask me, that makes them pretty pointless. But pointless or not, this particular prophecy caused me all kinds of trouble. The fairies get all worked up into a tizzy by that "where she goes, where she stays, where she stands, there shall the gates be closed" part, and they keep trying to get me onto their side, either by threats or by tricks. Except I don't want to side with any fairies. I just want to find my parents and get a chance to find out what being a normal person is all about.

Now, my idea for starting our search through the studios had been to join up with one of the tour groups. Jack, being Jack, had a different idea. He spent most of our last fifty cents on a clean shirt at the secondhand store and the rest on a bath at a flophouse. Then he just walked right through the front door of Metro-Goldwyn-Mayer, which is the biggest movie studio in Hollywood, and asked for a job. You could have knocked me over with a feather when he walked out again and said he'd gotten one. It seemed that the MGM back lot was so big, they needed boys like Jack to run scripts and messages and stuff to the different offices and movie sets there. One glance at Jack's mile-long legs had apparently sealed the deal. He was on the back lot now, and I was following after so he could sneak me in. We didn't figure we could wander around looking like the kids we were without somebody getting suspicious, so I had to pretend to be a secretary or something like that, and that's why I was all dressed up trying to appear older than I was, and wearing exactly one piece of clothing that had never belonged to anybody else: I had on my first and only pair of silk stockings. I wished I could stop being nervous long enough to enjoy them.

It all would've been lots easier if I could have just used my fairy magic. One of the things I can do with that magic is make people see exactly what they wish to see. But there's a problem: when I use my magic, the other fairies can feel it. This was really bad, because it wasn't just my parents those fairies were after. They wanted me too. So using magic was out. We were going to have to do this the hard way.

The sun was just starting to come up over the hills, but the trolley to Culver City was already full by the time it pulled into my stop. I had to hang on to a strap the whole way out, and I wondered if the high heels had been such a good idea. At first I stood there trying to paste a look on my face that said I did this every day. That didn't work so well, so I just concentrated on keeping my head down. I knew nobody was looking at me. Fairies weren't the only ones who lived in their own world. Everybody else on that rattling, squeaking trolley was reading the paper or a book, or just staring out the windows at Los Angeles rolling past. Nobody knew me from Adam's off ox here, and they cared even less about me. But that didn't matter. My layers of disguise from the mission store felt paper-thin over the Callie LeRoux underneath, and a whole hive's worth of questions was buzzing around inside my head. Like, what happened to girls who were screwy enough to try to sneak into movie studios? Probably they just got thrown out, maybe with a stern warning, and the boys who helped them get in were fired. On the other hand, the studio had all kinds of walls and fences around it, plus security guards sitting in these white houses at the gates. Maybe they'd arrest me. Us. Maybe we'd end up in jail. Did they send you out on the chain gang in California?

When I get nervous, I start to lose my hold on my fairy half. See, like all fairies, Seelie or Unseelie, my inborn magic means I can grant wishes. But magic always has another side. The other side of being able to grant wishes is that if I'm not careful, I feel any wishes being made around me. And everybody on that trolley wished for something. They wished for fame, and better jobs, and love, and for that guy the next desk over to get what was coming to him, and for a better seat on the trolley home. The fairy part of me wanted to grant those wishes. It'd be fun, and the people would be happy, and I'd get to feel all that happiness, just as clear as I could feel all those hungry wishes. I could draw the feeling inside me and use it to fill up my magic with fresh power. Then I could do anything I wanted. Anything at all.

I shoved that idea back down and tried to find something else to think about while we bounced and rattled and clanged over the rail crossing. I settled on making up a second letter to my mother. Mrs. Constantine would want to see me writing another one, and I wanted to keep Mrs. Constantine happy so she wouldn't ask any more questions than was strictly necessary.

The next letter would start like this: *Dear Mama: Hope you are well. I promise I'll be seeing you soon. And guess what? Today I got to see a real movie studio!*

I'd tell her about Los Angeles too, if I actually wrote the letter. She'd want to hear about that. It was so different from Slow Run that it might as well have been on another planet. The dust storms that had wiped out Kansas and five or six other states never reached California. The hills blocking off the empty horizon were bright green. Coconut palms, live oaks, and date trees grew everywhere, and there were more kinds of flowers than anywhere else in the world. The buildings were all clean and new, and shiny cars and clanging trolleys filled the straight, paved streets. It was big and loud, suspicious and mean, beautiful, exciting, and confusing, and despite everything and everybody after me, I was in deep danger of falling in love with it.

But it wasn't love I was feeling by the time I climbed off the trolley at Overland Avenue. I was halfway to being sick and all the way to being exhausted from trying to keep my brain closed to all the wishing and feeling from the other trolley passengers. It only got a little better as they spread out onto the sidewalk, because they joined a whole river of other people who had their own wishes. People came from around the world to find work here, and their skin was every shade from pink to deep black and their eyes were as many shapes and colors as you could think of. They wore all kinds of clothes: suits or overalls, pretty dresses or hotel maid uniforms, long silk coats and pants on the men from China, smocks and sandals on the men from Mexico or the Philippines. The white ladies had big floppy hats on their heads to keep their skin from turning brown, the brown ladies wore big floppy hats to keep from turning black, and the black ladies wore prim hats and white gloves so nobody would think they were anything less than respectable.

The cars and trucks that rumbled down the street belched heavy smoke into the morning air, crashing their gears and blaring horns at drivers who didn't hit the gas quick enough when the light on the corner changed. It was going on nine o'clock. I tried to hustle down the sidewalk to get past the worst of the crowds, but the heels weren't making that real easy, especially when I had to duck around the people who stopped to grab their breakfast off the coffee cart before they filed into the office buildings.

The offices stood on the right side of Overland. On the

left side, all you could see was a tall fence, its white paint peeling off in big patches. On the other side of that fence waited the studios of Metro-Goldwyn-Mayer. Just thinking about it doubled those butterflies inside me. All the stuff they wrote about in the magazines and the gossip columns or talked about on the radio programs—stars, fame, and glamour—it waited just on the other side of this long white fence. Maybe I'd get to see them making a movie. Maybe I'd see somebody famous. Maybe Cary Grant, or Ginger Rogers, or even Ivy Bright.

But first I had to get through the gate. I lifted my chin, as though I walked past this fence every day and it meant nothing. Not that there was anybody left to see me. The sidewalk had cleared out, except for some men toting tin lunch pails and a raggedy bum hunched in the shadow of the fence.

"Spare a dime for a war vet?" I heard him croak as I got closer. "Spare a dime for a war vet?"

His big brown hands dangled on his knees, and he had his hat pulled low so the battered brim hid his face. A few withered apples sat on the sidewalk beside him, not doing anything to attract a second glance from the workmen hurrying past.

"Spare a dime for a war vet?"

I meant to pass on by. You could see bums like him slouched on every corner in Los Angeles. Some of them were just men out of work and scrounging, but some were out of their heads from cheap wine or whatever else they'd found. But then I noticed how his broken shoes were coated with gray dust. I knew about trudging across miles of dust, and about trying to get through with just what you had with you, even when that was nothing at all.

I had one nickel left in my handbag. It was supposed to be trolley fare back home, but I could get another from Jack. Now that he had a steady job, we usually had at least a few cents left after we'd paid for room and board. That made us lucky. It wasn't safe for me to be granting wishes just now, but I could spread what little luck I did have.

I laid my nickel down on the sidewalk and picked up one of the soft, sun-warmed apples.

"Thank you, miss." The bum tipped his hat brim up.

I stepped back before I could help myself. This man had been through something bad. It'd left behind a long white scar from his forehead to his chin, straight down over his left eye. That eye was milk white, shining wet in his wrinkled brown face, but his other eye was bright gold and amber, and that eye got a good look at me.

"You." The bum surged to his feet. "I found you!"

He was a tall man and bone thin. His ragged clothes hung loose around his whole body. He smelled like the dickens and grinned big and loose, showing me the gaps where his teeth had been broken off.

I stepped back again, ready to run, but I wasn't fast enough. His crooked hand shot out and clamped down on my wrist. "None of them could, but I knew, see, I *knew....*"

I wasn't about to wait around to hear what he knew.

I shoved that mushy apple right in his face, and when he jerked back, so did I. I whirled on my heel and stumbled up the street.

"Hey! Hey!" the bum shouted behind me. "Don't go in there! They'll spot you! They'll get you! Come back, Callie!"

The sound of my name almost made me break stride, but I clenched my fists and poured on the speed. He might've found me, but there was no way I was letting him catch me. Whoever he was. Since the fairies had found me that first time, I'd been threatened and tricked and followed, and I'd already come close to dying a bunch times more than is good for anybody.

The studio's side gate opened ahead of me, and I stumbled through, plowing straight into Jack.

"Jack." I stuck out one shaking finger behind me, and we both looked where I was pointing. But the bum was gone.

2

The Show Must Go On

"There you are, sis!" Jack said clearly. "I was getting worried."

Jack's the kind of boy who gets called "a long, tall drink of water." He was only sixteen, but he was eyeballing a finish line of at least six feet tall. His brown hair used to be all bushy, but when he got his studio job, he chopped it short and slicked it back. It seemed to me he was starting to look less like a boy and more like the man he would be, especially now that he wore long trousers instead of knee pants, and a button-down shirt instead of patched calico. That made me feel strange when I looked at him. I tried not to think about it too much, but sometimes it was real hard not to, especially when he got close to me or had hold of my arm, like now.

Except maybe he didn't need to be squeezing quite so hard while he pulled me up to the little white guard shack.

"Hey, Solly," Jack said to the man sitting inside, who was mostly hidden by his open newspaper. "My sister's here."

The guard turned down the corner of his paper with one finger. I smiled and swallowed and tried to look like I really could be related to Jack.

It was pretty plain that the guard wouldn't pay a plug nickel for any of it. The only thing that kept me from turning tail right there was the possibility I'd meet that bum coming the other way. Jack, on the other hand, stood there cool as cool could be. This was his best game. Once he had a story set in his head, Jack Holland could convince a snake it needed a new pair of socks.

Solly shrugged and rattled his paper. "She's gotta sign in just like everybody else."

"Oh, of course. Here, Callie."

I signed "Callie Holland" on the list Jack passed me. As soon as I finished the *d,* Jack grabbed me again and with a big wave pulled me past the swing-arm gate and into the back lot of the Metro-Goldwyn-Mayer studio.

"You okay?" Jack asked as soon as we were out of earshot of the guard shack. "You look like you're gonna be sick or something."

Truth was, I felt like I was going to be sick or something. I told Jack about the bum and how he'd known my name. At the same time, I knew I had to pull myself together. This might be our only chance to get onto the back lot. I could not afford to go to pieces, no matter what my knocking knees thought.

"Was he one of *them*?" asked Jack.

"I don't know," I said slowly. "He was awfully . . . broken to be a fairy." Fairies don't like ugly things. They want everything around them to be perfect, even their monsters. That's one of the reasons they like movies so much. Everything's always perfect in the movies.

"Okay, okay." Jack wiped his hands on his pants. "I'll tell Solly there's a bum hanging around bothering people. If he's still there, Solly'll run him off."

"No, don't. If it was one of them, he might magic the guard into letting him inside."

Jack saw the sense in this—which just goes to show how strange things get when there's magic hanging around. "Okay, we'll play it your way. So." He took a deep breath and gestured to the studio. "What do you think?"

I wasn't sure what I'd expected from a real movie studio. Maybe I'd thought it'd just be one big building with a whole bunch of stages inside, or that the world would turn all gray and silver and there'd be people in tuxedos and evening gowns with fame sparkling like fireflies around them. But we'd just stepped into a new city nestled inside the old. The air was full of shouts and engine roars and the smell of paint and hot concrete. Trucks rattled down straight streets, kicking up exhaust and dust. Men with their shirtsleeves rolled loaded crates and furniture from brick warehouses into trucks. The only hint that we were not really in Los Angeles anymore was the trucker who walked down a ramp carrying a big old battle-axe in one hand and a clown's head in the other.

"I think I don't want anybody here mad at me." I nodded toward that shiny-sided axe.

Jack chuckled. "You know what I mean, dopey. Did you feel anything when you came inside?"

When I get close to a fairy gate, I get this twisty feeling, like I'm inside a padlock while somebody's turning the key.

But I had to shake my head at Jack. "Nothing."

"Well, it's an awfully big place," he said. "And that bum tried to tell you not to go in here, didn't he? That *they'd* see you?"

"Yeah, but that could mean anything. He could've been thrown out on his ear by the guards once for hopping the fence or something."

"But he knew your name," Jack reminded me, and I really wished he hadn't. I mean, I knew going looking for the Seelies was looking for whole new worlds of trouble. I just hadn't thought we'd find them so fast.

"What do we do now?" I asked before I could start looking over my shoulder for the things that weren't there. Yet.

Jack made a face. "I gotta run some new script pages out to Copperfield Court, so I haven't got a lot of time. My lunch break's coming up, though. I can meet you, and we can take a real look around."

"But what about till then? Somebody's going to want to

know what I'm doing here." Mr. Mayer hadn't put up that fence and stationed guards at those gates because he was glad to let just anybody wander around his property. Movie people were different, but not that different.

"It's all jake." He had a special grin for when he was about to pull off a really good trick, and Jack used it now. "I got you a disguise."

My face scrunched up. "Another one?"

"This is different." Jack pulled a clipboard and a pencil out of the bag he had slung over his shoulder, like he was pulling a rabbit out of his hat.

"What are you, cracked? That's not a disguise!"

"It's the best there is." Jack pushed the clipboard and pencil into my hands. "If anybody looks at you, all you gotta do is act like you're making notes. Around here, there's always somebody making notes about something. Nobody ever asks what they're doing. They all just figure they're working for somebody else."

"You're sure about this?"

"Sure I'm sure. Now, I gotta get going with these script pages. I'll meet you at the Waterloo Bridge as soon as I can."

"Where?"

Jack pointed between a bunch of warehouses. "Head straight down Fifth Avenue. Bear left past the stock storage and the prison, and you'll see the lake and the cemetery. There's only one bridge, and—"

"If you say I can't miss it, Jack Holland, I'll bust you in the mush." I was scared, both about being turned loose all alone in this very strange place and about what might be sneaking along behind me. But I couldn't be scared or I wouldn't be able to do what needed doing, so I got mad instead.

Jack just shrugged. "Well, you can't miss it. It's the only bridge over the lake, and there's the cemetery on one side and a farmhouse on the other. If you have to ask anybody for directions, just tell 'em you're new and you're on an errand for Mr. Thalberg."

I nodded unhappily at my stupid little clipboard and stubby pencil. My feet hurt in those high-heeled shoes, and my skin was all prickly under the stuffed bra, which I was pretty sure had gone crooked.

Jack put his hand on my shoulder and smiled down at me. "Nothin' to it, Callie."

"Promise?" I asked. It probably shouldn't have come as a surprise that I suddenly had a fresh case of butterflies.

"Promise." Jack's smile got all the way into his blue eyes and lit some kind of lamp in there. "I really gotta go now."

Jack took off running and left me with the clipboard and pencil, the biggest movie studio in the entire world spreading out around me.

What could I do? I quick hitched up my bra, clutched the clipboard in front of me, and started walking.

I tried to keep my head down and walk like my shoes fit and I knew where I was going. None of it worked. I felt like I had a neon sign over me flashing PHONY! PHONY! But when I got to Fifth Avenue, I forgot about doing anything except trying to keep my eyeballs from popping out of my head. Because I was just about to walk into New York City.

It was all right there, big as life and in full color—the huge stone buildings, wide sidewalks, and fancy shop windows all tricked out with curtains and mannequins and gold lettering. There was even a cathedral with wedding-cake arches and stained-glass windows. Except I was pretty sure in the real New York they didn't cut the buildings off above the third story and just leave steel beams and scaffolding sticking out of the top. I was also pretty sure it didn't have train tracks down the middle for the black, hulking cameras sitting on carts. But then, I'd never been to New York, so what did I know? Maybe they had all that, along with people wearing clothes from a hundred years ago who sat around in folding chairs or stood smoking cigarettes and talking about the Dodgers and horse racing with guys in shirtsleeves and shovel caps.

"You there!"

I about jumped out of my skin. A red-haired woman wearing a black smock and carrying a huge black case planted her free hand on her hip and glowered down at me. "What're you doing?"

Panic jabbed me hard. I'd only been here ten minutes and already I'd got caught. So much for Jack and his disguise. They'd throw me out on my ear and I'd never get back in. Jack would lose his job and we'd never find my parents and . . .

"I . . . uh . . . I'm new," I stammered. "I'm on an errand for Mr. Thalberg?"

"Mm-hmm," the woman said, in that way that meant she didn't believe one word. But she was already looking back over her shoulder at a cluster of skinny young women with cinched-waist blouses, long skirts, and huge feathered hats standing around smoking and laughing. I could all but hear her thinking how she was responsible for them, not me. If I opened up that special spot deep inside me, I could nudge her just a little, make her forget she'd ever seen me. . . .

I gritted my teeth and squashed that idea down, hard. That bum—whoever he was—was still out there. I did not need to be splashing around any extra magic to help him find me again.

"Well." The woman shifted her grip on her case. "If it's for Mr. Thalberg, you'd better get moving, hadn't you?"

"Yes, ma'am." I got moving as fast as my feet could go.

A dirt alley ran behind Fifth Avenue. I hurried into it, and the world changed again. Not only were all those buildings chopped off at the top, but they were hollow up the back. On this side, a street from the biggest city in the country was nothing but a bunch of frames made from two-by-fours, plaster, and metal pipes. It was even busier back here than it was out front. Men swarmed up and down a maze of scaffolding. They hammered nails, tightened bolts, and hoisted up loads of boards, buckets of tools, and paint cans. They filled the air with shouts and curses and the sound of

ringing hammers. While the actors were having their ciga-
rette break, these men were building a whole city for them
to play in. Their work and pride and plans sank into my
skin like the heat of the sun. This was even stronger than
the wishes of the people on the trolley, because these people
liked what they were doing; they were working hard and
making something brand-new. I wanted to stop and turn my
face toward all that feeling and drink it in deep.

I didn't, though. I kept on going until I reached the end
of Fifth Avenue. Jack was right again. There was a prison
looming there, complete with guard towers and a long black
car parked out front. But the back was as hollow as Fifth
Avenue had been, and as soon as I was past that, I was out
in the country. There was a straight dirt lane lined with full-
grown live oaks, and three pretty front porches with bits of
houses behind them. A big green picnic meadow opened
up behind those jigsaw-puzzle houses. More men were cutting the grass. Others were on their knees pulling weeds. A
truck jounced by in a cloud of exhaust. One of the garden-
ers glanced up at me. This time I remembered to get my
clipboard up and scribble on the paper with my pencil. He
looked away again. Maybe there was something to this disguise of Jack's after all.

I didn't have to go much farther. Past the picnic meadow
waited the lake Jack had talked about. It was skinny and
twisty, and truthfully, it looked more like a river of oil than
any kind of lake. The Waterloo Bridge was a stone arch
stretching over that still black water and leading down to

the farmhouse Jack had mentioned. Unlike most of the other buildings I'd passed, the house had all four walls plus a roof. It looked almost real. But the graveyard right next to me was just plain trying too hard. The headstones and crosses were dotted around like they'd sprung up with the rest of the weeds. There was a battered statue of a lady holding some kind of miniature pipe organ, and a crouching angel with bald plaster patches on its wings where the gray paint had chipped off. A big old tomb complete with an iron gate and pointy roof backed up onto some full-grown trees.

Perfect.

I looked around to make sure nobody was watching and then ducked behind the tomb. Nobody'd bothered to water back here, so—carefully, on account of my new stockings—I settled down in some dirt and scrubby weeds that probably never got into any movie anywhere. I drew my knees up to my chest, trying to make myself as small as possible, and rested my chin on them. The smell of dust wrapped around me, familiar and comfortable in a funny kind of way. If anybody was going to come looking for me now, I'd see them first. All I had to do was keep my eyes peeled, stay still, and not lose my nerve. But the second I thought that, I thought about the scarred, ragged man outside the gate, waiting for me and calling my name.

Dear Mama . . . I started a new letter in my head to distract myself from thinking about those wrong-looking hands and that one milky eye. *You are not going to believe what it's like in here!* I kept my thoughts running along those lines, trying to work out just how I'd describe Fifth Avenue and the prison and the lake. But it wasn't good enough. I still heard a raspy voice and saw a pair of mismatched eyes that I felt like I ought to know.

I found you, he said, over and over. *None of them could, but I knew, see, I knew. . . .*

3

Gonna Trouble the Waters

I hate to admit it, but while I was busy keeping my eyes peeled for Jack, or anybody else who might be looking for me, I sort of fell asleep. By the time I got wise to this and jerked my eyes open, my stomach was growling, my neck was stiff, and night had fallen down around me.

I scrambled to my feet, blinking hard and knuckling my eyes. Dry wind rustled the tree branches, and the scrubby weeds brushed my knees. The only light left was from the few lampposts on the studio road and what city light could slide over the fence. One thing I could see way too clearly, though: all around me, the cemetery had perfected its spooky act. Headstones and stained crosses laid long shadows across the dusty ground. The carved lady turned her head away sadly, knowing me for a lost cause. The crouching angel was about to stand up and demand to know who I was.

But what really had the goose bumps running up my arms was that Jack had probably come and gone hours ago. I held my breath and strained my ears, praying for an angry, whispery voice calling my name. But there was nothing. Not even any footsteps. I was used to country quiet, the kind that's filled with buzzing insects and singing crickets. This quiet didn't even have that much to keep it company. There was just me and that thin, dry wind coming down from the hills.

I peered around the tomb. If this had been a movie instead of just a studio back lot, an owl would have hooted somewhere. The long, twisty lake was a wavering mirror, spreading ripples of lamplight and reflecting the arch of the Waterloo Bridge. The farmhouse on the other side was just a squared-off blob in the dark. Then I saw a gangly bit of shadow peel off its side and slide around toward the front. Even at this distance, I knew it was Jack.

I was so glad, I had to bite my tongue to keep from shouting. Instead, I crouched down and crept forward as quickly as I could. I ducked from tombstone to tombstone and up onto the bridge, where I could slip through the shadows cast by the fake-stone railings. Jack hadn't seen me yet. He was easing his way toward the farmhouse door.

I was about to whistle to him, but my throat closed around my breath. My stomach twisted and the hairs on the back of my neck all stood up to stare. The fairy magic in my blood and bones was telling me we weren't alone anymore.

Something new was close by. It was alive, and it was magic, and it was very, very hungry.

I jumped to my feet, teetered over that bridge, and didn't stop until I plowed straight into Jack for the second time that day. He yelped and spun, swinging his fist out, so I had to jump back.

"Holy cats!" Another time the look on his face would have been funny. "You scared me! Where've you *been*?"

I grabbed his wrist. "We gotta get outta here!"

Before I could get any further, voices drifted down the street.

". . . but why, Miss Markham?" whined a tired girl.

"I told you. There are some people you have to meet," a woman answered. Her voice was bright and stiff, like when you're trying too hard to convince someone you're happy. "Now, let me fix your collar—there's a good girl."

"But I need my sleep!" Footsteps scraped and pattered down the dirt road, coming closer. "I'll get bags under my eyes."

Jack and I dove into that farmhouse so fast, I swear we left a cloud of dust behind. Somebody had been using it for a storage shed, and we hunkered down alongside toolboxes, stacks of boards, and kegs of nails.

"Now, Ivy," the woman was saying, "you promised me you wouldn't argue. These are *very* important people."

I jerked my chin toward the back window. If we could climb out through that, we still had a chance of getting away without being seen. But Jack had already eased the door open and pressed one eye against the crack. I rolled my eyes, then came up behind so I could look over his shoulder.

A woman in a dark suit was dragging a girl who could have been about my age down the studio road. They passed under a lamppost, and the girl glanced back over her shoulder, like she hoped to see somebody coming after them. When I got a look at her face, I blinked, and blinked again.

I knew that girl. Heck, everybody in the country knew that girl. She was Ivy Bright, "the brightest little star in Hollywood," as it said on all her posters. Not that she looked like her posters just then. Her famous long golden curls needed a good brushing, and her tam-o'-shanter with its big pom-pom on top had slipped too far to one side. She struggled to shove the hat back into place while Miss Markham pulled her stumbling to the foot of the Waterloo Bridge.

"I've brought her," panted Miss Markham to the empty dark. "Just like I promised."

I got the feeling of something live squirming just out of sight. Jack gripped my hand, but he wasn't looking at me. He was staring out at the bridge.

An eyeblink ago, the Waterloo Bridge had been empty. Now a woman walked on it, as though she'd just strolled up from the other side, except she hadn't. She'd come straight out of nowhere and darkness. She was dressed in darkness too, but on her it sparkled. A glittering silver veil covered her hair and pale face.

This was bad. This was fairy magic. It was what we'd come to find, but not like this.

"Yes. You've kept your part of the bargain, Ruth." The sparkling black-and-silver woman stepped off the bridge. "Hello, Ivy."

"H-hello." Ivy Bright shoved her tam into place again, but it slipped right back down.

"Oh, dear, so pale." The sparkling woman clicked her tongue. "It doesn't suit you at all, Ivy. But there's nothing to be worried about." Tenderly she resettled Ivy's tam. This time it stayed. "We're just going to meet some new friends."

"I don't think I should. Mama won't like it." Ivy looked over her shoulder again, but no one was coming. The only people around were me and Jack, hiding in the dark, too scared to move. Outside, reality seemed to be sinking into Ivy. A single tear trickled out of the corner of her eye and sat shimmering on her round cheek.

Sparkling Woman crouched down to bring her eyes level with the girl's. "Don't be scared, Ivy, honey." She closed her hand around Ivy's. "We're not going far, and once we get there, you'll have so much fun you'll forget you were ever frightened."

I heard Jack swallow hard. He knew all about the kind of fun fairies had with regular people. It tended to end up with somebody being dead.

"You—you did say . . . ," stammered Miss Markham.

"Don't you worry either, Ruth. I haven't forgotten our bargain." Sparkling Woman straightened up and turned toward the lake. She didn't let go of Ivy's hand. "Brother!" she called. "You can come out now!"

Ivy glanced over her shoulder again. *Run,* I begged silently. *Run now!* But she looked back toward Sparkling Woman and Miss Markham, afraid to go, afraid to stay. And too late.

Deep inside, I felt how the world shifted around us, like somebody had turned its key. At the same moment, the water under the bridge sloshed hard. A bulky shadow waded out from the oily darkness to crouch on the bank. It might almost have been a man squatting there, but its man-shaped body was covered with gray hair. Tangled locks hung from his chin to his navel, long enough to brush the ground. Water beaded up in the snarls, glittering like the sequins on Sparkling Woman's dress. He had shiny silver eyes, and bits of dark weed hung from his beard and ankles. It didn't look like he was wearing any clothes.

"Rougarou's here." The hairy man grinned at Ivy and Ruth Markham. "We're all here now, hey?"

Ivy gasped and slapped her hand over her mouth. She tried to pull away, but Sparkling Woman yanked her closer. Miss Markham just stayed rooted to the ground, staring.

"Miss Ivy Bright." Sparkling Woman rested her hands on Ivy's shoulders to hold her in place. "Miss Ruth Markham, I'd like you to meet my brother. You may call him Rougarou."

"All here and all so pretty." Rougarou straightened up. A pond's worth of water sluiced off him, plastering his weedy hair tight to his body. He definitely wasn't wearing any clothes.

"What is this? What is that thing?" whispered Ruth Markham. "You said . . . if I just brought the girl, it would be you . . ."

"Do calm down, Ruth," said Sparkling Woman. "I can't do everything myself, now, can I?"

"This isn't funny!" cried Ivy. "You take me home right now!"

"Patience, Ivy." Sparkling Woman wrapped her arm tight around the girl's shoulders. "We're almost done here."

"What do I have to do?" Miss Markham spoke too fast, like she wanted to get this over with before she lost her nerve.

"Well, now, you've heard the expression 'sealed with a kiss,' haven't you?"

"I have to kiss him?" Ruth's voice rose to a squeak on the last word.

"Just one kiss, that's all, pretty lady." Rougarou grinned way too big for the size of his hairy face, and his teeth flashed white. "One little kiss for Rougarou."

"Pretend you're a princess in a fairy story, the one who has to kiss the frog," suggested Sparkling Woman. "You should be able to do that quite easily. You're an actress, after all."

"She's not an actress!" shouted Ivy, and for the first time there was some fire in her voice. "She's a *secretary*!"

"You be quiet!" snapped Miss Markham. "After this, no one will even remember who you are, you little brat!"

"I won't be quiet! You can't make me! I'll tell Mr. Thalberg! *And* Mr. Mayer! I'll—"

Sparkling Woman laid one long, perfect hand on Ivy's head. "Hush now, Ivy."

The girl's words cut off. Slowly all the fear drained out of her face. So did every other expression. She leaned against Sparkling Woman, as limp and staring as a rag doll.

Jack gripped my hand hard and jerked his chin sideways. He was right. We couldn't leave the brightest little star in Hollywood—or anybody else—to get taken for a ride by Sparkling Woman and her hairy brother. I squeezed his fingers back and nodded.

Outside, Miss Markham had her hand stretched out toward Ivy but didn't quite touch her. "Is . . . is she all right?"

"It's a little late for you to worry about that now, isn't it, Ruth? It's time to make up your mind," said Sparkling Woman. "If you're just brave for one tiny minute, you'll have everything you've wished for."

Her voice was so sweet and sure, you knew in your bones that whatever she said just had to be right. That voice could make you face monsters. If I hadn't already known Sparkling Woman was a fairy, that would have clinched it.

I let out a deep breath and opened the part of me that

controlled both my magic and my awareness of other people's magic. The strength of Miss Markham's wish slapped me hard. She wanted fame, power, and money—everything Ivy Bright had. Everyone would love her and need her, and for once she'd be calling the shots. The power of that wish reached out to the driving hunger inside Rougarou and lit the greed inside Sparkling Woman. But there was something else too. It was way far in the background and I couldn't quite wrap myself around it.

"Can you magic them?" Jack breathed.

"They'll feel it as soon as I try." They'd be after us in a hot minute too, throwing their magic around, and I had no idea how strong they were.

Outside, Ruth took one trembling step toward that dripping wet, hairy, naked monster. She didn't even glance back at Ivy. The monster grinned and spread his arms wide. "Bring your kiss to Rougarou."

"You'll have everything you wish for, and a little bit more." Sparkling Woman smiled underneath her veil. She kept one hand on Ivy's head. Ivy leaned against her like a tired girl against her mother, except her mouth dangled loose and open. "Just one kiss and it's all done."

Jack Holland can be a pain sometimes, and he's way too good at twisting people around his thumb, but he's nobody's coward. He set his jaw and scooped up a fistful of nails from the nearest keg. There's one thing fairy magic can't get around, and that's iron. Even a little piece, like a nail, could put the kibosh on a whole lot of power.

Jack sucked in a deep breath and kicked open the plywood door.

"Hey! Ugly!" Jack charged onto the bridge like he had the whole U.S. cavalry behind him.

Rougarou whirled around, scattering drops of water and clumps of hair. "Who—?"

"Wasn't talkin' to you!" Jack reared back and pitched a handful of nails like he was on the mound for the Yankees. They hit Sparkling Woman square between the eyes. She reeled backward, clutching her forehead. Without her to lean against, Ivy crumpled to the ground.

By the time Sparkling Woman stopped moving, she wasn't pretty anymore. Or a woman. Or even human. Her smooth skin and sparkly black dress turned rough and lumpy like crocodile hide. The silver veil turned to lanky gray hair hanging in twisted knots across her face. Her feet splayed out into webbed claws, and when she opened her mouth to scream, it was full of needle-sharp teeth and a really nasty long gray tongue.

Rougarou waved his hairy arms and bellowed like a disappointed freight train. Jack pitched another load of nails at Sparkling Woman, hitting her square in her crocodile face. He turned on his heel and took off running back toward me and the house, tossing nails behind him like iron bread crumbs. Ruth screamed and screamed some more. She was wishing she was gone, but she couldn't make her feet move. That was okay, because she was wishing, and that was what I needed. I got behind that wish and put my shoulder to it.

It was heavy and I had to lean in. Something was dragging on it, and on me. I clenched my fists.

Be home in bed. Be home in bed. Be having a bad dream.

For a split second, Ruth Markham was there screaming. Then she was gone. Something inside me snapped shut. It had worked. I'd done it. I could feel it. This very moment, Ruth Markham was waking up screaming her head off in a dingy one-room apartment she shared with a girl named Gertrude who worked the perfume counter at Schwab's drugstore.

"Who did that?" shrieked the crocodile creature that used to be Sparkling Woman. "Show yourself!"

I had no plan to do any such thing, but then I saw Ivy still huddled in a heap on the ground.

I cussed. It was Ruth's wish I'd used, so it was Ruth I'd magicked. I hadn't gotten the spell big enough to cover Ivy. She was out good and cold, so she couldn't wish anything. And here came Jack running across the bridge with Rougarou behind him.

I fumbled in the nearest toolbox, came up with a hammer, and staggered out the door. I was shaking like a leaf in a high wind, but if Jack could lead a charge, so could I.

The crocodile woman screamed something, and Rougarou spun around again, but I pushed myself into a tottery run. I had the hammer out in front of me like a bayonet, and I plowed straight into Rougarou's stomach with all the strength I had left.

Something went *crunch*!

Rougarou flailed around, bellowing. I staggered back. His hair left slime trails all across my skin. The hairy man dove into the lake and vanished beneath a huge cloud of steam and bubbles that came complete with the stink of burning hair and rotten leaves. I got him good, but I didn't have time to enjoy it. The crocodile woman was still there, and she was standing right beside Ivy.

"Now who might you two be?" she said. Her voice hadn't changed a bit. It was still all silky and sophisticated, the kind that should belong to a lady at a cocktail party. Her eyes hadn't changed either. They stayed big, beautiful, and way too close to human in her crocodile face.

At her feet, Ivy rolled over. I bit my lip and forced my hands to stop trembling. If I could keep this woman's attention on me, maybe Ivy would wake up enough to make a new wish. I could already feel Jack wishing she was gone, but I was awfully shaky and he wasn't concentrating. Not his fault. Rougarou was crawling back out of the lake, his silver eyes shining and his mouth open to show all his sharp white teeth. It was kind of distracting.

"Come, come, tell me. Who are you?" The fairy woman turned all the power of that beautiful voice toward me. Even looking at her lumpy crocodile face and twisty gray hair, I felt how pretty she was and how much I wanted to do what she said.

"Who wants to know?" Jack dodged close to me, digging his hand into his pocket. He blanched and I knew the nails were all gone. I'd dropped my hammer back in the grass somewhere. We were facing down the crocodile woman empty-handed.

"Oh, where are my manners? You can call me Amerda."

"Pleased to meet you, Amerda," I said with what Mama would have called my Sunday manners. I wasn't about to tell her either of our names. Not only was I kind of famous in fairy circles, but names have power, so you don't want to go giving yours out to just anybody. "Now you can take yourself out of here."

Amerda laughed. "Why would I leave my home?"

"This ain't your home."

"That's where you're wrong, little girl. This is my home, and *you're* trespassing."

"You want to make something of it?" I snapped.

"Why, yes, I think I do." Amerda raised her hand.

Jack was wishing again. He was wishing Rougarou and Amerda were gone, gone for good, shriveled up dead for preference. Now *there* was a wish I could take a solid hold of. But Ivy picked that moment to push herself upright.

"Who're you?" The little movie star blinked up at me. "What're they doing here?" She blinked again, and this time she got a good look at what "they" were.

Ivy Bright wailed at the top of her lungs. She grabbed my arm to yank herself to her feet, and almost pulled both of us over in the process. Amerda opened her crocodile mouth and laughed. Ivy clutched my neck and bawled.

"What is she? What's she want? Help! Somebody, help! *Help!*" She was screaming right in my ear now, and my hold on Jack's wish slipped away.

One glance at Jack was enough to tell him we'd better have a backup plan. He saw at once what it should be, and so did I. This time we moved together

Jack charged again, head down, elbows out. He hit Amerda square in the stomach, and they both toppled to the ground. I grabbed Ivy Bright and dragged her into the farmhouse. Jack jumped to his feet and barreled in after us. He slammed the door, and I kicked over one of the kegs, spilling nails across the threshold. Outside, Amerda howled and cursed.

"What . . . what . . . what . . . ?" Ivy choked out.

"Shut up!" I grabbed her by the shoulders and shook. "You want to get out of here, don't you?"

She sniffled and blinked through the flood of tears. "Y-yes."

"Wish," I told her.

"What?"

"Wish! Wish you were home! I can't do it if you don't wish!"

"I wish I was home!" It was shaky and she only kind of meant it, but it might just be enough. I wrapped her and that wish up in her own fear and pushed hard, and she was gone.

The door wrenched open, and the shapes of Amerda and Rougarou filled the doorway. The hairy man moved to step forward, but Amerda hissed a warning and pointed at the nails.

I blinked at them as stupidly as Ivy'd blinked at me. My strength was gone. There wasn't even enough left to hold me up, and I fell to my knees.

"Callie!" Jack grabbed my arm to keep me from dropping onto my face.

Amerda and Rougarou froze at the threshold.

"Callie?" rasped Rougarou. "Did he call her Callie, my sister? Did he?"

"He did," Amerda breathed, and her hunger swirled around my head. "Oh, that he did."

Jack was trying to haul me to my feet, grab hold of a two-by-four, and keep his eyes on the monsters at the same time. I was trying to remember where my feet were.

"Callie," whispered Amerda. "We've got ourselves Callie LeRoux. The Bad Luck Girl herself. The Prophecy Girl. Why don't you come here, Callie?"

She had one of my names, and my brain had gone fuzzy. I leaned toward her. Jack dragged me away, retreating toward the back wall of the house, but I kept pulling hard against him. I didn't want to, but I couldn't help it. I couldn't think straight. I couldn't even see straight.

Then, outside, a voice so deep it could have come straight out of the earth said a very rude word.

4

Fit the Battle

To my surprise, Amerda smiled all over her crocodile face. "Why, Paul!" She turned toward whoever'd spoken outside. "There you are at last!"

Without her calling my name, I was able to stumble with Jack toward the back of our flimsy fake farmhouse. Rougarou leaned as far as he could over the pathetic heap of iron nails, and that was awfully far. He had long arms too, and he stretched them all the way out, so we could see fingernails like dirty sickles.

"I thought I made it clear I wasn't having anything to do with you people," said the man outside to Amerda.

"Oh, you did. And we heard you. We were just on our way, weren't we, my brother? You need not worry about us anymore." Rougarou snapped his teeth at us and jerked his chin. His meaning was clear, to me anyway. If we made any noise, that man out there was dead.

Jack looked at me, and I looked at Jack. We got the message. But listening to folks who are already trying to kill you is never a good idea. Jack set his back to the wall and hefted the board in his hands like a baseball bat. "Help!"

"Whoever you are, help!" I added for good measure.

"What the hell are you doing?" shouted the man. "You've got *kids* in there!"

"This isn't your business anymore!" snapped Amerda.

Apparently Paul out there didn't agree. I couldn't see what happened, but it made Amerda scream, loud and high, which got Rougarou to whip himself around and run. This left me and Jack with nobody watching us. Jack shoved up the sash on the nearest window and cupped his hands. I let him boost me out the window and fell hard on my knees. He vaulted through behind me, and we took off.

We didn't get far.

Amerda screamed again. I couldn't understand the words she used, but I also couldn't feel the ground under my feet anymore. Jack and I flew backward through the air. We slammed into the dirt at her feet, and before my head stopped spinning, claws dug into my shoulder. Pain followed a split second later, and this time I did the screaming. Jack was on his feet, ready to swing his board, but a man caught hold of his shirt collar and jerked him back.

I don't know what I was expecting "Paul" to be, but this man wasn't it. He was just about the biggest, blackest Negro I'd ever seen in my life. He was dressed in a fine white shirt, dark trousers, and suspenders, but what I really noticed was that he wasn't running away or screaming. In fact, he'd put himself between Jack and both the fairies.

"Now, Paul." Amerda dug her fingers into my shoulder. She'd put her pretty face back on, so she was the sparkling woman we'd first seen, but her crocodile claws still pressed needle-sharp into my skin. "There's no need for any more trouble. We've each got ourselves one. What could be more fair?"

"Let her go!" Jack yelled, and tried to duck back in front of Paul, but Paul just stuck out an arm to block his way.

"You heard the boy," said Paul, not even noticing Jack was pushing on him. "Let her go."

"Oh, no." Amerda's claws nestled closer into the hollow of my shoulder. If I tried to move, she'd tear a chunk out. "Not this one. Not even for you, Paul dear."

"Please, mister—" Jack began.

I cut him off. "Run, mister. Just . . . get him out of here." These two would probably keep me alive because of what I was, but if they got their hands on Jack, he'd be dead. Jack wasn't even part fairy. They didn't need him for anything. It was plain they had some kind of history with this Paul, but Amerda would kill him too, just to keep her claws on me. I could feel it.

Rougarou had his own ideas, though. He crouched down like a runner, his long, tangled hair puddling in the dust around his big feet. "Let Rougarou have Mr. Paul." His eyes glittered in the pale street light. "Let Rougarou wrestle him down. Rougarou will bring them all back to the Seelie king. We be fed and free forever, sister mine!"

"Now there *is* an idea." Greed slowed down each word. Amerda laid her fingertips on her chin, making a big show of thinking it all over. "What do you say to a little wager, Paul?"

"No!" I shouted. Amerda's claws broke my skin, and I squeaked. "Don't do it. I'll be okay. Just run. Please, get out of here!"

Jack didn't pay me any mind. Right there in the middle of being scared for my life and his, and for the life of this Paul guy, who knew too much and not enough at the same time, I wanted to roll my eyes. Brave was one thing, but Jack was downright dopey.

Amerda sighed and shook her head. "There'd be no need for any of this if you'd just accepted my offer, Paul. I wouldn't even have known the girl was here." She smiled down at me, all soft and pretty. The effect was kind of spoiled by my being close enough to see how jagged her teeth were. "In a way, you've done us a tremendous favor."

"Don't listen to her!" Amerda was trying to pull a fast one. She wanted Paul to think it was his fault Jack and I were in this fix. He hadn't been here to see Ivy Bright. He didn't know what was really happening.

That was when Paul surprised me again. He crouched down until his gaze was level with Jack's. "Has either of you promised anything to this . . . woman?" he asked. "Anything at all?"

"No, mister," said Jack. "Nothing."

Who was this man? How'd he know about fairies and promises? And why couldn't he figure out he was supposed to be scared out of his mind by now? He was as bad as Jack. "Mister, you don't understand."

"You're correct. I don't understand. But we'll sort that out later." Paul straightened up again. Standing beside him, Jack looked like a wheat stalk sticking up next to an oak tree. "Right now I'm going to finish this."

He folded his hands behind his back. "Now, Miss Amerda. I don't believe either of these children wishes to go with you, and as neither seems to be of your family, I see no reason why they should have to. Do you?"

"Only that I've got my hands on this one, Paul." Amerda shrugged, and her claws dug in further. Blood trickled out slowly under my suit jacket, and I tried not to wince. "And I've grown so fond of her, I simply can't bear to let her go."

"What if I told you she was mine?"

I bit down hard on both my lips.

"Oh, no, *really?*" Amerda flashed a delighted smile and shook me. Pain sent bright sparks all up and down my arm. "I never suspected. Perhaps I should have. It would explain her being here, wouldn't it? *Such* a small world."

She was buying it. She thought I was related to this giant. Was she that stupid? No. She was that greedy. With all that passed for heart and soul under her fairy hide, she wanted to bring me back to her folks, and that made her stupid. Paul knew it too, and he was using it.

"And what if I told you I'd let you have my girl free and clear if your brother there can beat me in wrestling?"

Oh, no, no, no. Don't do this. Stop him, Jack. Stop him! Just a minute ago, I thought he knew about fairies and promises. Fairy promises aren't like human promises. On their side, they can't break them any more than they can hold on to black iron. On the human side, if you try to break the promise, they will come after you, and they will keep coming until one way or another the promise is kept.

"Please, please, please stop." But it was like my voice didn't reach all the way up to Paul's ears. Jack wasn't helping either. I could tell by the way he curled up his fists he wasn't going to make a move. I dug down deep for my magic, but all I found was more shakes.

Paul patted Jack's shoulder once and stepped forward.

"Stakes," hissed Rougarou. He was starved. Hunger billowed around him like the smell of wet rot. He wanted pain and he wanted fear. He'd munch them down and be filled. Paul's fear would taste so sweet. My stomach heaved. "What are the stakes for this little game?"

Paul wasn't paying any attention to the hairy man. He walked in a slow circle, scraping a ring in the dirt with the heel of one shiny shoe. "If you throw me, I give you my girl," he said. "If I throw you, you leave these children be, and you and yours never bother me again."

"Done!" cried Amerda.

Slowly, with more dignity than I'd seen from a lot of men walking down the street, Paul took down his suspenders and stripped off his shirt. He tossed it to Jack, who caught it, I think because he didn't know what else to do. Paul's skin gleamed. He had arms like a boxer's and hands that could have unbent a horseshoe after he'd pulled it off the horse. Rougarou grinned and crossed into the circle. Paul stepped over the line to join him. He bent his knees and put his arms out, looking like a football player waiting for the tackle.

He didn't have to wait long. Rougarou bellowed and threw himself straight at Paul. Paul didn't even try to get out of the way. Rougarou plowed his head straight into Paul's stomach, and Paul grabbed the hairy man around the waist and twisted. The monster hit the ground, and Paul dropped himself down to land right on top. Amerda hissed, and her ugly brother lashed out with one foot, and that was when we found out Rougarou could grab hold of things with his hairy toes. His hands caught Paul's wrists and his toes wound around Paul's ankles. Rougarou rolled over backward, aiming for the circle's edge. But Paul wrapped his big hands around the monster's elbow and dug both thumbs into the joint. The monster bellowed and dropped him. Paul rolled over onto his shoulder and came up into his crouch again, hands out, teeth bared in a grin that made him look every bit as fierce as Rougarou.

Amerda had her attention glued to the fight. A thin trickle of spit ran from the corner of her perfect, smiling mouth. In the ring, Rougarou and Paul circled around, sizing each other up, looking for openings. Rougarou feinted, left then right, fast enough to be a blur in the dark. Amerda laughed.

This time Paul didn't wait for Rougarou. He charged, and Rougarou got him by the waist, whirling them both around. He lifted his muzzle high. He was going to bite Paul on the back of his neck. I screamed. But Paul swung those huge fists, and Rougarou hollered. Paul twisted and punched again, and Rougarou's grip broke. Trying to cover his head, he backed away from Paul, right toward the circle's edge, Paul's fists driving him out of bounds.

Amerda frowned. She lifted her free hand to her mouth, pursed her lips, and blew across the palm. A cloud of dust spiraled up from the ground, straight into Paul's face. Paul fell back, choking. Rougarou stuck out a foot and caught Paul right behind the ankles. Paul stumbled out of the circle and fell to the ground.

"You cheated!" I cried. "You're a cheater!"

"But I never said I would not." Amerda straightened up until she was almost as tall as Paul. "Your man was careless, and he lost you, little Callie." She cupped her hand under my chin and smiled down at me. Her hidden scales scraped against my skin, and she showed me all her crocodile teeth.

"No, no," croaked Jack. "It can't be."

"It's not." Paul pulled himself up onto his knees and spat dust.

Amerda swung around, but she didn't let go of my chin. "What's that?"

"As it happens, she's not my girl."

A light came on inside me, like he'd thrown a switch. At the same time, Amerda's jaw dropped.

"What?" She hissed out the word, all long and slow and deadly.

"She's not my girl." Paul climbed slowly to his feet. He wiped the back of his hand across his mouth. "She's nothing to me. I have no power to give her away."

"But you said—"

"I said, what if I told you she was my girl? But I didn't tell it to you, and you didn't ask who my girl was. Or if I even had one," he added with a grin that managed to be cheerful and dangerous at the same time. "You said you would take my girl as our bet. Well, whoever Miss Callie here may be, she's not my girl and was no part of our bargain."

Amerda hissed, long and hard. "You think you're so very clever. But you do have a girl. You have a wife, you have—"

"Might be a problem, if . . ." Paul pivoted on one heel and wrapped his tree-trunk arms around Rougarou's waist. The monster wasn't ready for it, and Paul lifted him high. He held him there for a minute silhouetted against the deeper dark, and all I could think of was Samson from the Bible. Then Paul slammed the monster down so hard he bounced.

"I threw your man. *I* win."

"You cheated!" shrieked Amerda.

"I never said I would not," Paul replied calmly.

Amerda swelled up until the sparkly disguise stretched

thin and the crocodile face showed through underneath. She let go and stalked forward, her anger at Paul blinding her to everything else. Jack darted forward and grabbed my hand, ready to run. I tried to latch on to a wish, something, anything, but it was all too heavy and slick and my shoulder hurt too much.

Paul just stood where he was, letting Amerda come right up to him. She lashed out, claws curled, but her hand stopped two inches from his face like she'd hit an iron wall.

"You've lost, Amerda," Paul said calmly. "You and your brother. You can't touch me."

Rougarou climbed to his feet and howled.

"You think you're so very clever." Amerda backed away. "The gallant knight riding to the rescue of the pitiful little girl. You have no idea what kind of creature you've just tried to save."

She screamed, and she and Rougarou were gone. Whatever bubble of quiet she'd been holding us in burst and all the city night noises came flooding back. The world was almost normal again, with Jack holding my hand and this giant stranger who'd just saved our lives looking solemnly down at us both.

5

He's Comin' Back to Call Me

"Who are you?" Jack whispered finally.

"My name is Paul Robeson."

"Paul Robeson!" Now it was my eyes trying to pop out. "You sing on the radio! You're one of my mama's favorites!" I remembered sitting with Mama in the Imperial's parlor and listening to the deep voice rolling out of the radio, so strong it felt like it could sweep away all the troubles the Kansas dust storms had rolled in. This wasn't dance music or blues. This was what they called spirituals: deep, serious, slow, beautiful music. I'd never heard anything else like it.

"You'll have to thank your mama for me." Mr. Robeson smiled, charming and easy. My cheeks heated up.

Jack remembered to hand Mr. Robeson back his shirt. "Thank you," he said as he took it. Lines of sweat ran down Mr. Robeson's face and chest, and he was breathing hard. But if he was hurt, he wasn't letting on any. He just buttoned his shirt and pulled his suspenders up as though he did this kind of thing every day. For all I knew, he did. I'd've believed anything about this man right then. "Now, I've got a question for you, young lady," he said as he finished tucking his shirttail in. "Did I hear your name was Callie LeRoux?"

"Yes, sir."

He bent down and looked at me close and hard. I didn't know what he was looking for, and I tried not to squirm, but it wasn't easy. I'd lost my hat somewhere and torn my gloves, and my stuffed brassiere was a lopsided mess. I really didn't want anybody looking at me right now, let alone somebody this famous who'd just saved my life and Jack's. "I knew a piano player back in Harlem who went by the name of LeRoux," he said finally. "Any chance you might be related?"

There are words that root you to the spot. Jack's eyes went round. It felt like a long time before either one of us could remember we spoke English. "My papa was a piano player," I croaked.

"Thought so. You look a bit like him."

Was it possible? I still couldn't get my head around the idea that this man knew about the fairies. Could he really have met my papa? A sick, horrible feeling crawled through me, because I'd had people try to trap me like this before, and I did not want Mr. Robeson to be another trap. I didn't think I could stand it if he was.

But he didn't say anything more about my papa. "Let's get you two out of here before Amerda comes back with reinforcements."

Mr. Robeson strode off back toward the prison and New York City. Jack and I looked at each other, each of us trying to see if the other had a better idea. Neither of us did, so we followed him.

I'll tell you what, that man had some long legs. Even Jack had to trot to keep up with him. I'd gotten my breath back, and at least some of my brains, enough to start wondering about what I'd heard go by between him and Amerda.

"How come the Seelies know you, Mr. Robeson?"

His face went hard. "They made me an offer to come sing for them sometime back, and I turned it down."

"You turned them down?" squawked Jack. Nobody turned the fairies down. They could make all your wishes come true, or at least make you think they had come true. All the fame and fortune Ruth Markham thought she was getting for handing over Ivy Bright? She'd have it. She might not live very long after she got it, but she would have it.

"You get around a little, you find out that people who offer you the whole world usually want everything you've got in return. I gave up believing that kind of promise a long time ago." The anger in those softly spoken words sent shivers down my spine. "Anyway, the Seelies, as you call them, seemed to take it as a kind of challenge, and they've been sending their people around after me ever since. Amerda was their latest attempt, and you walked into the middle of it."

Which meant Amerda hadn't really wanted Ivy Bright at all. She'd just been trying to set things up so that Mr.

Robeson would jump in and try to save the brightest little star in Hollywood. Except Jack and I got there first.

And got caught, I added to myself. *And now they know who I am, and that I'm hanging around the movie studios.* My head felt seasick, and a giggly little thought in the back of my brain started up another imaginary letter. *Dear Mama: Guess what . . . ?*

We were back in New York by now. The hollow, unfinished buildings with their jagged tops and their long shadows fenced us in. I didn't like it here anymore. Those fake buildings could all be hiding more monsters. Without thinking about it, I crowded a little closer to Jack.

Mr. Robeson looked the whole long way down at me. "Now, suppose you two tell me how you came to draw the attention of Amerda and her kind."

"I, um, well . . ."

"I work here," said Jack quickly. "I'm a script boy." His head must have been spinning too. Usually Jack makes up much better explanations.

Mr. Robeson's face screwed up, like we'd just offered him a rotten lemon. "And I suppose you wanted to get into pictures?" he said to me.

"No! Nothing like that. I mean, I *am* looking for work, but not acting work. Kitchen work, maybe. Housekeeping, things like that."

Mr. Robeson squinted down at me, trying hard to figure out the story behind what we were telling him. I wasn't so sure he liked what he was figuring either. I bit my lip. I didn't really want to talk about any of this. Not with those buildings and all their holes and hiding places around us. Anybody might be listening, and for us "anybody" covered a whole lot of ground. Mr. Robeson saw me looking at that fake New York and he nodded like he understood. He didn't ask any more questions, but he did pick up the pace, so Jack and I were all but running to keep up. That was okay by me. Amerda and her brother might not be able to touch us, but sure as the California sunrise, they had Seelie kin. Those kin had other kin and friends and maybe a few enemies on the lookout for some fun. They could put their heads together and find a way around the bargain Mr. Robeson had made. After all, they'd only promised to leave him alone, not us. They could all turn up spoiling for a fight any second now.

It came home to me cold and ugly that Jack and I had made a mistake walking in here without a real plan. We'd been putting that off until we actually found the Seelies. Well, now we had found them. Problem was, they'd found us too. Fear leaned in on me again and brought all my shakes back.

We finally reached the gate to Overland Avenue. Solly was gone. Instead, the shack was occupied by a black man reading what looked like a schoolbook.

"Good evening, George," said Paul. "Does Michael have the car out?"

"Evenin', Mr. Robeson. I think so. You need to go

someplace?" He eyed me, then Jack, then me again. He didn't like whatever he was thinking. I was pretty sure I didn't like it either.

"These two need to be driven back home."

"Oh, sure. Lemme call over." George picked up the phone and dialed. Mr. Robeson took me and Jack each by the arm and led us toward the gate.

"Now," he said firmly, "you will go straight home and into your rooms. You will not stop for anything or open the door to any strangers."

This was a little too much for Jack, who'd been on the bum pretty much since he was twelve. He pulled himself up as far as he could and tried to look tough. He went a fair way toward doing it too. "Listen, we really appreciate your help, Mr. Robeson, but it's not like we're babies or anything."

"No, you're not. But you are in danger and you need to take care. And stay out of here." This last was said to me. "If you're really looking for work, you can come see me tomorrow morning. I'm staying at the Dunbar. Maybe I can find something for you."

Jack was making a face, and I got the feeling he was hoping I'd refuse. I wasn't sure why, though. Mr. Robeson might just be a regular human, but he could fight off the Seelie fairies and twist a bargain so tight they got lost in it. If we told him about my parents, he might be able to help.

"Yes, sir," I said. "Thank you."

Before I could say anything else, a big white Cadillac

pulled up to the gate. The chauffeur who climbed out was a bent old man in a gray suit and peaked cap, but he gave Mr. Robeson's hand a hearty shake like they were longtime friends. "What is it I can do for you tonight, Mr. Robeson?"

Paul explained how we needed a ride. Michael agreed right away and gestured us into the back of the white car. We scrambled up onto the plush seats. I was used to cars that choked and popped when they started, but the Cadillac just cleared its throat politely as Michael pulled into traffic.

"Holy smokes!" I flopped back in the seat. "You ever see anybody like that? I mean anybody?"

"Nope, I never." Jack took off his cap and scrubbed his hair. "I wonder what his story is," he added in a whisper, so Michael wouldn't hear. "Do you think he could really have met your pop?"

I wondered too. He sure hadn't told us anything like the whole story. But then, we'd been pretty skimpy with our own set of details, so I guess I couldn't blame him. "He's got something going for him," I whispered back. "Otherwise he'd be singing for the Seelies, not wrestling 'em."

"I guess." Jack looked out the window for a long time at the city lights going past. "Do you think Ivy Bright's okay?"

Guilt closed my mouth. I'd almost forgotten about Ivy, the original bait for the original trap. I'd sent her home, but she'd been tricked and magicked and scared. None of that could have done her any good.

No way, no how was I going to go using any magic right

then, but I did open up my inside eyes to peek a little, just to find out if there was any magic flying around the vicinity. Just a quick peek couldn't hurt, I told myself.

Unfortunately, it didn't do a whole lot of good either. All I felt was city—no magic, no fairy gloating. That could mean something, or nothing at all. There was just no telling. But from the way Jack was holding his face, I figured this was not the time to try to explain all that. "I think she's okay," I told him.

"Good," Jack said softly.

We both had too much to think about to talk after that.

Michael let me off in front of Mrs. Constantine's boarding-house and headed out to take Jack back to Ma Lehner's. We had to stay in two different houses. In the City of Angels, where they've seen just about every shade in God's paint pot, not even Jack could convince any woman who advertised "clean and respectable accommodations" we were brother and sister. Women like Mrs. Constantine had reputations to protect, so they looked at you a lot closer than the guard on any gate.

I climbed up the creaky steps to the crooked porch. Whatever old Mr. Constantine had done for a living, he couldn't have been much good at it. If he'd left his widow any kind of money, she wouldn't have had to take in boarders like me. I had a hunch Mr. Constantine did not exist, or that he had never married her. She could have pegged the

Mrs. onto her name to keep up appearances. But my mama had done the same thing, so who was I to get snooty about that?

I was so tired, all I wanted right then was to get this stupid, lopsided stuffed bra and my ruined stockings off and crawl into bed. I turned the knob and pushed on the front door, but the door didn't open. I stared. Slowly it occurred to me that it was after midnight. Mrs. Constantine locked the door at twelve on the dot, and if you weren't on the right side of it, it was just your tough luck.

I dropped onto the porch swing and buried my face in my hands. The car and Jack were long gone. I was going to have to stay out here all night, and then Mrs. Constantine'd kick me out in the morning, because I wouldn't have any kind of good reason for being out past curfew and she had been clear about this being a *respectable* house. She'd been real nice, and she'd been looking after me just like you would a person who was real to you, not just a stranger in a back room. I didn't want her thinking I was a liar, or a tramp. Tears pricked my eyes. It was a little thing after all that had happened, but it was also that last straw everybody talks about. Especially when my shoulder hurt so bad where the crocodile woman had gotten hold of me. Because of that stupid prophecy and my parents and maybe a whole bunch of other things I didn't even know about yet, she and Rougarou and all the other Seelies were out there someplace, making plans about how to come get me, and I couldn't even get into the house to hide under the bed. ·

"Dear Mama," I whispered to my hands. "I'm sorry. I'm trying. I really am, but I don't know what to do."

A porch board creaked.

"There she is," said a soft, familiar voice. "Callie LeRoux. There she is."

6

Come to Keep Me Company

The porch creaked again. From around the corner of the house, a shadow slid along the warped boards, and a man's silhouette followed it.

"Is this what you want, Callie LeRoux?" It was the bum, the one who'd tried to stop me on the way to the studio that morning. His crooked hand opened with a jerky, painful motion to show a door key lying on his palm.

"Here. I'll make it a present to you." He held it out.

I'd've as soon touched a live rattlesnake as anything this man had to give. "You get outta here! I'll scream and have the whole neighborhood down on you." That might have made a better threat if I'd been able to talk louder than a whisper.

"Sure you will, sure you will," the bum crooned. "Because you don't know me yet, do you, Callie?" Then, to my surprise, that raggedy man swept off his broken-down hat and began to sing. *"Let him go, let him go, God bless him . . ."*

The song plowed straight through my brain, tossing up memories left and right. I was in a dusty honky-tonk. A lean man at the upright piano coaxed "St. James Infirmary Blues" out of the keys. Later, that same man in evening clothes and a flowing cape stood beside my Unseelie grandparents and looked down on me with a big, fake smile on his face. Later still, he stood in the middle of fire and ruin and gunshots, with me as good as dead, and he laughed about it.

"Oh, no, no," I whispered. I wanted to back away, but there was no place to go. He had me, trapped, alone in the dark. *"Shake!"*

"Now you see me." The bum bowed low. His white eye gleamed like a pearl in the porch light. "Your uncle Shake. What's left of him, anyway."

"But . . . but you're dead." Last time I'd seen Shake, a boardwalk amusement park had been burning down around him, and I'd whacked him hard upside the head with a cast-iron frying pan. That kind of thing tended to make a person dead in a hurry, even a fairy. I'd gotten out, of course, and so had Jack, but we'd had help from outside. I just plain never stopped to think that Shake might have gotten out too.

"Oh, no. Not dead. No more than you are."

"No thanks to you!" My fists bunched up. Fear took it on the lam and left anger behind, spoiling for a fight. "You get out of here, or so help me I'll magic you into the middle of next week!"

"Now there's your father's daughter!" That big, sloppy grin split Shake's scarred face again. Three of his front teeth were nothing but jagged stumps, and a couple others were flat-out missing. He'd been hit in the face, hard, and there was a dent in his skull that pushed his forehead out of shape. "Don't you worry, Callie. Things have changed. I want us to be friends. Best of friends."

Before I could think of any kind of answer to that, the porch light snapped on overhead, and we both froze.

"What on earth is going on out there?" Mrs. Constantine's voice sounded over a flurry of snapping of locks on the other side of the front door. She appeared on the threshold in a pink housecoat with her hair all knotted up in white rags.

"Callie LeRoux! What are you doing out this time of night? And who is this . . . fine gentleman?" She crossed her arms and blocked the door, all the while looking Shake up and down like the cat had not only dragged him in but took a few good chomps out of him in the process.

"Oh, um, ah . . ."

While I sputtered like a fool and wished Jack was here, my uncle shuffled up to my side. Before I knew what was what, he had his hand on my shoulder. His bent fingers felt thick and heavy and too cold to be normal. Something sharp dug into my mind and I felt just a little magic welling up, like blood around a splinter.

"Mrs. Constantine?" Shake held his hat over his breast.

"How do you do? Lawrence LeRoux. I understand you've been looking after my niece Callie since she's been in town?"

As Shake spoke, Mrs. Constantine's eyes went fuzzy, like she wasn't quite seeing what was in front of her. Which she wasn't. I knew just what she was seeing because Shake was pulling it out of me along with the magic. Whether I wanted to or not—and I really didn't—I was conjuring up a vision of a well-dressed man holding a new snap-brim fedora as he smiled politely at my landlady. He had shiny wingtip shoes on his feet and a leather suitcase beside him with stickers on it for places such as St. Louis and Chicago.

"Mm-hmm." Mrs. Constantine pasted a frown on her face, but now only because she thought she should. The anger had drained away as the illusion took hold. "Well, Mr. LeRoux, where're you in from?"

"Kansas City." Shake stepped us into the front hall so smoothly I wasn't even sure how it happened. "What a charming house," he said, and Mrs. Constantine puffed up with pride. "I am so sorry to have to disturb you at such an hour, but the train broke down on the way across the border. Callie had come to meet me at the station. Wound up asleep on a bench, poor girl." He shrugged.

"Land sakes." Mrs. Constantine shook her head in sympathy. But then, because she didn't want it to look like she was letting anybody off the hook too easily, she added, "Callie, why didn't you tell me your uncle was coming today?"

I opened my mouth, searching for an excuse, but Uncle

Shake squeezed my shoulder hard. It was a good thing it wasn't the one Amerda'd gotten hold of, or the noise I'd have made would have startled everybody. As it was, I understood what he was trying to signal. He'd already got a spell around Mrs. Constantine. If I tried to say something different now, she might not believe me. Even if she did, once I broke the spell I'd still have to try to get away from Shake and throw him out of the house and the neighborhood. Then I'd have to explain to my landlady how things had gone so far that this broken bum could have said even once that he was my uncle. I wasn't sure I could do any of that, because my legs were going all shaky again and my other shoulder was starting to set up a whole jazz band's worth of pain. Plus, with this magic leaking out of me, I was putting myself in a spotlight. If Amerda and the Seelies had set anybody on my tail, they'd follow the feel of magic like a hungry cat following the smell of fish straight to the market door.

I had to stop this whole thing, fast, and the fastest way was to go along with it.

"But I did, Mrs. Constantine," I said, feeling every bit the liar I was. She didn't deserve this. She'd been nice to me. "You saw the letter when it came. I said he'd be arriving on the twelfth, and you said you'd have a room for him."

"So you did!" Mrs. Constantine slapped her forehead, as if she was really remembering something, instead of just finding the new idea Shake and I had put into her mind. "I'd forget my head if it wasn't screwed on my shoulders.

Well. You just rest yourself in the parlor while I get your bed made up, Mr. LeRoux."

Mrs. Constantine bustled into the house and up the stairs. Shake steered me through the brocade curtains to the parlor. The big cabinet radio was the only new thing in the room. It was sure newer than the pair of sofas, the four armchairs, and the card table with its mended leg. There was a grand piano covered with silver-framed photos of a plump, pretty little girl, who I had a feeling was Mrs. Constantine's daughter. Miss Patty played that piano sometimes. I could have too, but I didn't dare. Music brought out the magic in me even faster than people wishing.

The curtains dropped shut behind us. Shake let go of my shoulder and groped for one of the saggy armchairs. It was clear he was in pretty sad shape, but I wasn't in the mood to feel sorry for him.

"What'd you do to me?" I wished I could shout, but I held my voice to a whisper. I couldn't risk anybody else waking up.

"Just used a little of your magic, Callie." Shake sat down slowly and carefully, like an old man. "Nothing to get on your high horse about."

"Are you cracked? Slinging my magic around! They'll find us!"

"Who will?"

"The Seelies! Every time I make a wish they're all over me!"

"That's because you don't know what you're doing."

He had the nerve to shake his head at me. "My magisterial parents have taken my power, but they didn't take my brains and my skill. No one beyond our Mrs. Constantine felt a thing."

"You promise?" I hated how scared I sounded when I said it.

"I do." He turned his amber eye to me as he looked me up and down. That eye had both light and darkness behind it, midnight and starshine all mixed up together. "Hmmm. I would have thought Shimmy would have done better by you."

"You leave her out of this. She didn't have any time to teach me much of anything because we were busy running away from the vigilante man *you* set on our trail!"

All the twisted good humor disappeared from Shake's scarred face. "You kept me from my throne. It should have been mine when your father abdicated."

"That's not my fault!"

"No," Shake agreed. "But I wanted you to die just the same."

Shake—whose real name was Lorcan deMinuit—was my papa's younger brother. Papa quit his job as heir to the Midnight Throne so he could marry my mama. This should have left Shake next in line to become the big boss for the Unseelie fairies. Problem was, I'd been born before Papa could finish with whatever passed as paperwork with the fairies. According to their law, that made me, not Shake, next in line for the throne. It turns out fairies can't break their own laws any more than they can break a promise. As long as I was alive, I was first in line to take over the Midnight Throne, and there wasn't a thing Uncle Shake could do about it. Except kill me.

I started to throw up my hands, but my right shoulder pulled and the pain sparked hot.

"You're hurt." Shake leaned forward. "Who hurt you, Callie? What have you been doing?"

"It's none of your business!"

"Shhhhhh!" Shake held up one broken finger to his lips. "Here comes Mrs. Constantine."

I heard her rustling on the other side of the curtain a second later.

"Your room's all set, Mr. LeRoux." Mrs. Constantine came back into the parlor. "That'll be seven-fifty for the week, meals included. Cash. In advance." Which just goes to show you the limits of fairy magic when it's facing a city lady running her own boardinghouse.

"Of course."

Shake had hold of me again, and he wasn't even touching me. My magic bled away into him as he dug into his pocket and brought out a handful of nothing. He handed that nothing to Mrs. Constantine. My landlady took it, counted it, folded it neatly, and tucked it into her housecoat. "That's fine, then. I'll show you up."

I followed them up the stairs. I spent the whole climb promising myself I'd find a way to get Mrs. Constantine her money, or at least make up to her for helping Shake push his way into her house. Of course, that'd have to be after I found out what he was actually doing here.

"Laundry is picked up on Thursdays," Mrs. Constantine was saying as she pushed open the last door on the right, the one directly across the hall from mine. "Sheets are changed every Monday. No smoking in the rooms. No callers except in the parlor. No visitors of any kind after ten. This is a *respectable* house."

The rooms at Mrs. Constantine's were about as barebones as you could ask for—one old brass bed, a mishmash of worn-out furniture that would have been up in the attic of any house that could afford better. But everything was clean as a whistle and the roof didn't leak. Considering that before this I'd spent a stretch sleeping in rail yards and chicken coops, it counted for a lot.

"This will do splendidly, Mrs. Constantine." Shake looked around the room with his amber eye. I wondered where he'd been sleeping lately. I told myself I didn't care, but I never was much of a liar. "Again, I sincerely apologize for getting you out of bed at this hour."

"Well, these things happen, Mr. LeRoux. I'll wish you good night now. I'm sure Callie can show you where everything is."

"Yes, ma'am," I agreed. I wanted her out of there. I had more than a few things left to say to Shake.

Mrs. Constantine left, and I shut the door behind her and shot the bolt. Then I turned on my uncle.

"No more games, Shake. What're you doing here?"

"I could ask you the same thing, Callie. You shouldn't be within a hundred miles of the Seelie territory."

"I've got to find my parents!"

"What a coincidence. I also want to find your parents."

"Oh, sure you do. You want to kill them too?" How had I even let him come near me? Why hadn't I magicked him the second I recognized him?

"I told you, Callie, you got me all wrong. I want to help them, and you. I want to see you on the Midnight Throne." He gave me his sloppy, broken-toothed grin. "Just like you're supposed to be."

I waited to feel his magic wrapping around me, all warm and cozy, trying to get me to believe what he said. But it didn't come. It wasn't possible he was telling the truth, was it? Slowly I stepped forward. I made myself look at his scarred face and milky eye, his lopsided head, and down, to his fingers.

"What happened to you?"

"You did, Callie."

"What's that supposed to mean?"

Shake sighed. "Well, for some reason Their Majesties weren't too happy that I tried to kill you."

This surprised me. Their Majesties, my grandparents, weren't exactly the squeamish type. They certainly hadn't shown any hesitation about dancing Jack to death—which was something we were going to have a little talk about, just as soon as I got over being terrified at the thought of them.

"If I'd finished the job, maybe they would have thought I'd done them a favor," said Shake, like he knew what I was thinking. Which he just might have. "But blood's thicker, as they say, and then there was the little matter of this prophecy regarding your power over the world gates. So I had to stand trial, and it did not go well. They marked me as a traitor." He touched the scar that ran across the lid that drooped over his milky eye. "And they broke my hands." I winced. I couldn't help it. When I'd first met Shake, he'd been playing a piano. I remembered how graceful his hands had been then, and how his slow, lazy music made you want to listen all day. Now those hands didn't look like they could hold a spoon, let alone play a piano.

"I have since been cast out to walk the mortal world." Shake smiled broadly. "Let that be a lesson to you, Callie. When you set out to challenge the Midnight Throne, don't you dare to fail."

"Yeah, well, I hope you don't expect me to feel sorry for you." I tried to fit the mad back into my voice. I didn't want to feel anything for him. He'd hurt me and scared me and just told me to my face he wasn't a bit sorry. But at the same time, I couldn't help thinking how the fairies collected beautiful things and beautiful people. They probably thought making someone ugly was worse than straight-up killing him. And the king and queen of the Midnight Throne had done this to one of their sons. "I'm just the one you tried to murder," I said, almost as much to remind myself as to remind him. "Why should I care what you—"

"Okay, okay, Callie LeRoux." Whatever magic he'd taken from me must have been wearing off, because the wobbles had crawled back into his voice. "Have it your own way. Now I'm tired, tired, tired. *'Been walkin' all day and I'm nearly done . . . ,'*" he crooned, and flashed that big gap-toothed grin again. "We'll continue this so-pleasant conversation in the morning, isn't that right?"

I knew what I should be doing. I should be magicking him out of there, the way I'd magicked away Ivy Bright and Ruth Markham. The problem was, I didn't have any wishes, or anything else to feed the magic, and Uncle Shake wasn't the only one who was tired. There was something else too. An idea was putting itself together in the back of my brain. It wasn't a good idea. In fact, it looked awfully dangerous.

"In the morning. Right." I turned to go.

"Callie."

I stopped. My uncle moved faster than I would have believed. His hand closed around my bad shoulder, and I felt him dig into my magic and I yelped in pain. Then the pain was gone and he backed away and fell into the chair.

"You can go now," he wheezed.

I left him there. I crossed the hall to my own room and shut the door. Miss Patty's snoring hitched once and then settled in for the long haul. On the other side, Mr. and Mrs. Jones rolled over in a chorus of creaking springs and heavy-duty snoring. I took a deep breath, and another. I tried to tell myself that this new, bad idea was from Shake, not from anywhere inside me. It didn't work.

I changed out of my dress and finally got that stuffed bra off. I looked at my shoulder in the mirror. Four dark, scabby dots stood out in a neat line just below the collarbone. There was a lot of blood smeared around them, but the dots themselves were little more than pinpricks. I shrugged. This time it didn't hurt.

I washed my shoulder with water from the basin I kept on the dresser. I pulled on my too-big secondhand nightgown. My silk stockings were ruined, but I hung them carefully over the back of the chair anyway. I lay down on the bed, setting up my own mess of spring creaks. *City crickets,* I thought, and closed my eyes. I opened them again. I stared at the streetlight working its way through the curtains, and at those torn stockings hanging like a pair of baby ghosts over the back of the chair. I told myself I was too tired to pay attention to some raggedy idea that was way too dangerous to work.

That raggedy idea wasn't listening. It just kept picking up more pieces from around my brain and sticking them onto its sides. It grabbed hold of how I didn't know what to do next, even though we'd found the fairies, and how Uncle Shake might really mean it when he said he wanted me on the Midnight Throne, and how he knew how to use magic in ways the Seelies couldn't catch hold of. Last of all, it sussed out how I knew exactly what Shake wanted from me, and the way I could give it to him. In return, I could make him tell me all the things I didn't know, including how to free my parents.

My idea used all these bits to make itself bigger and better, while I stayed awake and watched.

7

Shall We Dance?

It took until the sun rose over the Los Angeles rooftops, but I finally found a way to make my raggedy idea back off. Before I did anything else, I was going to talk to Mr. Robeson. He knew plenty of important things about the Seelies, like how to stay free when they were after you. Plus, he'd already saved me and Jack from them once, which was one hundred percent more times than my uncle had. Maybe I could even find a way to tell him about Shake without mentioning that he was my uncle. The idea of explaining to Mr. Robeson how I was part fairy made my stomach squirm and start looking for a back door.

I told myself over and over again while I got dressed that this was the best plan, trying to settle it down in my head. It wasn't easy. From the beginning, Jack and I had been on our own. We'd gotten used to hiding and to keeping secrets.

The thought of telling someone else what we were aiming for was awfully slow to take root.

I was back in normal clothes today—a brown skirt I'd hemmed up so it wasn't too long, a white blouse that was only a little too big, white socks, and almost-new shoes. I caught myself taking my own sweet time braiding up my hair. I knew as soon as I finished I'd have to do something about Shake. If he was even still there. Which he might not be.

That idea dropped like a brick into my mind. Shake could have snuck away while I was trying to figure out how not to have to do any kind of deal with him. He said he didn't have his magic anymore and that we should be one big happy family now, but that could just be a fresh batch of moonshine. He could be anywhere, doing anything. *Anything.*

I shot across the hall to bang on Shake's door.

You better be in there. You just better! At the same time I had no idea what I'd do if he wasn't.

"What on earth!" Miss Patty stuck her head out her door. "Callie? What's wrong?"

"I . . . uh . . ."

Shake's door opened too. He slapped his cold hand down around my wrist. Before I could do more than yelp, he'd siphoned off enough magic to pull on his disguise like other folks pull on their bathrobe.

"Callie. What is the matter?" Shake looked like he was

dressed in a good dark suit, a clean blue shirt, and a straight black tie. He saw Miss Patty and smiled at her. "Good morning, ma'am. Lawrence LeRoux. Sorry if we disturbed you."

"I . . . uh . . . it's breakfast time . . . Uncle Lawrence," I mumbled. "I didn't want you to be late."

"I appreciate that, Callie, but there's no need to raise the roof about it. Do excuse us, ma'am." He smiled once more at Miss Patty and, still holding my wrist, steered me into his room and shut the door.

I shook him off and backed away until I was up against the wall.

"You have got to stop calling attention to yourself," scolded Shake—or Lawrence, or Lorcan. He was piling up names faster than he was piling up disguises.

"You don't tell me what to do!"

He didn't even flinch. "Somebody's got to; otherwise you're not going to make it six feet from this door now that the Seelies know you're here."

"I don't need your help. We've been doing just fine."

He shrugged. "Probably you're right. Probably I need you much more than you need me. So, what are you going to do about that?"

Which was a really good question, and I hated him hard for saying it out loud.

"I've got to go talk to somebody." I sure didn't want to tell him what I was planning, or about the idea that had built itself up so big in my head the night before. That didn't leave a whole lot I could tell him. "You stay here until I get back. You don't go anywhere, you don't talk to anybody, and you especially don't magic anybody."

"I've told you, Callie, without you, I can't lay any spells at all. That's gone from me."

"I know what you said. Why should I believe you?"

Shake was silent for a minute, as if this was a brand-new idea. "Very well." He held up his hand. "See for yourself."

I stared at him. "What are you talking about?"

"Come into my mind. You know it's within your power. See for yourself what I am doing here."

I didn't doubt I could do it. When I opened my magic, I could feel people's wishes and wants. The idea that I could hear thoughts wasn't that much of a stretch. But I saw the starlight sparkling in the back of Shake's amber eye, and all of a sudden, memory took hold. I saw my mother, standing in the kitchen, arms folded. It was right after the banker had left. He'd been trying to get her to put up the Imperial as collateral for a new loan.

Come into my parlor, Mama muttered, *said the spider to the fly. . . .*

"No," I told Shake. "You're not getting hold of me that easy." He'd already proved he could siphon off some of my power when I didn't want him to; what was he going to be able to grab if I opened all the way up to him?

"Callie, Callie." Shake's fist shook as he closed it. "You have to trust me."

"I don't *have* to do anything. You're nothing but a liar. You lied your way right in here!"

"Your landlady did that to herself. She wished I was a respectable man, someone who could make the rent, and so I was."

"When I met you back in Kansas, you said you were my papa!"

"I never did. I may have let you think I said it, but I never out-and-out said it myself. *We* are very good with words, Callie. We have to be in order to survive being near humans. But lies . . . that's different. Every lie is a new story, and that kind of creativity is difficult for us."

I shook my head. I didn't want to be talking about this, and I especially didn't want to think about how humans might be dangerous to fairies. That did not sit well at all. Neither did the idea that my inability to lie might be a consequence of my fairy half. "You just stay here, and don't do anything until I get back," I muttered.

"Am I allowed breakfast? After you made such a fuss in the hallway, it will look extremely odd if I don't put in an appearance."

I gritted my teeth. "Okay. But you go straight back to your room afterward."

"I am your obedient uncle and servant, Callie."

There weren't words enough in Webster's dictionary for how much I did not believe that "obedient" bit.

* * *

Shake and I were the last ones into the dining room. Mrs. Constantine was bustling around, laying out ham, eggs, biscuits and gravy, milk, and coffee so her guests could help themselves. Not that everybody ate all that. Miss Whitman just had a half grapefruit and coffee, because she was an actress and had to watch her figure, she said. Mr. and Mrs. Jones kept to toast and butter and maybe a slice of ham. Miss Patty, though, she ate everything that came her way. She was the personal assistant to Miss Gina Lords, who was starring in a new picture this summer, and Miss Lords sometimes kept her running around all day and didn't remember to give her time to get lunch.

"Good morning, good morning!" said Shake as we took our seats at the table. He proceeded to introduce himself to one and all as my uncle Lawrence LeRoux. He shook hands with Mr. Jones, bestowed a sweet smile on all the ladies, and settled down to enjoy Mrs. Constantine's breakfast.

I don't think I've ever seen anybody eat so much, not even Jack after we'd been on the bum for a week getting from Kansas City to Los Angeles. Shake didn't even have to help himself after the first biscuit. He just talked so much sugar to the ladies at the table, they were all batting their eyelashes at him and urging him to take another helping, even Mrs. Jones. Shake joked with Mr. Jones too and asked him about his work in dry goods and what he thought about California politics and the latest crisis in Europe. Before long, the whole table had decided Shake was a long-lost friend.

While Shake worked his way through a fourth ham slice, I couldn't seem to manage to do more than cut my biscuits into little pieces and push them around in puddles of gravy. I didn't dare look up. Somebody would see that the only person at the table who wasn't glad Shake had joined them was his niece.

"Callie." Mrs. Constantine came out of the kitchen, a fresh pot of coffee in her hand. "Your friend Jack is here. I put him in the parlor."

I threw down my napkin and ran out without an "excuse me" or a backward glance.

"Callie! I got great news!" shouted Jack as I came through the curtains. I glanced back over my shoulder, waving at him to keep it down. Jack just rolled his eyes and grinned at me. He sure didn't seem any the worse for our late night. In fact, he looked ready to wrestle bears or monsters, whichever he could find first. "I got a telephone call from Ivy Bright!"

"You did? How'd she know where to find you?"

It was pretty plain this wasn't anything close to the reaction he'd hoped for. Jack's face went sour as he shrugged. "Asked at the office, I guess. That doesn't matter. What matters is she wants to meet you."

"Me? What for?"

"Dopey! She wants to say thank you. I don't think she remembers exactly what happened, but she knows somebody tried to kidnap her and *we* saved her." He pulled himself up straight and proud, every inch the conquering hero. "This is your chance, Callie. If she likes you, she can get you a job on the lot, just like that." He snapped his fingers.

I thought about properly meeting the most famous girl in the country. Then I thought about how I'd kind of already met her in the first place. "I don't know, Jack. . . ."

"What don't you know? You need a job, don't you?" Jack's salary was having a hard time stretching to cover two rooms and two boards, plus streetcar fares and clothes and all the other little expenses that seemed to keep marching in.

"Mr. Robeson said he could get me a job," I reminded him.

"He said *maybe,* and he didn't say it was with the studio. It could be hotel work or something. That won't get you any closer to finding your folks, will it?"

Something in the way Jack said all that dug under my skin. He spent a lot of time acting like he knew more than I did. Sometimes it was true, but sometimes it wasn't. "Yeah, well, it might not be a good idea to have me hanging around where the Seelies can come calling anytime they darn well please." That stopped him in his tracks, and I admit I kind of enjoyed it. I would have enjoyed it more if the thought hadn't come out of my conversation with Shake. I did not want to start trusting what my uncle told me. "Besides," I said before Jack could start up again, "we got a problem."

I told Jack about Shake. All the excitement that had

been brimming over in him drained away. So did most of the color in his cheeks, which turned a kind of sick yellow shade. "You let him in here?"

"I didn't let him. He just sort of got in, and then once Mrs. Constantine saw him, there was nothing I could do."

"You coulda called the cops or . . . or something."

"And tell them what? He hasn't done anything."

"Except try to kill us!"

"Callie?" Right on cue, Shake pushed his way through the parlor curtain. I guess he'd gotten worried about how long I'd been gone. "Who's your young man?"

"You know good and well who I am, mister," Jack answered, soft and low. The friendly kid vanished. This was the tough Jack, the Jack who'd been a bootlegger, ridden the rails across the country, and even been on a chain gang. You didn't see this Jack a whole lot, and you really didn't want to.

"So I do." Shake smiled, all sly and secret, as he sat on the nearest sofa and crossed his ankles. "But you understand the importance of keeping up appearances, don't you? I wonder, what can you two have been talking about in here for so long? Callie's breakfast has gone stone cold."

"It's none of your business," snapped Jack. "You shouldn't even be here."

"Where else should I be?" Shake asked with a fake, patient smile that could have gotten a rise out of Mahatma Gandhi. "She's my niece, after all. Who else is going to take care of her? You?"

Jack's fist balled up. For a second I thought he was going to knock out a few more of Shake's teeth.

"Don't." I got in front of him. "He's trying to get to you." I turned around and walked over to Shake. I needed to show I wasn't afraid. It didn't matter who he was related to; he wasn't pushing me around. I leaned in close and whispered in Shake's ear, "You better get back to your room. You don't want Mrs. Constantine finding out what you really look like, do you?"

I straightened up. Shake was looking at me, first with his good eye, then with the scarred eye. I had no idea what he saw, but eventually he sighed and got to his feet.

"If you insist," Shake said. "Be careful today, Callie. I can't promise I'll be able to do much once the Seelie court gets hold of you as well."

I really didn't like the way he said that. It sounded too serious and too certain. At least my shivers waited until the curtain fell closed behind him before they started running up my spine.

"You've got to get away from him," said Jack behind me.

My shivers agreed with him, but that wasn't one of the choices any of us had right now. "He can help us. We don't know enough about the Seelies, or the Unseelies, or anybody. He knows everything about them."

"As if he'd ever tell us the truth."

"He's going to be after us anyway. He's mad at his folks and he wants to get back at them. He thinks he can use me to do it. So he's not going to do anything to get me too mad." Yet.

"I don't like it," Jack muttered. But I could tell he knew I was right. I decided not to tell him about my other idea, the one I'd had the night before. I might not have to use it, and if I didn't, then there was no point in giving him something else to get upset over.

"I don't like it either. But as long as he thinks he's got a chance to bring me round, he'll stay put, and at least we'll know where he is." I tried to smile at him, and kind of did. Jack blew out his cheeks and shoved his hands in his pockets.

"Okay, we'll play it your way. We better get going, though. Miss Bright's waiting to meet you."

Miss Bright? When'd that famous little screamer become *Miss* Bright to Jack? "I can't. I've got to meet Mr. Robeson at the Dunbar."

"You can meet him later. This is important."

"Why? She doesn't know anything, and she can't do anything. Mr. Robeson knows how to get around the Seelies."

"What do you mean, she can't do anything? She's a huge star! She can get you a job, Callie. Right on the lot. We know there's a fairy gate sitting smack under the Waterloo Bridge. Once you're set up, you can go through it, right into their country to find your parents. This is exactly what we came here to do!"

I opened my mouth and shut it again. He was right. The gate was there. I'd felt it last night. I'd been so caught up in worrying about Shake, I hadn't gotten anywhere near the idea that I could just go through the gate. Maybe this was why the fairies were in such an uproar about me. Maybe they didn't like the idea that I could just sneak in on them.

Where she goes, where she stays, where she stands, there shall the gates be closed. That prophecy had been chasing after me, with the Seelies and the Unseelies figuring they knew what it meant. Maybe it was time to make it mean what I wanted it to mean.

"It can't be that easy," I whispered.

"Course not," said Jack. "We'll figure the rest out once we're on the other side. Now come on. If Miss Bright gets mad, she won't want to help you, and we're back to having to try to sneak you past the guards again."

This all felt wrong, but I couldn't think how. I mean, Jack was right about the gate, and about how much Ivy Bright could help us if she wanted to. I could talk to Mr. Robeson later. Maybe I could even use Mrs. Constantine's telephone to leave a message at the Dunbar for him. It'd be all right. Mr. Robeson would understand once I'd had a chance to explain everything. Everything I could explain, anyway. He'd still help us. It'd be all right.

And I sure couldn't stay around here with nothing to keep my worried mind occupied. Not with Shake sitting in his room, smiling that patient smile and waiting for me to believe him just a little too much.

8

Nice Work If You Can Get It

This time, when we got off the trolley, Jack and I walked through the studio main gates, right under the archway with the carving of the roaring lion. We also had to get out of the way as an open-topped car roared past us and screeched to a halt by the double-width guard shack. The woman who leaned across to laugh with the guard looked familiar, and might even have been Katharine Hepburn, or Olivia de Havilland, or Jean Harlow. The urge to get nearer so I could stare properly took hold as strong as any magic spell. Fame will do that if you let it get too close.

"Mr. Holland? Miss LeRoux?"

I am not proud to admit that hearing someone call us made me jump and set my heart hammering.

"That's right." Jack put one hand on my arm to steady me.

A white man in a gray chauffeur's uniform tipped his

cap to us. If he noticed me trying not to be startled, he pretended he didn't. "I'm Sumner, Miss Bright's driver. Miss Bright would like to invite you to join her for breakfast at her bungalow. I have the car waiting for you." He gestured toward a long black Rolls-Royce. The silver lady hood ornament gleamed in the morning sun.

Jack and I raised our eyebrows at each other. Then Jack puffed out his chest and pulled on his most grown-up manner. "Of course. However, we do still need to sign in."

"Miss Bright has already taken care of that." Sumner pulled a pair of cardboard passes out of his pocket. "If you'll come with me?" He opened the door of the Rolls and bowed us inside.

The seat was soft as a featherbed, and the tinted windows dimmed the California sun, leaving the inside cool even though the day was heating up fast. If the Cadillac last night had politely cleared its throat as it moved, the Rolls purred with a deep and contented sound. Jack grinned and sat back like he owned the car and the studio. I wished I felt half as good. For me, being in that big, heavy car felt like being wrapped in cotton wool. I didn't like not being able to see the outside clearly through the darkened windows, or feel who passed by out there. They could be anybody at all—human or Seelies or Unseelies or Uncle Shake—and I couldn't tell.

This was a shame because it was probably the finest car ride I'd ever had in my life. Sumner drove so smoothly through the studio streets, it was like we were standing still while the world eased past us. I even found myself starting a fresh letter to Mama in my head.

Dear Mama: Guess what? Today we got to see Lot No. 1 at Metro-Goldwyn-Mayer. It's really different from Lot No. 2, more like a regular city. It's got office buildings, warehouses, and garages. It's even got street names, like First Avenue and Third Avenue and Main Street.

Nobody on this side of the studio grounds wore costumes or dragged cameras along. We were part of a whole stream of traffic just like we would be on a regular city street. Trucks and cars passed people heading into buildings with names such as Film Services or Production and Sound Department. But no matter how I tried, I couldn't relax. I felt like I was inside a set of boxes tucked one inside the other—us inside the car, inside the studio, inside the city. I couldn't help wondering how many more boxes down we were going to go, and how we were ever going to get out again.

Jack gave me a concerned glance, but I shook my head. I couldn't explain what was eating at me, and even if I could, I wasn't going to talk about it where a stranger could hear.

"Miss Bright has her own house right on the lot," Jack said by way of conversation, and, I think, to try to distract me.

"That's right, sir," said Sumner from the front seat. "It was given to her by the great comedienne Miss Marion Davies after she and Mr. Hearst moved over to Warner

Brothers. Miss Davies said she wanted to be sure Miss Bright had a real home, not just an apartment or hotel suite. And here we are."

Sumner pulled the long car into the driveway of that real home, right there on A Street. It was the very latest model of Los Angeles houses: two stories tall with beige stucco walls, arched windows, and that red bumpy tile roof that's supposed to be a Spanish style.

"Looks just like the movies," I murmured.

"You ain't seen nothin' yet." Jack grinned as Sumner came around to open the car door and bow us out. One short second later, the bungalow's front door banged open.

"You're here! Oh, I knew you'd come!"

The Ivy Bright of this morning was nothing like the pathetic little thing from last night. She'd gotten herself all cleaned up, put on a pink dotted-swiss dress, and tied her golden curls back in a matching ribbon. She grabbed me, hugged me, and planted a big kiss right on my cheek, every inch the bubbly girl she played in the movies. I didn't even have a chance to catch my breath, let alone say anything, before Ivy had me by the hand and was dragging me into the house and through the foyer to the sitting room.

"Mama, Mama!" she cried. "This is the girl I was telling you about, and this is Jack Holland—he works in the script department. Callie, Jack, this is my mama, Olive Brownlow."

"How do you do, Callie? Jack?" Mrs. Brownlow was fair-skinned and golden-haired, just like her daughter. Well, not just like. I had the feeling it took a lot of trips to the beauty salon to keep Mrs. Brownlow's bobbed hair that shade of yellow and that precisely waved. Her pale face was perfectly made up, and her peach-colored silk suit with coral trim had probably been tailor-made for her.

"I can't tell you how grateful I am to you for helping Ivy." Mrs. Brownlow gave me a soft, cold hand to shake, and I caught myself wondering if she'd been sick lately. Where Ivy's blue eyes sparkled with life, her mother's looked tired, even though it was just barely nine in the morning. She reminded me of somebody, but I didn't have a chance to think who, because just then a squared-off, dusky-skinned woman in a plain black dress and starched white apron stepped into the room.

"Excuse me, Mrs. Brownlow, but if she's to be on time for school, Miss Ivy needs to have her breakfast." The woman had one of those voices that let you know the owner regarded time as precious and wouldn't stand for any waste. This effect was helped by the way she peered at us over the rims of her thick-lensed glasses.

"Oh, of course, Mrs. Tully." Ivy's mama blinked at Mrs. Tully and then at us, as if she was digging deep for the proper words. "You'll have some too, won't you?"

I planned to say I'd already had mine, but Jack, as usual, got his words out first. "Yes, thank you, Mrs. Brownlow, Miss Bright. We'd love to."

"Isn't he just the sweetest!" Ivy clapped her hands. "You call me Ivy, silly. We're all going to be best friends!"

As if to prove it, she looped one arm through mine and one arm through Jack's and pulled us close together.

"I'll join you. . . ." Mrs. Brownlow got to her feet.

"Oh, but, Mama, you've got that meeting with Mr. Raymond in publicity, don't you?" Ivy said. "You were just telling me about it."

Mrs. Brownlow frowned, thinking hard. "Oh, yes. Of course. Mrs. Tully, have you seen my bag?"

"Here it is, ma'am." Mrs. Tully went to the hall table, picked up a little beaded purse that had been dyed to exactly match Mrs. Brownlow's suit, and handed it over along with a pair of white gloves. "Sumner will be waiting for you out front."

"Yes. Thank you. I'd forget my head if it wasn't screwed on my shoulders. Don't be late for school, Ivy."

"I won't, Mama." Ivy skipped over and planted a kiss on her mama's cheek. I watched Mrs. Brownlow leave and Mrs. Tully close the door behind her. Memory poked at me. It was trying to tell me something important, but Ivy was talking again.

"Mama has to meet with a lot of people. She manages my career." Ivy grabbed Jack's and my hands as she breezed past and pulled us into the dining room. A long table, complete with lace runner and silver candlesticks, stretched right down its middle. You could have sat a baker's dozen guests here and still had room in case any family dropped in at the last minute. This morning, only one end was set with blue willow pattern dishes, crystal glasses, and grapefruit halves in glass bowls. There was a funny wire rack in the middle with toast triangles stuck in it.

"Please sit down." Ivy sounded at least as grown-up as Jack. "Orange juice?"

"Yes, thank you," said Jack. I nodded. Ivy made a little gesture to Mrs. Tully, who came over and filled all our glasses. My stomach still felt kind of queasy, but I'd never had orange juice before and didn't want to miss my chance. It tasted sweet, tart, and bright all at the same time, and before I knew it, I'd finished the whole thing. Mrs. Tully gave me the fish-eye, but she filled my glass again. She was looking at my hair and how browned up my skin was. Mrs. Tully backed away to stand next to the big sideboard, but she didn't stop watching me from behind her horn-rimmed glasses. She saw. She knew. The brightest little star in Hollywood was sitting down to breakfast with a black girl, and Mrs. Tully most definitely did not approve. My spine stiffened right up. Who was she to be looking down her nose at me?

"I'm sorry there's not more food," Ivy was saying to Jack as she dug a spoon with a jaggedy tip into the big pink grapefruit. "I can only have grapefruit and toast in the mornings because I have to watch my figure, for the camera. They're awfully strict about my health," she added in an undertone. "Once I snuck a whole box of gingersnaps into my room. Tully about had a fit when she found the crumbs in my bed!"

Jack laughed like this was the funniest thing he'd ever heard, and Ivy giggled.

I drank some more orange juice. "Must be hard going to school and being in movies at the same time."

"Oh, no. The school's on the lot. Right next door, as a matter of fact. All the studio kids go there. Miss MacDonald, she's even stricter than Tully, so none of us get out of line." Ivy giggled again. I wondered what it was like to find every little thing so funny. "Where do you go to school, Callie?" she asked.

"I'm done with school." She didn't need to know I'd only gone for a couple of years back in Kansas before the dust storms closed the school, and the entire town of Slow Run, for good. Jack was rolling his eyes toward Ivy. I swallowed. The orange juice suddenly tasted sour. "Actually, I'm, uh, looking for work."

"You are?" cried Ivy. "Movie work? You're so pretty, I bet the camera loves you."

Me? *Pretty?* Nobody ever called me pretty. Maybe the giggling wasn't so bad after all. . . . I stopped that thought in its tracks. If I started letting Ivy Bright flatter me, I'd be looking as goofy as Jack before long.

"Um, no," I said. "Nothing like that. I worked at my mama's hotel before. I can clean and cook and—"

"Cook? You can cook?" She blinked those big blue eyes at me like I'd just said I could fly.

Jack jumped right in with both feet. "Callie's a terrific

cook! There's nothing in the world she can't make taste good. And her cakes! They're better'n anything you get in New York, or Paris even."

As if he'd know. But it was nice of him to say, anyhow.

"That's wonderful!" exclaimed Ivy, but then she frowned down at her grapefruit. "I'd love to be able to cook. Or do anything real."

"I'd love to be able to make millions of people like me," I said back.

"Oh, you're so sweet, Callie." That got me another big hug. This one almost tipped over both our chairs. "I just knew we'd be friends! And I know what we can do! You can come stay here and be my personal cook! Mama's been saying I shouldn't have to eat in the commissary with everybody else, hasn't she, Tully? She says it's important for my health and complexion that all my meals are made specially."

"Yes, Miss Ivy," agreed Mrs. Tully from her post by the sideboard. "That's exactly what she said to Mr. Mayer only yesterday."

"There! You see? You'll do it, won't you?" Ivy grabbed both my hands. "I mean, we'll say you're my cook, but really, you'll be my friend. We can talk about . . . well, about *everything*. I've never had a real friend before. Just the other girls in the pictures, and they always move away or get fired or something. Even Miss Davies." Ivy's lip trembled.

I knew about being the one left behind. I'd seen a whole

town pack up and leave me and my mama stuck where we were. And Ivy had every right to be scared after what had happened to her last night. She didn't have magic of her own, or anybody like Jack to stand up with her. She at least deserved to know what was going on, but we sure couldn't talk about it with Mrs. Tully and her evil eye hanging around.

Mrs. Tully wasn't the only one tossing me hard looks. Jack rolled his eyes, bobbed his head, and did everything short of sending up a signal flag to say I should agree to Ivy's plan. The problem was, I didn't want to, or at least the goose bumps that were all standing up on the back of my neck didn't.

"I, um . . . I'm sorry, I need to talk to Jack for a second." I didn't wait for an answer. I just grabbed Jack's hand and dragged him out into the front garden with its masses of red and orange flowers.

"We're in!" I'd never heard anybody crow and whisper at the same time, but Jack managed it somehow. "I knew she'd help!"

"Jack, I don't know about this. . . ."

"What's the matter? You need a job, and you need to be in here. This is perfect."

I had an answer. It was scratching at the edges of my thoughts, but I couldn't get it to come any closer. "I don't think Mrs. Tully likes me," I said lamely.

"So what? She doesn't have to like you. Besides, she's just the housekeeper."

That scratching in the back of my head got a little harder. It wasn't like Jack to dismiss somebody so fast. Especially on account of their job.

"I'll have to tell Shake. And Mr. Robeson," I said.

"Oh, I guess."

"What do you mean, you *guess?*" Jack actually sounded sulky, and I couldn't for the life of me figure out why. What the heck was wrong with having somebody around who could actually help for a change? Somebody we could trust?

"I just don't like the idea of them knowing too much about Miss Bright, that's all." Jack kicked at a loose stone. It rattled across the courtyard and bounced into the flower bed. "I mean, she's already had a bad time. She shouldn't be getting mixed up in any more fairy business. She might get hurt."

"Mr. Robeson's not going to hurt her! He's helping us!"

"Are you sure?" he shot back. "Mr. Robeson brought those Seelies there in the first place, and he didn't save Ivy, *we* did. We would've gotten out of the rest of it just fine without him."

"What is the matter with you, Jack?"

"What's the matter with *you?*" he shot back. "The last time you went and trusted somebody who just walked up to help us, you nearly got killed!"

So that was it. This was about Shake. I wanted to shout at Jack that this wasn't like that other time and he didn't understand anything. Except he did. He'd been there with me. And that wasn't all. I did have Shake stashed back at the boardinghouse, and I'd come here without being a hundred percent sure he'd stay put. Could I really complain it was Jack who didn't take the situation seriously enough?

Besides, what if he was right? What if Mr. Robeson was just another pretty distraction from the Seelies, a way to get in good with us so they could stab us in the back later?

Jack stepped close. He put his hand on my shoulder. The grown-up mask was gone. This was just Jack. He'd run with me, fought for me, and stuck by me through dust and nightmare and California sun. "You do what you've got to, Callie, but be careful. We don't know anything about anybody here."

I nodded, but something inside me was breaking into pieces. Before I could find any more words, the bungalow door eased open and Ivy peeked out, blinking.

"Well? Will you do it?" she whispered. "Please say you will, Callie."

I didn't want to. Something was not right about this place. I didn't like the way I felt cold standing under the California sun, or the way the heavy, sweet smell of the roses and bougainvillea was getting in and smothering the doubts scratching at the back of my head. I didn't like the way Jack was talking, or Mrs. Brownlow's soft hands and vague eyes. I really didn't like how much was coming at us and how fast it was moving.

I looked from Ivy to Jack. Now he looked worried, and I didn't like that any better. I tried to remind myself that we needed to be here. We'd found a gate into fairy country, which was what we'd come all this way for. And it was in the golden mountains of the west, right where we'd been told to look. My parents were somewhere on the other side of that gate, in the house of St. Simon where no saint ever came. If I turned down Ivy Bright, we'd have to start all over again looking for another gate, if there even was one anywhere nearby. Either that or I'd have to do something really risky, like try to get Shake to help me find one, and I couldn't trust him to help me find a lost safety pin.

I squared my shoulders and managed a smile. "Sure. I'd be glad to come cook for you, if it's okay with your mother and everything."

"Mama will love the idea, don't worry about that! And I'll take care of everything with the studio. Oh, this is going to be perfect! I'm so excited!" Ivy ran out into the garden to hug me again, and I felt my ribs start to give way. This time it was Mrs. Tully who saved me.

"It's time for school, Miss Ivy," the housekeeper said from the doorway.

"Oops." Ivy giggled. "I'm sorry, Callie, Jack. You'll be all right on your own, won't you?"

"We'll be fine," Jack told her. "I've got to get to work anyhow."

"Oh, that's right! I'll probably see you on the set later. Let me get my hat. Tully will show you your room, Callie, won't you, Tully? You can move in, and we'll see each other after my shoot this afternoon. Then we'll really talk!"

Room? I was blinking after her and starting to wonder if this was how Mrs. Brownlow had gotten that permanently vague look on her face. Jack stepped up close to me so his arm brushed against my shoulder.

"Something's not right here, Callie," he whispered. "It's more than the gate and . . . and what happened last night. We've got to find out what."

Now that sounded like the Jack I'd come so far with. Some of the worries crowding inside me eased up. Before I could answer him, though, Ivy Bright came running back out. She pushed straight past Mrs. Tully as she planted a floppy-brimmed white hat over her curls. With one last giggle, Ivy looped her arm through Jack's. He looked startled, then he looked worried, but while I watched, he smoothed the worry away and turned his biggest, best smile on Ivy Bright. I knew what he was thinking. He was thinking he'd have her eating out of his hand inside five minutes. He just might too.

The gate clanged shut behind Jack and Ivy, leaving me standing alone with Mrs. Tully and her sharp eyes. She had a long nose as well, and she looked all the way down it to where I stood trying not to fidget.

"Well, come on." Mrs. Tully turned on her heel and headed back into the house.

"I . . . um . . ." I hurried to follow her. "I wasn't planning on staying here, Mrs. Tully. . . ."

"It doesn't matter what you were planning." Mrs. Tully's

square heels clacked on the tile floor. "You're here now and you might as well make yourself useful. But I warn you." She pointed one finger straight at me. It was as long and sharp as her nose, and I had the really strong urge to back away. "Miss Ivy's health and appearance are very important to the studio. Your job here will be the same as the rest of ours—to make sure Ivy Bright remains in good spirits and ready to work. Is that understood?"

"Yes, ma'am," I said, trying to keep my voice from going sulky. This woman had the power to make my life unpleasant. She might even be able to get Mrs. Brownlow to fire me before I'd really been hired. I could not start out this business by getting her any more set up against me.

"You can have the attic room. Come along."

I went along. Ivy Bright's bungalow was a lot bigger than it looked from the front. Mrs. Tully led me up a broad, curving staircase and down a central hall with stucco walls, brick-red tile, and small wooden tables covered with little silver and gold knickknacks. There were all kinds of fancy paintings on the walls too, including three portraits of Ivy in different costumes I recognized from her movies. Mrs. Tully unlocked the last door at the end of the hall, revealing another staircase. This one was steeper, narrower, darker, and a lot stuffier. I followed Mrs. Tully up, thinking about bare boards and spiderwebs and piles of old junk—all the stuff you find in attics in the movies.

That was when I got my next surprise, and for a change,

it wasn't anything bad. The attic of Ivy Bright's bungalow really was a guest room. There was a pretty little bed with a carved headboard and a white spread. The walls were decorated with Mexican scarves, and Indian rugs covered the floor. The dresser, wardrobe, and rolltop desk all matched the bed. A telephone waited on the nightstand, and round windows like portholes had been opened to let the breeze in. It even had its own bathroom, with a bathtub.

Mrs. Tully saw my jaw flap open and lifted that long nose. "We do not have anything second-best here," she announced.

"No, ma'am. Um . . . can I . . . can I use that telephone?"

She looked down at me like I'd just forgotten to wipe my feet. "All calls go through the studio switchboard. So be careful what you say on the line. Whether they are supposed to or not, the operators listen. We most emphatically do not want gossip spread concerning Miss Ivy. Is that understood?"

"Yes, ma'am."

"You'll want to see the kitchen now." It was not a question, and Mrs. Tully was already marching down the stairs.

Not having anything second-best applied to the kitchen as much as it did to the guest room. The counters were solid silver. I'd read about silver counters in a "Homes of the Celebrities" article in *Movie Fan* magazine, but I'd never in a million years thought I'd see one for myself. Copper pots and pans hung from a rack overhead. There was an electric refrigerator instead of an icebox, and yet another telephone hung on the wall. The stove looked so brand-new, I wondered if it had ever been used at all. In fact, everything in there was so new, it felt like it had been magicked into existence just that morning, and just for me.

I tossed that idea on the heap with all the other unpleasant thoughts I'd been collecting since I got out of bed.

"Your duties will include the marketing and cleaning. All bills will be submitted to me for approval." Mrs. Tully stationed herself in the doorway like she thought I might make a run for it. "Miss Bright always dines at six. Lateness will not be tolerated. Is that understood?"

And that was the last straw. I had not made it this far just to have some dime-store queen of the housekeepers try to put me in my place.

I turned around and planted my hands on my hips. "Listen, I don't know what you think I'm after, but I got enough problems without trying to break into pictures or be anybody's new best friend. I'm taking this job because I need a job. Is *that* understood?"

"*Well.*" I wouldn't have figured Mrs. Tully could have thrown her squared-off shoulders back any further, but she managed. Just as I was wondering how to tell Jack I'd set the world's record for shortest time on the job, her thin mouth bent into an actual smile. "You've got some starch in your craw. You'd better be careful how you use it, Miss Callie.

You and I don't mean *that* around here." She snapped her fingers hard. "As long as that girl makes money for Mr. Mayer, if she takes it into her head she doesn't like either one of us, we'll be gone before you can say 'knife.' You see how it is?"

"Oh, yes, ma'am. I got that one all figured out."

"Good." Mrs. Tully cocked her head, and I got the impression she was really seeing me for the first time since I'd walked into the house. "You might just do after all, if you can keep one more thing in mind."

"And what's that?"

Mrs. Tully moved closer, and I swallowed as the cloud of soap and talcum powder scent wrapped around me. "Mrs. Brownlow," Mrs. Tully said softly and urgently, like she was afraid someone might hear. "Mrs. Brownlow has a delicate and nervous disposition. Miss Ivy's being constantly in the public eye has been very difficult for her. You must not under any circumstances upset her or pay attention if she says something a little odd. If she seems to become agitated in any way while she's with you, you come tell me, so I can call the studio doctor. Do you understand?"

I didn't, but it didn't matter. There was only one way I was going to answer. "Yes, ma'am."

Mrs. Tully let out a long breath that might just have been a sigh of relief. "Very well. As soon as Sumner comes back, he'll take you to your hotel so you can pack your things."

She clacked out of that shiny new kitchen and I

slumped against the counter. Questions flooded around me until I was neck deep in them. Mrs. Tully was so clear about the importance of Ivy Bright, about Miss Bright's health and spirits and how important she was to the studio. So where had Mrs. Tully been when Ivy was hauled off by Ruth Markham? Come to that, where had Mrs. Brownlow been? She was managing Ivy's career in addition to being her mama. How'd someone with a nervous disposition like that let her girl out of her sight after dark? My mama'd had a nervous disposition too, and my mama'd never have done anything so careless.

There was something fishy going on in this house, and I had plunked myself right down into the middle of it. I had to find a way to straighten out everything that had happened and get a good look at it. If I didn't, I was never going to figure out what I should really be doing. Including what I was going to tell Mr. Robeson. I hoped he wasn't waiting for me. I hoped he wasn't angry at me for not turning up like I said I would. I tried to remember how right Jack had been about being fooled by someone who seemed to be helping us, but I couldn't get my heart into it. This wasn't the same. I couldn't have explained how, but it just wasn't.

A breeze swirled through the checked curtains; it smelled of green things and hot concrete. I felt a million miles away from the world, and it was not a good feeling. In this house in the middle of this city that was busy cranking out money and movies, I was alone.

"Dear Mama," I whispered under my breath. "I'll be there soon, Mama. We'll find a way." I wrapped my mind around those words and held on tight. Because if I forgot what I was really doing here, I'd be worse than alone. I'd be lost.

9

Just a Simple Walk

"Well, well, a job already." Shake leaned against the lop-sided dresser and watched me pack my battered case. "You do work fast."

I shrugged. I needed to get this done. Mr. Sumner was waiting for me out front, fighting a losing battle to keep the neighborhood kids from climbing all over the car's fenders. Except I didn't just need to pack up what few things I owned. I needed to figure out what I was going to do about Shake. Mrs. Constantine was only letting him stay because we were family. The long list of people she didn't let rooms to included single men, and there wasn't enough magic in the Unseelie court to make her think she'd changed her rules. I couldn't exactly turn up back at Ivy Bright's bungalow with my fairy uncle in tow either, but I just as sure couldn't leave him out here to do as he pleased.

"Jack says it's perfect." I folded up my nightgown and laid it down next to my old yellow dress.

"Ah, yes." Shake nodded solemnly. "The young Mr. Holland."

"What about him?" I snapped, and Shake had the nerve to look startled.

"Did I say anything about him?"

"You wanted to. Jack's my friend and he's saved my life, unlike *some* people," I added, just in case he didn't get the whole point. "You leave him alone."

"I'd be glad to, but since you insist on keeping company with him, I don't think I can."

All the anger and worry I'd been trying to keep ahead of caught up with my good sense and shot right past it. "You lay a finger on Jack—you so much as look at him funny—and so help me . . . !"

"All right, all right, Callie. Calm down." Shake spread his crooked hands. "I won't do anything to hurt your Mr. Holland."

Which might have been a fine answer coming from an ordinary person, but this was Shake talking to me. "Promise," I said.

That one word took all the relaxation out of his skinny frame. He stiffened, as though he'd just heard an alarm bell ring. "I've got no reason to hurt him, Callie, or you."

"Oh, no. That's you trying to change the subject." And I was not falling for it this time. *"Promise."*

Shake went quiet for a long, slow minute. The longer he

stayed quiet, the farther the lid drooped over his white eye, and all at once he looked tired and old, older than anybody had a right to look. "Very well. I promise to take no action that will hurt your Mr. Holland."

"Okay." I pulled the silk stockings I'd ruined off the back of the room's one battered chair. With a twinge of guilt at the waste, I wadded them up and threw them into the trash basket. There'd be other stockings someday, once I got out of this mess. Problem was, I didn't feel like I was any closer to getting out of it. I looked around for something else to pack, but there wasn't anything.

Shake had settled onto the edge of the chair. His back and shoulders were bowed and his broken hands dangled between his knees. He looked the way he had out on the street: like a bum without home or hope. *It's for show,* I tried to tell myself. But I couldn't stop seeing the scar on his face or his broken fingers. Those were real things. Something deep inside me said the exhaustion and hunger that drew his skin tight across the bones of his face were real too.

"I wish you'd decide to trust me," he whispered. "I really do want to help you."

"Then how about a straight answer? If you haven't got any magic anymore, how come you found me before anybody else could?"

Shake turned his head back and forth, looking at me with his amber starlit eye, and then with his milk-white scarred eye. After he'd taken a good long look, he nodded.

"All right, a straight answer. I may not be able to cast enchantment now, but not even the king and queen could change my nature. I knew what you were wishing for most, and I followed that wish."

"How'd you know what I wish?"

"I felt it in you when we met." A proud little grin across Shake's tired, hungry face. It made me think of Jack when he'd just been especially clever, and I wished I could bury that thought somewhere else. "It took a while for me to understand you really do want to free your parents, not just your father but your mother too. The king and queen"— he jerked his chin toward the door, as if they waited in the hall—"never worked it out. I could have told them, of course, but they weren't going to listen to me." His voice went soft under the weight of anger and memory, and that milk-white eye glittered as bright as the one full of starlight. For a moment I felt something sharp under my own eye, like a knife point, and I winced. "They're trying to sniff out your ambition, grab hold of the texture of your scheming." Shake's little grin spread and grew into a full-blown smile, and that smile had nothing to do with any polite feeling. "They don't know to look for your love."

"Why wouldn't they figure I love my parents?"

"Love is not natural to us, Callie," said Shake. "Not the deep, lasting love that humans know. Ordinarily, love for us comes slow and passes quick, like ripples on a pond."

Cold trickled down my spine. I told myself Shake's "us" didn't really include me. I was only half Unseelie. I had just as much human in me. Of course I loved my parents. It didn't matter that sometimes the only thing keeping me from turning around was that I had nowhere to turn to. That was just on bad days, when things got hungry, or lonesome, or just plain hard. It didn't count.

"Your grandparents, my parents, think you want to be a princess, Callie." Shake's words poked at me, searching out a soft spot. "That's the only reason they can understand for what you're doing. They believe you want to take their place on the Midnight Throne and that you don't intend to wait for them to make way for you."

That yanked me right out of my private worries, and I was glad to go. "The king and queen think I want to *kill* them?"

"Can you blame them? Especially after you went and set fire to their earthly palace and summoned a train to run over the Kansas City gate."

"The train was an accident," I muttered.

"You've got a way of creating really big accidents, niece Callie." Shake chuckled. "They've got a name for you around the Midnight Throne now, you know. You're not the Prophecy Girl anymore. They call you the Bad Luck Girl."

Bad Luck Girl. Those words didn't just poke; they sank straight in. Amerda had called me that, and I'd been able to let it go past. But it was different when Shake said it. It hit too close to home.

I'd always been afraid I was a jinx. I never talked about

it, not with Jack, not with anybody, but I'd always felt it. When I got near people, bad things happened. If it wasn't for me, Mama wouldn't be kidnapped. If it wasn't for me, Jack wouldn't be in danger all the time. Mrs. Constantine took me in, and now she was being magicked into believing whatever Shake wanted, whatever I wanted. Shimmy'd died because she'd tried to catch me and then help me.

I had a lot of experience not thinking about things, and I used it now. I needed something to distract me, and it needed to be something big. I made myself look at Shake. He was in the mood to talk about family, but there was only one person out of all my Unseelie relations I really wanted to know about.

"What was . . . what is my father like?"

"Your father?" Shake repeated slowly. He leaned back on that rickety chair and crossed his legs, making a great show of thinking hard. "Your father was different from the rest of us," he said. "We all like humans, of course, but he was enthralled by your kind. He spent as much time in your world as he did in ours. I did try to warn our parents that he was absorbing much more than music to bring home."

"Did he . . ." I bit my lip.

"Did he what?"

I shook my head and snapped the catches on my case shut. I was *not* asking this question.

As it turned out, I didn't have to. "You want to know if he loved your mother," my uncle whispered. "You want to know if he even *could*. Isn't that it?"

"Yes." Tears pricked, as bright and sharp as the anger.

"Look at me, Callie."

I did look at him, right in the mismatched eyes.

"I said that *ordinarily,* love for us is fleeting. Your father was never ordinary. He did love your mother. Our parents couldn't say or do anything to change it, and believe me, they tried every trick in their book. He was perfectly prepared to give up everything to be with her."

I believed him. Maybe it was just because I wanted so bad for what he said to be true, but I did believe.

"What . . . what's his real name? Mama called him Daniel, but that can't be it."

"Oh, now, Callie, you know with us that's a very serious question."

"I know. I also know you keep saying you want me to trust you."

Shake didn't speak for a long time after that. Finally he said, "You understand I am putting him in your hands if I tell you. You could well be used against him."

"I know your name," I reminded him.

There was another long pause as he thought that one over. "Donchail," Shake whispered at last.

Now that I had the name, I knew I'd never lose it. My father was Donchail deMinuit, and he loved my mother.

"Thank you," I said, and I really meant it. For the first time he'd given me something I could hold on to. Maybe it wasn't much, but it was lots better than the aching nothing I'd had so far.

Shake nodded once, accepting the words. His starlit eye narrowed, and my insides set about tying themselves into sailor's knots.

"You found something in there." Shake jerked his chin toward the window this time. He meant the studio. "What is it?"

"I don't know," I mumbled. "Maybe nothing."

"Callie, Callie." Shake leaned closer. "I just gave you something of great value, and this is how you pay me back?"

"This ain't about paying back."

"Isn't it?" He was giving me his smile again, the one that looked so clever and so similar to one of Jack's. It was creepy and wrong, and he was doing it on purpose. I knuckled my eyes. I had so much I needed to hold on to. I had to figure out what to do with Shake, and I had to get back to the studio so I could find out what was going on around Ivy Bright, and I had to find my way through the gate to my parents. But my head was too tired to keep its grip on even one of those things. I needed time—time to sleep and time to think—but there just wasn't any.

"There is, though," answered Shake.

"What are you talking about?" But I already knew. I'd been wishing for time, and he'd felt it.

Shake chuckled again. "Poor Callie. She needs so much, but she doesn't even know what she's got. Stop pretending you're human, little niece of mine. You are a queen-in-waiting among the Unseelies. You can have all the time you need."

"I don't understand."

"You're tired, Callie. You need to rest. Open yourself a gate and step outside, and stay for as long as you want."

I stared at him. I knew my magic could open a gate in time. I'd once opened a window that looked back a hundred or so years. But I'd never thought about being able to get past time altogether.

"How?" I probably should have just told him to be quiet, but I had to admit, he had my curiosity going.

"Let me show you."

"You can't open gates." That was supposed to be something only I could do, which was what all the fuss was about in the first place.

"But you're going to let me inside, and then I'll be able to show you how your power works."

This was not good. In fact, this was really bad. I'd refused this idea before, and I should do it again this time, no matter how tired I was, no matter how badly I needed to understand my magic. "You just want something from me," I said, but my voice wasn't anything like as strong as it should have been.

"Of course I do. That doesn't mean I can't teach you how to use your powers as well."

I wished I wasn't alone. I wanted Mr. Robeson there, or Jack. I needed an anchor to keep me tied to the memory of all that Shake had done to us. The problem was, I wanted more than that. I hated not knowing about my magic. It felt like a bad dog on a short chain inside me. I didn't have any real idea what it was going to do when I let it off that leash. I really was tired too, all the way from the roots of my hair to the soles of my feet. The thought of having time enough to sleep sounded sweeter than anything I'd heard in days. All those things got together and ganged up on the rest of my sense.

"Okay," I said to Shake. "Show me."

My uncle smiled until his mismatched eyes twinkled. He held out his crooked hand. It was still cool and weak. If I squeezed even a little, I'd break those bones all over again. That nasty idea didn't linger long, however, because something else was happening. Something new pricked my mind and started worming its way into my veins, down deep into my blood. Not something, I realized. Someone.

Walk with me, niece. Let me show you your true world.

This person inside my head wasn't any broken bum called Shake. This was my uncle Lorcan deMinuit, a scion of the Midnight Throne. I was finally hearing his true voice, the voice that could call up magic as easily as whistling and twist it into any shape required. I had a voice like that inside me, as soon as I was ready to use it.

My uncle leaned lightly against my thoughts. He made them shift, slowly, so I could feel the change and follow it. One move at a time, we found the key in the pocket of my magic. We brought it out and set it into the lock of the world. I turned it, we turned it, and the world twisted around us. Lorcan tugged on my hand and on my thoughts. Together we moved. We stepped sideways, turned in place and rounded a corner, and stepped down. My mouth went dry and my ears popped. Everything shifted and blurred. I couldn't tell if we'd really moved or not, because I couldn't see anything. Then I could see too much.

Shake and I still stood in that dingy boardinghouse room, but now I could see under it and through it. I could see the stained plaster walls, but also the lath and frame beneath them. I could see the boards that frame used to be, and the logs the boards used to be, and the trees the logs used to be. I could see the street, and the dirt roadbed underneath it and the blank dry ground under that—all the states of existence for this single place, all stuffed one inside the other.

My mouth wouldn't move, but my thoughts still shaped the question. *What is this?*

We've moved betwixt and between. I felt the smile in Shake's silent words. *You've opened a gate from the human world, and now we are between all worlds.*

I didn't like this. Nothing felt solid or remotely real. I couldn't even feel the floor beneath my shoes. People flickered in and out of my vision like fireflies. I didn't dare look up to see all the skies shifting overhead. *Seeing* didn't even seem the right word for what I was doing. The world came straight in through my skin. I knew the texture of the path we'd traveled to get here, and how the places where the motion was the fastest were warmer than the places where the states of being were stuffed most tightly together. Slowly, fear bled away, to be replaced by something close to excitement.

What's that? I asked, looking toward a patch of shadow. That shadow was neither flickering with motion nor stuffed tight with different states of being. It was something different.

What? came Shake's answer. *Show me, niece.*

There. I tried to focus on it. It felt warm to the touch of my thoughts and magic, like a stone lying in the summer sun.

Shake took hold of those ideas and turned them over to get a better look.

That's one of the thin places.

A thin place? It didn't feel thin, or like a place. It felt more solid than anything else around me. It felt loose too, like I could wrap my hand around it, lift it up, and move it aside.

The mortal and fairy worlds are in constant motion. They rub against each other, and sometimes they rub each other thin. Sometimes a hole is worn between them, creating a natural gate that anyone can pass through. Some of these holes heal over quickly; others last a long time and are seized by one court or the other.

A picture of the Fairyland amusement park, where I'd first met my grandparents, formed in my mind, and I knew it had come from my uncle's thoughts. I countered with a picture of the Waterloo Bridge, and Rougarou crawling out from underneath. I felt him agree.

You can't see this hole, though?

No. I can't shape it either. But you could.

How?

How do we do anything? Reach out for it. Wish for it. Try, niece.

He was pushing me, almost daring me. Maybe I should have hesitated, but I wanted to understand, and here was a chance. Things that had been buried deep bubbled up to the surface. I wouldn't have to search for a way to power my magic. I wouldn't need music or wishes or strong feeling. Here I was the magic and it was me. I'd left the human on the other side of the open gate. All I had to do was reach out to that new piece of warmth and stillness I'd found. It was a hole and it was a door, and it led to the outside. I reached for the key, just as Lorcan had showed me, and held the key toward the lock. If I'd been in my regular human self, I'd have been taking a deep breath. I set lock and key together and made them twist. Easy as breathing, I felt the gate open wide, until I was looking out from betwixt and between to a whole new world.

A city waited on the other side of my gate. Its air wrapped around us, silent, heavy, and dense, but also as warm as the welcome of your best friend and filled with all the good scents there were. Golden trees spread their branches over towers of obsidian and silver. No stars burned overhead and no sun, only a blank indigo sky. But it wasn't dark at all. The whole world—the ground, the trees, the blossoms, even the stones—shone from the inside out with sweet golden light. I knew that light. I'd seen it before, but I couldn't remember when. It grabbed hold of me the way the sound of my father's name had. I wanted to melt into it, take it into myself, and become part of it at the same time. I stepped closer, and my uncle followed right behind.

Where is this?

Can't you guess, Callie? Uncle Lorcan's laugh sparkled through me. *It's our home.*

A wall stretched right up against the gate. It was about as high as my waist and its stones shimmered with the same golden light as the trees and the gleaming black towers. Vines twisted around and between the stones, shining green, gold, ruby, and emerald. As a fence, it didn't look like much. I could climb right over it. I didn't have to just see home; I could be home.

Then one of that wall's shining stones stretched and shivered. The twisted vine around it stretched too. There was a sharp pop and the stone opened a single eye, cold and clay-colored.

"Who's that?" The stone crawled out of the wall and squatted right in front of us, looking like a bullfrog with vines for legs and crooked arms. "Who comes knocking at my door?"

10

Then We Must Part

"Who's that?" the stone repeated. Its tongue ground against its teeth as it spoke. "Who's that come sneaking?"

Pop, pop, pop. The other stones jammed together in the wall opened their eyes. They were all the same cold clay color, and they all had the same long twisted limbs and grinding teeth and tongues.

"Who? Who?" They grated as they heaved themselves toward us. "Who? Who?"

"Shake . . ." I backed up.

But Shake stayed right where he was, and his amber eye flashed. I mean it really flashed, like someone had struck a match inside him. Now I knew why the golden light in this place looked so familiar. This was the light the fairies carried inside them, even when they came to the human world.

"Down, all of you!" my uncle shouted. "Down before the heir!"

The frog stones froze, except for their eyes. Those gray clay eyes all swiveled toward me. I felt their gaze like hail dropping against my skin.

"Her," said the first one.

"Her, her, her, her," echoed all the others. Their recognition hit as hard as their gaze did, as hard as their words did.

"Down!" Shake's order cracked over that flock of frog stones. His will pressed against them, forcing them backward until they hunkered down into their hollows. But they didn't go easily, and I could tell they didn't want to stay.

"Quickly now. I won't be able to hold them for long." Shake pushed me forward.

This time, though, I found the sense to dodge sideways. "Are you nuts? I'm not going in there!" The stones rumbled and strained. They ground their teeth together and pushed against Shake's commands. I could feel the hatred welling out of them, the way I felt their stares and their words.

"You're not going to get another chance like this, Callie. There are those here who will help us both."

"Help us do what?"

Shake rolled his one good eye in exasperation. "You want to free your parents? So do I. But we can't do it alone. Come on. I can take you to my friends." He reached for me again, but I yanked my hand away.

"You didn't say anything about this."

"I wasn't sure we'd find a thin place. There's no time to argue. Come with me, now."

My uncle was grabbing for my thoughts the way he was grabbing for my hand. He wanted to knot my wishes up with his. The problem was, the closer he pulled me, the better I could see what was going on inside him. I saw that Lorcan was scared. He was seeing faces—people made of sticks and twigs, or drops of water and pure wind. He saw animals with human faces and humans with horns and tails like Halloween devils and shining, tall, perfect people carrying bronze spears. He'd promised all these people he'd bring me back. He'd promised them power if he got to the Midnight Throne. That was how he'd got out into the human world. He hadn't been cast out at all. He'd escaped from wherever my grandparents had him jailed. All these people had helped him get free, in exchange for that promise.

Now he was stuck. Because we can't break our promises.

"You hoped we would find a thin place," I said slowly. "You brought me here on purpose."

"All right, yes. It doesn't change anything. There's help for us here, but you have to go *now*."

But while Shake was trying to tighten his grip, his hold on the frog stones slipped—not much, but enough.

"Her, her, her, her." The stones opened their eyes again, *pop, pop, pop,* their words and their eager anger going off like firecrackers, sending out sparks. "Send the word. Spread the word. It's her, her, her, and she's with him. Him, him, *him!*"

From root to branch and stone to stone, the warning

traveled like a signal down a telephone wire. Everything in this whole world that had its own little mind and thought and spirit—which was just about everything—was waking up. All those minds turned toward Lorcan . . . and me. None of them was happy, but all of them were hungry.

"Close the gate!" Lorcan shouted. "Close it!"

The stones bounded forward, shouting and hating. I scrabbled at the gate's edges, struggling to hook my magic around them. But the stones had jammed themselves into the gate. They were hungry and greedy. They wanted to get through, to see what was on the other side, to grab some of it up and take it for themselves. If they succeeded, if they got us, the king and queen might let them keep little pieces of us and anything else they scooped up from the other side of the gate, so they could change, grow, become new and stronger things. . . .

The first of the stones heaved itself toward me, tendrils reaching, teeth bared. I screamed and jumped back, but not fast enough. Twisting gold fingers tangled around my wrist, ice cold and steel strong.

Lorcan swore. He grabbed hold of the frog stone's fingers, and I felt a burst of magic. The stone screamed, and its fingers snapped. Shake howled with pain and effort as he caught me around the waist and hauled me off my feet, across the threshold, and into the betwixt and between.

Panic and anger knotted together inside me. I reached deep and held tight, pulled and twisted. The stones cried out. They wept and strained, but the world closed in front of them, and they were gone and it was just betwixt and between flickering around me and Lorcan.

And while I was standing there getting my head around the fact that I'd just almost gotten killed by a herd of living stones, Lorcan smiled.

Well, that was closer than I'd hoped.

I knew it! I knew you did that on purpose!

But all the outrage I could muster slid right off him. *I wanted to bring us help, and I hoped that when you saw your home you would be drawn to it.*

You tried to trick me! Again!

How did I trick you? You wanted time; I've given it to you. You wanted to know how your powers work; I've showed you.

I wanted time to sleep!

Then sleep. You know I will not let anything hurt you. I can't. I've made promises, niece, and you're a part of them.

I'm supposed to trust you after what you just did?

I did nothing. You did that to yourself. Sleep as long as you like. When you wake up, we step back through your gate. His thoughts pointed and mine followed. *Or when you've had the chance to think better of it, you will open another gate, and I will take you to meet my friends.*

He wasn't going to stop. He'd bully, cheat, trick, and coax until he got me there. The worst part was, part of me wanted to just give in and do what he said. I wanted to see more of the Unseelie world beneath its indigo sky. I wanted to find out if my uncle really had friends who could help me find my parents. But I couldn't do it. I didn't dare. Lorcan had been straight about exactly one thing since I'd asked him to show me my own magic: I did, in fact, know just what he was. I hadn't wanted to believe it. Now I had to do something about him before he dug his hooks in any deeper. The truly frightening part was, I had a plan.

I made the thoughts as small and whispery as I could. *How am I going to fall asleep here?*

Little niece, little niece, you know we can give such gifts to one another.

He was telling me he could put me to sleep. I felt him urging me to trust him. I'd sleep sweet and easy, and when I woke up, he'd show me how to walk to whatever world I wanted to reach, just like he'd shown me how to open the gate to betwixt and between, and to the Unseelie world beyond. We were family. I could trust him. I had to trust him. Everything depended on it.

We can send each other to sleep? I faced my uncle. *Really?*

Truly. He smiled indulgently. He thought his little niece was finally coming around, and maybe he was right.

Okay. I took a deep breath, and I reached down into my magic, where Lorcan was already waiting. *Go to sleep, Uncle.*

Both his eyes flew wide. He tried to pull away, but he was too late. I knew what sleep felt like—the warmth and the slow drift into comfortable darkness. I raised all of that and passed it over to Lorcan. Because he was already inside my blood and bone, he had no chance to get away.

"Oh, very good," Lorcan breathed. "Didn't think you had it in . . ."

His eyes closed, and he was snoring, sound asleep in a place outside of time.

I turned toward the gate I'd opened from the human world. I moved through it, and back around the corner and stepped up, and I was inside the world again. I pulled the gate shut. The lock turned and I opened my eyes, which I hadn't realized I'd closed. I was in my dingy boardinghouse room. I was also alone.

I'd done it. Just like the prophecy said I could. I'd opened a gate where none had been before, and I'd closed it again. But I hadn't made it go away. I could feel its warmth and shape at my back. I'd feel it every time I walked into this room from now on. I could feel something else too. I could feel Shake, my uncle Lorcan. Awareness of him sat heavily in the back of my head. He was asleep, yes, but he was also waiting for me to return, and if I didn't, he'd wait forever.

My stomach lurched. All at once I was shaking like a leaf. I was hot. I was cold. I was weak as water. I was too full of energy. One feeling was stuffed inside the other, and they were all stuffed inside me, like I'd carried back all the contradictions from betwixt and between and now they were fighting it out with my everyday self. I'd almost fallen deep into a home that saw me as a danger. I'd opened and closed gates between worlds. I'd put my uncle to sleep without knowing whether I'd be able to wake him up again. And according to the clock on the dresser, I'd done it without even one full minute passing by in this room.

I bolted down the hall and made it to the bathroom just in time to be sick in the sink.

Somebody was banging on the door.

"Callie? Callie, is that you in there?" called Mrs. Constantine. "Are you all right?"

"I'm fine. I just . . . I just need a minute." I grabbed the edges of the sink and tried to stop the shakes. I looked up at myself in the mirror, blinked, and looked again. Had something changed around my eyes? I leaned closer. They looked brighter, shinier, maybe. I tried to tell myself it was my imagination. It didn't come close to working. I'd changed. I'd stood on the threshold to my fairy home, and I'd let something into me, or maybe out of me, and I was not going back to the way I used to be.

I turned away fast and fumbled with the knob. Mrs. Constantine filled the hallway.

"Fine, she says!" My landlady snorted. "When she's whiter than a sheet. Have you had anything to eat today at all?" she asked abruptly.

That question caught me off guard. "I . . . um . . . not since breakfast."

"I thought so. Where's that uncle of yours?"

"He's . . . he's out calling on the trade."

"Hmph." She frowned down the hallway. "Well, then, you'd best come along with me, young lady!"

The next thing I knew, I was being marched into the kitchen and made to sit in a chair. Mrs. Constantine turned her back on me and began bustling about, pulling bread out of the larder and cold cuts out of the icebox, talking the whole time about how nobody could be expected to do any kind of job when they weren't feeding themselves properly and how I ought to have more sense, a great grown girl like me. She muttered and banged around that kitchen like she was giving orders to her pots and pans. Considering that I'd just seen my uncle ordering a bunch of rocks around, I really didn't want to think about that, because it made me dizzy.

Mrs. Constantine slid a bologna and cheese sandwich and a glass of milk in front of me. "Now you eat that. You're not going to be doing anyone any good if you're starved."

I didn't want to eat, and then all of a sudden I did. I really was starving, which probably wasn't normal after a person had just been sick, but I couldn't help it. I wolfed down two bites of sandwich before I felt Mrs. Constantine's frown, and remembered to slow down, chew, and show some manners, even if this was the best-tasting sandwich I'd ever eaten.

I'd expected my landlady to be angry when I told her I was leaving before my week was through, but once I told her the reason, she puffed up so far, she nearly busted the seams on her work dress. She made me promise I'd come back when I got a day off to tell her all about Ivy Bright and life at the studio. She already had Miss Patty for movie gossip, of course, but Miss Patty only worked for a new starlet, not a world-famous star the way I did now. But this was past wanting the studio gossip. This came from the same part of her that made sure I wrote my mama and kept to the rules of the house so I wouldn't get hurt. Mrs. Constantine was still looking out for me, the way she'd done since I washed up on her doorstep.

"Mrs. Constantine?" Sumner knocked on the back door. "Miss Callie, we need to get going, or—"

"The girl's not going anywhere until she's finished her sandwich," announced Mrs. Constantine. "So you may as well come in and have one too."

Mr. Sumner looked at me and my sandwich. I knew he wanted to protest, but there's nothing stronger in this world than a woman in her kitchen when she's got the need to feed.

I guess Mr. Sumner knew that too because he just took off his cap. "Well, I guess that's how it'll be, then."

Mrs. Constantine made him a sandwich, then did up one for herself. We all sat at that table. I kept my mouth busy with chewing and let Mr. Sumner and Mrs. Constantine's conversation wash over me. They talked about prices and work, and where each of them came from and how they'd gotten where they were. It was as steadying as the good bologna and bread, all normal and comfortable. Friendly. As simple as that word sounded, I felt it bone deep right then.

"Well, now, Mrs. Constantine, I thank you for that," said Mr. Sumner when he pushed his plate away. "But I do have to get Miss Callie back."

"I'll go get my case." I climbed to my feet. But halfway to the door, I stopped and turned. "Mrs. Constantine?" My landlady looked up at me, the remainder of her sandwich halfway to her mouth. "Mrs. Constantine, if you could wish for something, anything, what would it be?"

I thought she'd laugh. The question sounded ridiculous, but it didn't feel ridiculous, and her face stayed serious. I don't know whether it was magic or this little space of friendship we'd set up in her kitchen over sandwiches. She set the sandwich down and looked at her big rawboned hands. "I'd wish to hear from Sophie, I suppose," she said. "Just to know she's all right."

I wasn't surprised. I could have guessed it, but she had to say it. She had to wish. I opened my magic and saw her Sophie. She was in a cold-water flat in New York. She was working hard cleaning rooms, and wishing she hadn't run away. She was wishing she could find the nerve to call home, and wondering if her mother would even talk to her, especially after she found out about the baby.

I nodded, muttered a good-bye, and hustled up the stairs to get my suitcase. I wanted to be out of the house before the phone rang.

11

The Folks Back Home

When I got back downstairs, Mr. Sumner took my case. He had to shoo the latest group of kids off the running boards before he could open the car door for me. The Rolls pulled smoothly away. The boys chased after it, cheering and waving. I tried not to feel Shake's extra weight in the back of my head. I told myself it wasn't like I'd done anything permanent to him. I'd get him out as soon as I could figure out what to do about him. It was only fair anyhow. He meant to trick me; I'd just beaten him to it. But nothing eased that weight off my mind, and I was sure nothing would, not until I let Shake go.

I swallowed and tried to concentrate on what I needed to do next.

"Mr. Sumner?"

The chauffeur chuckled as he eased that big car around

the corner onto South Central. "Just Sumner, Miss Callie. What can I do for you?"

"Could you take me to the Dunbar Hotel?"

"Why would you want to go there?" Sumner shot me a glance in the rearview mirror.

"There's somebody I've got to see. It's important, and personal." Mr. Robeson was a singer and they toured around a lot. I had no idea how long he'd be in town. If I was going to talk to him, I'd have to do it soon. But there was more to it than that. Given all that had happened just today, Jack and I might be in over our heads this time. We needed a friend. A real friend.

"Well . . . I guess it won't do any harm. But make it quick, all right? If I'm not back on the lot to drive Mrs. Brownlow around, old Tully'll have my hide."

"Mine too." I made myself smile the way Jack did, or the way Ivy did. "Miss Bright always dines at six."

Sumner chuckled again. "We'd both better be quick, then."

As he spoke, I felt Shake roll over in the back of my mind. I clenched my fists to try to keep from twitching. It sort of worked.

The Dunbar wasn't the biggest hotel I'd ever seen, but it was done up fine, with plenty of marble, dark wood, and fresh flowers. To one side, doors opened on a restaurant with white cloths on the tables and a set of smells coming out of the kitchen that made me hungry all over again. On the other side, matching doors led to the nightclub. They were closed, but you could hear the music clearly anyhow. Big, brassy horns slid into a river of jazz with a long piano line rolling underneath. After a couple of bars, it'd break off to the sound of laughter or cussing, then start up again. The folks crossing the lobby or standing at the desk were all turned out in their best. The men sported sharp hats and the ladies stylish dresses, and every last one of them had black skin.

I walked through that grand lobby feeling strange, like I'd put my shoes on the wrong feet. I'd never lived anywhere with lots of Negroes. I was used to thinking about all the places I couldn't go if anybody found out my papa was a black man. I'd never thought about how black folks—how we—might make new places where we could be ourselves.

The clerk on the desk had light brown skin and his hair was arranged in gleaming curls. He looked me up and down carefully. My mission-store clothes didn't seem to fit too well right then.

"Can I help you, miss?" he asked in the kind of voice that meant *This better be good.* I straightened up and met his eyes. No matter how fine, the Dunbar was a hotel, and if there was one thing I knew, it was how to behave in a hotel.

"You can call Mr. Robeson's room and say Callie LeRoux would like to speak with him."

"One moment, please." The clerk picked up the house phone and dialed.

While I waited, I watched the lobby around me. I liked

being here. I liked the way the smell of good cooking and the music wrapped around me, bringing the feel of the people with them. The halting jazz was filled with the satisfaction and frustration of making something grow, bit by bit, note by note. I wondered what it'd be like to work in a place like this, where I wouldn't have to worry about my coarse hair or my skin, which turned too brown in the sun. I didn't think much about my own life. There'd never been time for it. I'd always had something or somebody else to look out for, even before the Unseelies and their magic had barreled over my world. But right then I wondered. I knew how a hotel ran. I was a good cook. What if one day I came back here and got a job? Or . . . what if I opened my own place?

It came over me like a burst of light. I could make a place too. We could even do it together: me, Mama, and Papa. It'd be a supper club, one of the fancy places where all the ladies wore their best gowns and the gentlemen dressed in black tie. We'd call it LeRoux's, or better yet, the Midnight Club. Papa would play the piano and lead the band. Mama would run the kitchen, turning out the best food for miles around. I could help her, and hostess, and maybe sing with the band on Friday nights. Nobody would have to hide who they were or who they were with when they came to the Midnight Club. Everybody could eat and drink and enjoy the music right out in the open.

The force of that sudden dream rooted me to the spot. It was too strong. It was like starvation. Once it was inside, there wasn't room for anything else.

"Miss? Miss LeRoux?"

I shook myself and turned back to the clerk. He didn't frown, exactly, but he pretty much had me pegged for the hayseed I was. "I'm sorry, Mr. Robeson isn't in. Would you care to leave a message?"

"Um . . . yes. Say Callie LeRoux is sorry she missed her appointment this morning but she would like to speak with him as soon as he's available." I told the clerk where I was staying. He didn't even bat an eye at the studio address, just took it all down and tucked the note into one of the pigeon-holes behind the desk.

I thanked him and walked out of there, still dazed from the dream of a future that had washed through me.

Dear Mama, I thought, in the way that was fast becoming a habit. *Dear Mama . . .*

But I couldn't get any further. I didn't know how to compress my dream into words. It was all too big and too new. I drifted back out to the waiting car, not seeing what was in front of me. I barely heard my own answer when Sumner asked where I wanted to go. It was like being be-twixt and between all over again. Nothing was solid except this new idea of the Midnight Club.

Sumner drove me to the grocer's, the baker's, and the butcher's to pick up what I needed to stock Ivy's pantry. I'd hardly ever seen so much food in my life, at least not food I could afford to buy. A day before, I would have been paralyzed by my choices. Now, though, I walked between the bins and past the counters, and thought about whether what I saw would fit on the menu for the Midnight Club. I even peeked in at the fishmonger's. I'd only ever eaten catfish, and only knew one way to cook that. But Mama would know how to use all these other kinds they had laid out on beds of crushed ice. One of our games at the Imperial was to get down her cookbooks and make up menus for the day the dust storms eased and the guests came back. Memory of that game got tied up in the daydream, and I was able to start my new letter, writing in my imagination as though I really was setting up the club.

Mama, do you think we should have filet of sole or turbot? And what about oysters on the half shell? Do you think the china should be plain white with the club's name on it, or should we use the white-on-black motif? I wasn't entirely sure what a motif was, but I liked the way it sounded.

By the time Sumner pulled into the bungalow's driveway, I was too busy setting up the tables in the Midnight Club and writing notes to Mama to care that Mrs. Tully was there at the door, ready to watch my every move while I unloaded my groceries into that brand-new kitchen. Or that it was getting on toward dinnertime and Mr. Robeson hadn't called yet. I wasn't worried about how I still needed to find a way to explain to Jack about everything that had happened at Mrs. Constantine's, or even that I still had no idea what I was going to do with Shake when I woke him up. My idea of the Midnight Club swallowed up everything else. It was like I'd discovered a whole new country, one where I could finally be happy.

I did not quite forget I had work to do. If anything, all my dreaming and letter writing made it easier. After all, at the Midnight Club, we'd have to be ready to cater to movie people, so I'd better practice while I could. Fortunately, that brand-new kitchen came with cookbooks. I decided that for the sake of Miss Bright's health and complexion, we should have a light supper—Waldorf salad, chicken almondine, and creamed spinach, with poached pears in crème anglaise for dessert.

The clock in the dining room chimed six. Mrs. Tully sailed through the door just as I was tucking the serving spoon into the bowl of creamed spinach and laying the tongs on the dish with the chicken.

"Well." She looked over the rims of her glasses at my spread and sniffed. "That might just do."

"Thank you, Mrs. Tully." I figured she wasn't used to paying compliments and was starting small.

"Miss Bright and Mrs. Brownlow are in the dining room. Let's get this out." She picked up two of the chilled plates heaped with the Waldorf salad: apples and walnuts in mayonnaise set out on a lettuce leaf. I grabbed the other plate and followed her into the dining room.

Mrs. Brownlow sat at the head of the table, wearing the same vague smile she'd had on when she left that morning. Next to her sat Ivy, and next to Ivy sat Jack. My heart lurched hard. He'd been in the house this whole time and hadn't bothered to come around to even say hello to me. He'd stayed out here with Ivy. At the moment, Ivy was leaning so close her head was almost on his shoulder, and he was giving her his biggest grin as she looked up at him and giggled. And here I was bringing in their dinner like a maid.

"Oh, Callie!" Ivy covered her mouth. "There you are!"

As if I could be anywhere else. I was her *cook,* wasn't I? That's what she'd asked me to be. Jack turned his head, still grinning, but that grin was for Ivy, not for me.

"Hey, that looks terrific!"

It was everything I could do not to slam the plate down in front of him.

"Waldorf salad! Callie, you're so clever!" cried Ivy, like I was some kind of trained poodle. "Look, Mama, Callie's made us Waldorf salad! Your favorite!"

Mrs. Brownlow blinked down at her plate. "Why, yes. I was just saying so, wasn't I? It looks delicious." She groped for her fork and began to eat.

"I told you Callie could cook anything, didn't I?" Jack reminded the room at large. He gave me a wink, but I could barely stand to look at him.

"Mmm." Ivy smiled back around her bite. "Aren't you going to sit down, Callie? You've been working so hard, you must be tired."

"I . . . no . . . I've got something on the stove." I ran back into the kitchen.

I got there and just stood. Anger flooded all the places where I'd been happy a minute earlier. I didn't even know why I was angry. There wasn't any reason to be. So Jack hadn't come in to talk to me. So what? Maybe there hadn't been time. Maybe they'd just walked into the house and sat down at the table. Nothing real had happened. Jack had been laughing with Ivy. That was all. What was there to be angry about?

The door swung open and Mrs. Tully came in. She took one look at me and shook her head. "You're going to have to get over that if you intend to stay on."

"What?" I said, as though I'd lost my ability to understand English. I realized I'd been expecting it to be Jack who walked through that door. But Jack hadn't shown. Again.

"If you start being jealous of Miss Bright, you're not going to last a week."

"I . . . but . . . I'm not jealous."

Mrs. Tully didn't even start to answer that. She just helped herself from the bowl of leftover salad and dug in the silverware drawer until she found a fork. "You'd better eat while you can." She pulled a stool up to the counter. "I'm sure if she's allowed, Miss Bright will keep you and Mr. Jack busy tonight playing best friends."

"I'm not hungry." I also couldn't take my eyes off the door.

"No more than you're jealous." Mrs. Tully sniffed again. "Our place is in here, Miss Callie. We take care of them, and we do not start thinking of them like friends, ever. That's the only way we survive." She chewed for a moment. "You're lucky, as it happens. Your friend out there is going to learn that the hard way."

You don't know the first thing about me, or Jack. It's all for show. Jack's just charming Ivy because we need her. That's all. I just forgot for a second. He's going to come in any minute now to check on me, and he'll give me one of those big winks.

But Jack didn't come in. He stayed right at the table with Ivy and Mrs. Brownlow, while Mrs. Tully and I carried the food in and took away the empty plates. Oh, they exclaimed over it all and said thank you and please, just like they should. Mrs. Brownlow remarked that each dish was her favorite, or she did as soon as Ivy reminded her, but there was a distance between them and me, because I was working and they weren't. Not that it was any too comfortable in the kitchen either, with Mrs. Tully eating the leftovers and not saying anything.

I tried to think about the Midnight Club again. I tried to start another page of the letter to Mama in my mind. But I just couldn't. I couldn't even go out there again. I told myself I wasn't hiding. I was letting Jack know that if he wanted to talk, he'd have to get back here. I wasn't going out there to watch how well he was making moon eyes over Miss Bright, even if it was just for show. I had important things to tell him, but if he wanted to hear any of them, he had to come to me.

So Mrs. Tully carried out the dessert plates and I stayed

in the kitchen, cleaning until there was nothing left to clean and flipping through cookbooks without reading anything. I wasn't sure I was going to be able to keep from crying. I couldn't even get my feelings to make sense to me. I wasn't in love. It wasn't like I wanted to kiss anybody or anything, and it was a sure bet nobody wanted to kiss me. Jack couldn't be part of any dream of mine. I'd known the whole time he had only come with me because he wanted the adventure, and to write a story about it. Jack wanted to be a writer. That was his big dream. Sure, we'd helped each other out when we'd gotten into trouble, but that's what you do when you're in trouble. So what if I'd imagined a room for him over the Midnight Club, where he could have a desk and a typewriter? That was just a stupid, babyish daydream, same as the rest of it. I had no business thinking about a normal life. I wasn't normal, and all the wishing in the world wasn't going to change that.

None of this scolding made me feel better. It just started me wondering about what I'd done, and how, and what else I could do. I'd used my magic to get my own way before. Not that I'd ever try to wish Jack into looking at me the way he looked at Ivy. That wouldn't be right. I wouldn't even think of doing it, even if I knew for sure I could. Which I didn't. So there wasn't any point in starting to think about it.

The sun had gone down outside and the windows over the sink were blank, black mirrors. My reflection looked sad and sullen. I didn't like the way it kept catching my eye, or

SARAH ZETTEL

the way my eyes looked a little too shiny for their own good. I went to twitch the curtains shut.

And froze. I wasn't alone in that reflection. A grand woman with dark skin dressed in a shimmering gold dress and wearing a diamond tiara in her hair stood beside me.

Hello, Callie, my dear.

12

Come Callin'

I whirled around. No one was there. I looked back at the window reflection. There she was.

The queen of the Midnight Throne waited in the darkness of the windowpane. I'd only seen her once, but I'd never mistake her for anyone else. She was my father's mother, and Shake's mother. My grandmother.

"What . . . what are you doing here?" I croaked. *How'd you get here without me feeling it? How'd you even find me?*

I am only here in spirit, my child. And I followed your wish.

It took a minute to realize she'd answered the questions I'd thought, not the one I'd asked out loud. It took a minute longer to realize what she was talking about. My daydream of the Midnight Club hadn't been just a daydream. It had been a wish about my future, and I'd been wishing it for hours. My grandparents could feel wishes at least as well as Shake. Of course they'd been able to track it down.

Don't berate yourself, my dear. You are not used to your own powers yet.

I opened my mouth, then closed it, and concentrated on thinking. *Don't call me dear!*

Her sigh sent a long ripple of sorrow right down the center of my brain. *I know you are angry with us, and perhaps you are right to be. We mistook the importance of young Jack to you. Because of your father's obsessions, we feared . . . but never mind that. I need to give you a warning.*

About what?

Lorcan has escaped us.

Escaped? I repeated stupidly. Confusion blotted out a hundred images that threatened to flash to the front of my mind, where my grandmother might be able to get a look at them. Instead, I made myself see Ivy sitting with Jack. Anger and worry rose up fast and strong enough to drive thoughts of Shake into the background.

I felt my grandmother frown, and I knew I'd been right. She was trying to see into my mind, and not just what I wanted her to see either.

When we realized Lorcan had tried to kill you, we imprisoned him, she told me. *It was only his royal blood that spared him from a death sentence. But we should not have been so lenient. He tricked his guards and escaped. We know he intended to come for you, granddaughter. Has he been here?*

The kitchen door swung open. I jumped and whirled around. It was Ivy. She twisted her hands together and blinked her big blue eyes.

"I just . . . I just wanted to say good night, Callie."

"Yeah," I said, trying to get my breath back. Behind me, I felt my grandmother's presence waver. "Okay. Good night."

Ivy looked around. "Was Tully in here?"

"Um, no, just me. And Fannie Farmer." I picked up the nearest cookbook and waved it toward her.

"Oh. Okay. Well, good night."

"Good night."

Ivy left slowly, like she wanted to say a lot more. I was torn between the urge to shove her out the door and the urge to run after her. I thought I heard Jack's voice out front, but I couldn't hear what he was saying, and I couldn't exactly go out there while my grandmother was still haunting the window glass.

You must come home, granddaughter. Grandmother's image grew more solid, strong and heavy as crystal, and just as hard. *You are alone, unprotected and untrained. You do not have the strength to stand against a member of the royal house if he decides to work against you.*

My head spun. I gritted my teeth and took a minute to list all the ingredients in the Waldorf salad, because I couldn't have Grandmother getting in far enough to see what I had been doing and how much working Shake had already done.

I'm not going back there. I tried to shape each word clearly. *I've got too much to do right here.*

Then let us come to you. Open the way for us, Callie.

Can't you just come through? They had before. They knew where the holes were. They'd even built up palaces around them.

You are in the Seelie territory, Callie. It is warded against us. But you could let us in.

So there it was. I should have known. She didn't want me back. She didn't want me safe. She wanted to use me.

Yes. Callie, you are the only one who can control the gates. That is why we need you, not just as heir to our throne, and that is why we will always work to keep you safe.

Yeah, yeah, I get it. They'd keep me safe all right, so they could keep me right under their Unseelie thumbs.

Let us through, granddaughter. I felt her pressing close to me, even though her reflection hadn't moved at all. *Let us help you.*

Like you helped my papa? I snapped back.

We cannot reach him, Callie. But you can. Open the way for us, and we can lead our forces across. The Shining Court will not keep him from us any longer.

They had an army? Why hadn't I thought about that before? They ruled a kingdom. Of course they must have an army. I didn't need to play house with a giggling little girl and sneak into the Seelie country. I could meet the Seelie king as the princess I was, at the head of a whole fairy regiment. I could *demand* that the king give my parents back.

But then what? If the Unseelies had an army, the Seelies would too.

You must not fear them, Callie. They are weak and without honor. My grandmother's thoughts dug at mine, trying to get in and turn me around until I saw things her way.

They're weak and without honor, except they're strong enough that you wanted your son to marry one of them, and now that they've kidnapped him, you can't get him back.

That was a mistake, and a trick. But her words came too late. I'd caught her off balance.

Must've been one whale of a good trick.

You do not have to decide this moment. She said it as though she was granting me a huge favor, but it wasn't enough to cover the impatience trickling out of her. *If you wish your father to remain in captivity while you attempt to make up your mind—*

Oh, no you don't, Grandmother. I cut her off. *That one's so old, it's growing whiskers.*

Her silence was cold and thick. Mrs. Tully could only dream of sending out silence like that. But there was something else too. Grandmother was sad. When we'd gone walking betwixt and between, I'd felt the reality of my uncle. I felt the reality of my grandmother now, no matter how much she tried to drive it down into the depths of her silence: she regretted what was happening.

Callie, I have lost both my sons. I don't want to lose my granddaughter. Please. Let me help you.

I have to think about it.

Callie . . . There were tears behind my name, but I gritted myself tight against them. I reached into where my magic waited and thought about closing the window, about locking it. It wasn't easy. I didn't have any wish but my own to work with, and she wasn't using a gate. She was using my own head and the blood connection between us. I'd never been taught how to work this kind of magic. There wasn't a key I could turn or a gate I could get hold of. I had to find the thoughts and the strength to block her out. It gave Grandmother plenty of time to feel what I was trying to do, and all that gentle sadness was gone, as though it had never been.

Think carefully before you reject us, granddaughter. Your uncle, when he finds you, will not be so forgiving.

She was gone, and I was back to shaking. I pressed both hands on the counter and leaned against them, hard. My stomach tried to be sick for the second time that day. I swallowed, and swallowed again. I closed my eyes like I thought that would help. But nothing would help now. They'd found me. My grandparents knew where I was, and they could reach into my head and see what I was thinking. How would I ever hide from them again?

But that wasn't what was really setting its hooks into me. What was really bad was that Shake was the only person who could possibly help me fight off my grandparents if they took it into their heads to come and get me. But I'd sent him to sleep in the betwixt and between, and there was no way I could imagine him waking up in a good mood.

I made myself straighten up and ran both hands over my hair. The only reflection in the window now was mine, too pale, thin, and confused, without even a trace of magic silver in my eyes. I needed to get Jack. Right now. This changed everything, and we had to figure out what to do.

As calm as I could, I walked out into the empty dining room. "Jack?"

"Tully sent him home!" snapped Ivy. "When she knows we've got *plenty* of room!"

I followed her voice into the living room. But Jack wasn't there either. Just Ivy, Mrs. Brownlow, and Mrs. Tully. Ivy and Mrs. Tully were all but nose to nose, staring each other down. Mrs. Brownlow sat on the couch, her hands clasped and her forehead wrinkled in concentration.

"We are not having a strange young man staying overnight here!" Mrs. Tully said firmly. "What would happen to your reputation?"

Ivy let out a little scream through clenched teeth, stomped her foot, and then let a tear trickle down her cheek.

Mrs. Tully didn't budge an inch. "I'm sure your mother agrees with me. Don't you, Mrs. Brownlow?"

Mrs. Brownlow made a fluttery gesture. Whatever she was reaching for, it wasn't there, and her hand fell back into her lap. "Yes, of course. We can't let strangers in. They might take my daughter away."

That's when I felt the pressure against my mind. It wasn't just tension. Magic swelled in that room, like air inside a balloon. I clapped my hand over my mouth and swallowed again. I'd known something was wrong in this house, and now I knew what it was. The Seelies weren't just waiting out there on the back lot. They were in here with me. Except I couldn't tell who the fairy in here was. There was no direction to the magic I felt now, and I didn't dare open myself up to it or I'd give myself away.

Ivy gave another wordless, closed-mouth scream and rushed out of the room. The magic rushed away, as if the balloon had suddenly popped. Mrs. Tully straightened, satisfied.

"Come along, Mrs. Brownlow." She put her arm under Mrs. Brownlow's elbow and lifted her up. "Time to get you to bed."

"Yes, of course," replied Mrs. Brownlow. "I was just saying so, wasn't I?"

Tully murmured her agreement. She looked back at me over the rims of her heavy glasses. In the dim light of the living room, her eyes looked like black holes in her head. I couldn't tell whether they were human. I couldn't tell anything. "Do you have something to say, Miss Callie?" Tully asked.

"No, ma'am," I whispered.

"Then I'm sure you should be getting yourself to bed too." It was anything but a suggestion.

"Yes, ma'am."

Tully steered Mrs. Brownlow toward the broad staircase. I watched them leave, and felt the remains of the magic brush past my skin and escape into the garden. I wished I could follow it.

Instead, I hurried through the kitchen and up the back stairs to the second floor, then up the attic stairs. As I put my hand on the light switch, a shadow moved in the corner. I jumped and stuffed my fist in my mouth to smother the scream.

But it was Jack, stepping into the light where I could see him, with his hands out. My bones went soft as Jell-O on a hot day.

"Tully said she sent you home," I said stupidly.

"She did." Jack stuffed his hands into his pockets and let his eyes go all wide and innocent. "And I went. But I came back to tell her the lock on their back door's busted."

I blinked. "That's not safe," I said seriously as I switched on the lamp. "Anybody could just walk in."

"All the way up those old servants' stairs. I mean, just think about it."

We held steady for another half second before the tickle of laughter inside got too strong. It was a long time before we were able to stop giggling and shushing each other.

"I wanted . . . I wanted to make sure you were okay," said Jack when he had his breath back. "You weren't looking too good at dinner."

The leftover giggles were gone just like that. I dropped onto the edge of the bed. "Jack, we are in big trouble." I paused. "And I think Ivy is too."

I told him what had happened to me that day: that I'd been taken betwixt and between by my uncle, who'd tried to railroad me into going into the Unseelie country with him; how I'd put Lorcan to sleep and left him behind there; how my grandmother had chased down my wishing; how I'd gone into the living room and found Tully, Ivy, and Mrs. Brownlow in the middle of a cloud of magic.

By the time I was finished, Jack was sitting beside me, and he was so pale, his freckles stood out like dots of ink on his skin.

"Yeah," he croaked. "I think that qualifies as trouble."

"Yeah," I agreed.

Jack's face twisted up, and his mouth worked itself back and forth a few times, like he had to say something really unpleasant. "Could . . . could Ivy be a fairy? Maybe she's an Unseelie being kidnapped by the Seelie court, like they took your pop?"

"If she's Unseelie, what was she doing letting herself get hauled off without fighting back?" I shook my head and then tried not to hear the sigh of relief that rushed out of him. "And Ruth Markham didn't have any kind of magic around her. I'm positive," I added, before he could ask.

"So that leaves Tully," said Jack. Ivy Bright was pretty and talented and famous. She was just the sort of person the Seelies would love to get hold of, and Tully ran her house. Tully could have opened the door for Ruth and ordered Ivy to go with her. She could be magicking Mrs. Brownlow into a half dream to keep her from noticing what was going on.

There was something else too. Fairies could disguise everything about themselves anytime they wanted, except for their eyes. But their eyes they could cover up, say, with the sagging brim of a battered hat. Or a thick pair of glasses.

"Except the Seelies from yesterday were trying to catch Mr. Robeson," I reminded Jack, and myself. "Ivy was just the bait. If they'd been planning to take her away, why bother with trying to trap him too?" Could Amerda and Rougarou be that greedy? I shook my head again. The scene we'd stumbled into with Amerda and Rougarou had never really added up. The problem was, the more we learned, the less sense I could find in it.

"And what about Mrs. Brownlow?" I said out loud. "What if the scatterbrain bit's all an act? She could have handed Ivy over to Miss Markham, and who would have said anything?" There was definitely something not right about Olive Brownlow's eyes. I'd thought they were just vague and cloudy, but I hadn't taken any kind of a good look. There was another possibility. Mrs. Brownlow could be a half-blood like me, with just a little fairy shining out through her otherwise human eyes.

Jack and I sat there for a long time, searching for something useful to say and coming up with a great big goose egg. If I opened my own magic, we'd know more. But I'd also be waving a red flag and shouting, "Here I am!" And then what? I had no idea how many Seelies were nearby, or Unseelies either.

"You look beat," said Jack finally. "You should try to get some sleep."

I *was* beat. Too much had happened. My head felt over-stuffed with worry. "I can't. What if my grandparents are on the way?"

"But they said this place was warded and they couldn't get in," Jack reminded me. "Looks like the Seelies are good for something after all."

"Something." I gave him a small smile and stood up. "You should probably get out of here before Tully catches you."

"What're you, cracked? There's no way I'm leaving you here alone." He pulled the coverlet off the little white bed and grabbed up one of the pillows. "Dibs on the bathtub."

It turned out there was even a spare toothbrush in the medicine cabinet. Jack bedded down in the big claw-foot tub, pulled the coverlet over his head, and was asleep within minutes. Like always. They had yet to invent the place where Jack Holland couldn't find forty winks.

I lay awake for a long time in that comfortable bed listening to him snore and thinking about all the bad feelings I'd been nursing all day, none of which Jack deserved. Was Tully right? Could I really be jealous?

Could I be falling in love with Jack Holland?

I knotted my fingers into the crisp linen sheet. I told myself there'd be time to figure that out later. What was important now was getting through the night, which meant lying low and waiting it out. We could do that. We'd done it before. Come morning, we could figure out how to get not only ourselves but the brightest little star in Hollywood out of this messed-up house. Everything else would just have to wait . . . again. I squeezed my eyes shut.

Dear Mama, I thought toward the darkness. *I'm sorry. I'm really sorry.*

13

I My Loved Ones' Watch Am Keeping

Little niece.

The warmth of sleep cradled me close. One thought, then another, rolled under its dark quilt, but they didn't mean anything. An image drifted past in lazy, tumbleweed fashion. I didn't need to worry about that either.

Little niece. Little niece.

Who was calling me? I tried burrowing deeper under my covers, but it was no good. Something crawled right into the place where I was dreaming. Eyes opened underneath sleep's darkness, shining up at me: one amber and starlight, one milk white.

I knew you'd be back, said Lorcan.

I opened my mouth to scream, but no sound came

out. I struggled, but I had no sense of direction that would allow me to flee. The only things in existence were my uncle and me.

What are you doing here? I forced the words out of my confusion and anger.

I'm your prisoner, niece, Lorcan reminded me in a tone that was grim and gleeful at the same time. *You put your sleep onto me, and then you came into sleep yourself. Did you think you wouldn't find me here?*

No, I hadn't thought it. Not even once.

Well, you should have. His grin flashed out from the enveloping dark. His missing teeth made him look like a Cheshire cat who'd gotten in a barroom fight. *You know by now there're consequences to every enchantment.*

I tried to feel a way out, but slowly I had to admit there wasn't any. My uncle wasn't holding me here; I was holding him. If I wanted to get away, I'd have to let him go free.

You've got plans, niece. Shake loomed over me. I still couldn't see anything but his eyes and his teeth, but I could feel the cold of him. He was weak, broken, but that didn't stop him from being dangerous, and way too close for comfort. *They're bad ideas, bad ideas.*

How do you know?

Lorcan didn't even bother to answer. Of course he knew. I'd been asleep for hours, and he'd been here with me, watching my dreams and drifting thoughts like they were movies on the screen.

*You should be afraid, niece. The Seelie king will catch
you. He'll lock you up tight and draw your powers out of you,
and there won't be one damn thing you can do about it.*

Shows what you know, I shot back. I'd been running
scared for what seemed like forever, and I was getting plenty
tired of it. *You couldn't hold on to me. The Midnight Throne
couldn't hold on to me. There's no way the Seelies are worse
than all of you.*

Is that what you think? Maybe you should look here.

The darkness opened up. There was light all around me,
and the sound of voices and laughter. I didn't want to see
any of it, but I had no choice. You don't get to close your
eyes in a bad dream.

I saw a long, grand room, all carved wood and stone
with huge tapestries covering the walls. It could have been
a king's palace out of the movies. The night outside had
turned the arched windows black. Men and women, all of
them beautiful, most of them famous, filled the place, holding drinks and cigarettes. Smoke formed spiraling clouds
over their heads as they gestured dramatically. Their jewelry
and their clothing sparkled in the light of chandeliers and
candles. They talked and laughed easily with each other,
and a few were none too steady on their feet from the champagne the waiters kept pouring into their big glasses. One
man towered above the rest of them. He was built like a
mountain and had a mustache that drooped down over his
upper lip. I could tell in that way you can in dreams that this
was his house. It was his pride and joy and it wasn't even

done yet. It was growing, and he had plans. Great plans, and they'd come true soon enough. He'd always backed winners, and he was doing it now.

The mustached man raised his glass and clinked a fork against it. "My friends! My friends!" he called. The conversation and laughter faded away as the crowd turned to face him. "As you know, I've brought tonight's entertainment here to the Enchanted Castle at considerable personal expense and not a little bit of trouble. And I know you've come to look forward to their special performances as much as I have. So without further ado, ladies and gentlemen, I give you the royalty of the minstrel shows, Rags and Patches!"

Two servants threw the doors open, and there, wearing a baggy black-and-yellow checkered suit, stood my father.

I knew it was him. I would have known even if I'd been awake seeing him with daytime eyes. I knew it now, despite the fact that they'd made him up. He was a tall, lean brown man. It was hard to tell the exact shade of his skin, because somebody'd smeared black gunk all over his face and given his mouth a bright red clown outline. But they couldn't disguise his eyes. My father's eyes were the gray and black of moonlight and midnight, and swirled with the fairy light. They were my eyes when the magic shone out from me.

My father, the prince of the Unseelies, shook his boater hat like a tambourine, while he rolled those eyes and grinned a big, wide, stupid grin.

All the beautiful, famous people laughed and applauded

or raised their champagne glasses. Papa bugged his eyes out, like he couldn't believe he was seeing all these people waiting for him. The mustached man waved toward the musicians, and they struck up a jangly tune, all banjo and honky-tonk piano.

At the sound of the music, Papa gave an openmouthed grin and began to dance. He kicked up high and came down lightly. He high-kicked his way into the hall, leaning back so far he should have fallen over.

"I's gwine ta go down sout' for ta see mah Sal," Papa gurgled, shaking his yellow-gloved hands and hat as he strutted down the hall. The people laughed and they clapped.

"Singin' polly-wolly-doodle all de day!

Mah Sal, she is a spunky gal!

Singin' polly-wolly-doodle all de day!"

All at once, his feet shot out from under him. He flailed his arms but toppled over anyway and landed hard on his backside, blinking and staring.

The laughter redoubled. "Careful there, Sambo!" someone shouted.

"He's not going to get anywhere like that!" cried somebody else.

Now do you see? Shake was at my shoulder, whispering into my thoughts. *This is what they can do to one of us. He is of royal stock, and they've made him into their clown and slave. What do you think they will do to you, with your ignorance and your human weakness?*

Get out of my head!

Then let me go. Oh, but you can't, can you? You don't know what I'll do next. He grinned over me. *We're stuck here together, you and I.*

Papa had jumped to his feet and was looking all around him like a cat chasing its tail. "Who done dat? Who throwed dat banana peel down dere?"

But there was nothing to find, just more sharp, cruel laughter. It was still rolling through the hall when a woman's voice called from the doorway. "Yoo-hoo!"

The voice was too high and way too sugary, but I still recognized it immediately. I should. I'd heard it all my life. Papa knew it too. He jerked around, his grin growing wider and his eyes rolling huge and white. "Oh, it's *you,* mah sweetheart!"

They'd put Mama in a costume too. She was a ballet dancer, but her tattered tutu and white stockings had been patched with brightly colored calico. Her face was made up like a china doll's, all white with pink circles and a pink mouth. Her hair had been teased out and ratted so it stood in a ragged cloud around her face. She didn't dance in on pointe like a real ballerina, though. She clumped flat-footed, kicking up and stomping down, with her arms bent so her hands framed her face like she was shocked or afraid.

"Oh, mah sweetheart!" Papa went down on one knee and held his arms out. "Come give me yo' kiss!"

Mama's head jerked around and down. She stomped over to him, her torn toe shoes flapping on the stone floor. Her arm lashed out, and she delivered a ringing slap across

Papa's cheek. He staggered back, put his hand to the place where she'd hit him, and sighed happily.

The crowd howled with laughter.

How can they be doing this? Shake didn't answer me. I couldn't even feel him anymore. What I could feel was the whole tortured web of magic winding around my parents. Strings of enchantment tied them tightly—their wrists and ankles, the corners of their mouths, their eyelids, their tongues. The strings forced them to move like marionettes. They forced Mama to clomp clumsily about the stage, a dreadful parody of a dancing doll, tripping Papa, kicking him in the pants, dumping a drink over his head.

He just stood there, blinking and bowing and smiling, the champagne running down his face, cutting tracks through the blackface and making his clown makeup run as though his mouth was bleeding. I wanted to cry. I wanted to scream. Because as bad as being dragged around that stage was for Mama, for Papa it was worse.

Fairies want human love and imagination. They feel it and it works on them like alcohol on a drunk. I had to struggle every day to keep myself closed down so I wouldn't feel too much. Papa, though, was being held open. They'd gotten those strings around the magic that lived inside him and they'd wrenched it open. He could feel all the derision and contempt that filled the room. Every bit of it poured down his throat along with the laughter and the applause. He couldn't get away from these feelings. He couldn't stand against them.

It was killing him. I could feel that too. I could feel him. He couldn't shut out the music or the derisive emotions and it was bowing him down, wearing him away, leaving nothing but the broken, bug-eyed clown. Pretty soon there wouldn't be even that much left.

And they were using Mama to do it. My mama, who'd faced all the bad that life in the Dust Bowl could throw at her but who had held on, was being made to hurt the man she loved more than life and watch him as he weakened day by day. I reached down to my magic and pulled it out, groping for some way to shape it and send it out to them. I'd blow the place apart if I had to, but I'd wipe the smiles off all those people laughing at my parents. I'd start with the big man grinning in the corner.

But I couldn't. I wasn't there. I wasn't anywhere near them. I was only dreaming.

Dear Callie.

My thoughts jerked to a halt. Someone had said my name, right in the middle of this nightmare. Except it wasn't Lorcan.

Out in the hall, Papa'd gotten hold of Mama and thrown her across his knee. "I has you now, mah sweetheart! I will show you how much I loves you!"

Dear Callie.

Two soft words, a soft, strong, urgent whisper under the laughter and the jeering.

Dear Callie. I am glad to hear you are well and have found a good rooming house.

It's not happening. It's part of the dream. I stopped right there. Of course it was part of the dream, but this dream was real. I was hearing my mama.

I don't think I can tell you how much it's meant to get your letters. I think your plans for the Midnight Club sound just wonderful.

Tears spilled into my thoughts. All those imaginary letters had been wishes too. I'd wished Mama could hear me. And she had. She was tangled and chained in the Seelie magic, but we were still mother and daughter. There wasn't magic enough in the world to keep her from knowing I loved her. Now she was writing a letter in her own head, deep down under that enchantment. If the Seelies heard it at all, they probably thought this poor human woman was finally going crazy.

Mama had Papa's face in her hands and was looking straight into his eyes. *I hope you're staying wrapped up warm and taking care of your cough while you travel.*

"I loves you!" Papa burbled. "I loves you, mah sweetheart!" And he did. His love was searing and strong, and for that moment it swamped the anguish.

Then the enchanted strings jerked them together hard, so that they bumped foreheads, and again so that they bumped noses. The third time, they allowed their mouths to come together. A split second later, Papa jumped up, dumping Mama on the floor. He began dancing around in pain holding his mouth.

"Mah lip! Mah lip! She bited me!"

He staggered, pretending to be limp with pain. Mama clomped back out of the way, and Papa stumbled right into one of the guests, a woman who screamed; the man next to her shoved Papa back. He staggered again, reeling through the crowd. Suddenly they didn't find the act so funny anymore. The guests shrieked and scattered, spilling drinks on each other and sending genuine anger curdling through the room.

Somebody tumbled against the mustached party host, and he went down on his broad backside. I felt something slip, just a split second of concentration lost, and a split second more when he was covered over by everybody's attention and everybody's expectation that he would *do* something about this outrage.

Everybody's except Papa's.

"They keep me playing by the pool during the day," Papa breathed from where he sprawled flat on the floor. "I can't find where they keep—"

"You bastard!" roared the mustached man. He lashed out and kicked Papa in the ribs. Bright pain flared through Papa, and he rolled himself into a ball, still blinking and trying frantically to smile.

"Now, boss, now, boss, de darkie's sorry, he don' mean it, please, boss!"

But he did mean it. He'd created this scene on purpose so the magic would slip, just a little, just enough to get a message to me. I saw the starlight and midnight in his eyes as he scrabbled backward and the guests tried to pull the mustached man away. They handed their host a drink; they asked him what he'd expected from some darkie clown. Papa scrambled to his feet and grabbed up Mama's hand. They bowed and smiled.

They knew I was watching them. They knew I'd heard.

Pitiful, isn't it? Shake was back. I'd been so wrapped up in watching my parents, I'd all but forgotten about him. *And you're planning on coming in here and making it a trio.*

The great hall with its celebration faded to black. I wanted to dive after it, just to be near my parents again, but I didn't. As much as I could in that directionless dark, I faced my uncle.

You knew where they were. You've known this whole time.

He didn't answer.

And you weren't ever going to tell me, were you?

Still no answer.

Were you?

His smile was sharp as broken glass. *And I'm still not.*

I screamed. I lunged for him, but I had no body. I was thought and dream and darkness, and he was nothing but the light in his eyes and the gleam of his shattered teeth. I had no weapon but my anger, and Shake just laughed.

Oh, how sad, how tragic for my little niece! She thinks she can storm castles, but she can't even touch her old uncle when she's got him helpless. Whatever will she do?

"Wake up!" A new voice cut the darkness. Someone was shaking me. Jack. "It's a nightmare, Callie. Wake up!"

Yes, wake up, Callie, sneered my uncle. *It's only a dream, after all.*

"Callie! Calliope LeRoux!"

I could feel my body again, and find my eyes and snap them open. I could sit up too, and I could remember every single thing I'd been shown. Worst of all, I could feel Lorcan in the back of my mind, buried under my enchanted sleep and waiting for me to come back.

Jack let go of my shoulders. His face was worried. "Callie, what happened?"

"I saw my parents." I grabbed his hand and pulled myself up. "And we are out of time."

14

Gonna Steal Away

The sun was just coming up over the hills when Jack and I snuck down to the bungalow's second floor. I'd wanted to leave immediately, but Jack insisted we tell Ivy what was going on, because we might not be coming back. As much as I might have wanted to, I couldn't argue with that.

The hallway had six closed doors leading off it, but it was easy to tell which belonged to Ivy. A photo of her with her head cocked sideways, giving her biggest little-girl grin, hung on the door at the far end. Jack called the picture a "head shot" and said all actors had them.

He was also hanging back.

"What's the matter?" I whispered as I put my hand on the knob.

"It's her bedroom," he said. "I can't just walk in there."

"You just walked into my bedroom."

"That was different."

I rolled my eyes, but there wasn't time to argue this either. We needed to tell Ivy what she had to know, and then get out of there before the Seelies or my grandparents found us. And we had to do it all before I got so tired I couldn't stay awake and fell back to where my uncle was waiting.

I turned the doorknob as quietly as I could and tiptoed inside.

Walking into Ivy Bright's bedroom was like walking into a birthday cake. Everything—from the covers and the canopy on the bed to the curtains on the windows and the patterned rug on the floor—was as white and pink and ruffled as if it had been made out of sugar icing. Even the armchairs and vanity table had ruffly skirts and quilted seats. The fireplace had a pink-veined white marble mantel with a frilly lace runner that was covered with framed photos and gold and silver trophies.

Ivy sprawled in her bed, her hair all done up in white rags to keep the curl in. I'd have bet that nobody at *Movie Fan* magazine knew about that one.

I laid my hand on her shoulder. "Ivy? Ivy, wake up."

Ivy squeaked and grabbed hold of me. She had an amazingly strong grip and almost yanked me over as she sat up.

"What? What!" She blinked hard and knuckled her eyes. *"Callie?"*

"Shhhh!" I hissed urgently. "I don't want to wake up Tully."

Ivy frowned. "Tully sleeps with earplugs. You could bring an elephant through and she wouldn't hear. What time is it?" She peered at the pink clock on her dresser.

"I've got Jack outside," I said. "We need to talk to you, right away."

Her mouth and eyes went round. Then she giggled. "I'll get dressed."

"There's no time."

"But I'm in my nightgown. And my . . ." She tugged at her curling rags. "I'll be quick."

Ivy scrambled out of bed and ran for the bathroom. I groaned and sat, gently, in one of the ruffled chairs. I couldn't get the idea of sugar icing out of my head and was afraid that if I even touched anything, it'd snap in two.

Despite her promise to be quick, Ivy took her own sweet time. I imagined her in a ruffled pink bathroom, carefully taking the rags out of her hair, and gritted my teeth. What if Tully woke up early and found Jack loitering in the hall? We'd never get a second alone with Ivy again. We might even get thrown off the lot, and then what? I got up and wandered over to the mantel to look at the photos, trying to keep myself from shouting at Ivy to hurry.

The collection reminded me a lot of the pictures on Mrs. Constantine's piano. There was Mrs. Brownlow, smiling brightly with a little baby in her arms. As I moved along, the baby grew to a toddler, then a little girl with a huge bow in her curls and a perky smile for the camera. Then there were Ivy and Mrs. Brownlow in matching bathing suits by a swimming pool, and Ivy and Mrs. Brownlow standing on a terrace with a pretty blond woman and a big old man with a huge mustache.

My eyes stopped and slowly tracked back and looked again.

"Ivy?" I croaked.

"What is it?" She came out of the bathroom, tying the scarf on a pink and white sailor suit.

"Who's this?" I pointed to the picture of the man with the mustache.

She came up beside me. "Oh, that's Mr. Hearst, and that's Miss Davies with him."

"Miss Davies?" I said, hoping against hope I sounded just plain curious. I couldn't hear my own voice properly over the roaring of blood in my ears. "She's the one who gave you this house, isn't she?"

"That's her." Ivy touched the photo frame gently, like she was afraid it would break. "That was taken at San Simeon. They invite us up there a lot and . . . Are you okay, Callie?"

No. I wasn't. My jaw had fallen open and my lungs had stopped working. "San . . . San Simeon?"

Ivy shrugged. "It's Spanish. Practically everything in California is San this or that. San Bernardino, San Francisco, San Clemente . . ."

"St. Simon?" I croaked. *The house of St. Simon, where no saint has ever been.* I took the photo from the mantel.

"I guess." Ivy cocked her head at me. "Are you sure you're okay, Callie?"

In the golden mountains of the west, in the house of St. Simon. That was where my parents were being held prisoner. I had it in my hand. I'd seen it in the nightmare my uncle dragged me into. It had a broad balcony, with hills stretching out into the misty distance. It belonged to a Mr. Hearst and a Miss Davies, and Ivy Bright visited there all the time.

We'd come all this way, we'd been through so much, and here it was. The answer I'd been searching for had been one floor down from where I'd been sleeping.

This is not right. This cannot be right. I stared at Ivy. She frowned back at me and tried to take the photo out of my hand. I didn't wait for any more questions. I went and yanked her door open.

"We've been set up," I said to Jack.

Jack darted into the room and locked the door behind him. "What's happened?"

"Something's wrong with Callie!" Ivy grabbed hold of his arm and looked up anxiously.

Yes, there was something very wrong, but for a change it wasn't with me. We'd been played on a longer line than either of us realized. I snatched the photo back from Ivy and shoved it at Jack. "This was taken at San Simeon! *San Simeon,* Jack!"

Jack went white. He actually spoke some Spanish, and picked up on the name even faster than I had.

"Ivy gets invited up there all the time," I told him. "It really was a trap for us, and she really was the bait!"

"But how? How did they know where we were?"

"Wait! What's going on?" said Ivy.

"They played like they were kidnapping her so we'd see it and try to help and we'd all get to be friends and she'd invite us up to San Simeon." Shake had said my grand-parents didn't believe I really wanted to free my parents, but that didn't mean the Seelies had to be just as dumb. "We'd go because we'd think we were sneaking up on them, but they'd really be waiting for us!"

Jack slammed his fist into his palm and cussed a long blue streak. "I should have seen it before!"

"*Cut!*" bellowed Ivy.

Jack and I both jumped and stared. Ivy stood there, breathing hard, fists clenched and eyes bright with frustra-tion. "What. Are. You. Talking. About?"

I swallowed and glanced at Jack. He nodded. There really wasn't any point in trying to cover this up. Not even Jack could find a lie that would stretch far enough.

"How much has Jack told you about the Seelies?" I asked.

Ivy frowned. "A little, on the way home yesterday. How you escaped those awful Hoppers and that vigilante man, and made it all the way across Kansas looking for your par-ents. It was better than a movie," she added. "And believe me, I know what I'm talking about." For a second she sounded almost normal, not too babyish or too grown-up.

"Okay. Okay." I fought for calm. What I really wanted to do was run for the door. We had to get out of here, and now. But we owed Ivy. She needed to know what was going on around her, if only so she wouldn't be taken in by the same trick again. "It's like this. There are two kinds of fairies—"

"Seelie and Unseelie," said Ivy. "Jack did tell me that."

"They have to use gates to move between our world and their world. We knew they were holding my parents hostage somewhere, and we thought that if we could find a gate to their world, we might be able to sneak through it to find them. The Seelies like movie people. We thought they might have a gate in a movie studio, so we came here to look for one."

"We figured we'd start with the biggest studio and work our way on down." Jack perched on the edge of one of those ruffly pink chairs. He looked even more out of place in this room than I felt. "That's why we came to MGM. And we think . . ." He stopped, and I could tell he was trying to find some gentle way to break this to her. But there wasn't any way to tell someone her nightmare didn't really belong to her. "We think they knew we were coming and that's why they tried to kidnap you. It was a setup, see? So we'd stay and rescue you and we'd be friends, and you'd invite us up to San Simeon, and they'd trap us there."

Ivy wrinkled her nose, obviously trying hard to

understand. "But why would anybody *want* you to go to San Simeon?"

"Because it's one of *their* places," said Jack.

"How . . . how could you think that?"

"Somebody who knows told me that my parents are being held prisoner in the house of St. Simon, where no saint has ever been, in the golden mountains of the west, above the valley of smoke." I didn't bother with how I'd seen them there last night, being tormented to amuse the party guests. That was way more explaining than Ivy needed.

Ivy was quiet for a minute. I could feel her shifting things around inside her head, and as she did, her whole face changed. It was like a new girl was coming into focus, someone who was a whole lot different from the bubbly, babyish Ivy I'd been trying to get used to. This Ivy had been around a few blocks, if only on the back lot, and maybe had seen a few things.

And then that new girl vanished, leaving little Ivy with us, clasping her hands and all confused.

"I know it's a lot, Ivy," said Jack. "And believe me, I know it's hard to find out you've been used. It's not your fault. Really."

"No. No. It's not that. It's . . ." She took a deep breath. "So was that how those . . . monsters came and got me? Through a gate?"

"There must be an opening down under the Waterloo Bridge," I said. "And now you see why we've got to get out of here. If they think we're on to them, they won't wait for us to come out there. They'll come get us."

"But you can't just leave me!" she cried. "What if they come back and you're not here? What if they think it's my fault you found out?"

I hadn't thought of that. Jack's shoulders slumped.

"They tried to take her once," said Jack. "They might do it again, just to get at you. Us."

Anger bit down hard inside me. "Why would they?" I shouted, completely forgetting we were supposed to be keeping this conversation a secret. "They've already *got* my parents. How many hostages do they need?"

"As many as it takes."

He was right. They wouldn't stop, and I knew that. I just didn't know why they were so god-awful determined. So I could open and close the gates. How many gates did they need? What did they want with the human world anyway? The fairy world was so beautiful and filled with all that light and welcome and magic—what were any of them even *doing* here?

It was, I realized slowly, a question I'd never thought to ask. I'd been so caught up in trying to find my parents, and trying to keep from getting killed doing it, I hadn't stopped to ask why this was happening, not really. I mean, my grandmother had been pretty clear. She wanted me because of the gates and the prophecy. I didn't know much about prophecies, but I did know they didn't get started about small things.

"I'm afraid of them," whispered Ivy.

I didn't want to have to worry about her too. I wanted to break out of this ruffled sugary room and run all the way up to San Simeon, wherever that was, and bang on the doors. I wanted to let all this magic bubbling inside me loose, because I was strong. I had power. I could hurt them all, grant wishes that would have them wishing that they'd never taken my parents, that they'd never been born. I could do it. I could feel the power inside. I could feel the fear and anger close by, just waiting for me to grab them up and put them to work. I could do it. I could.

"Callie. Callie, stop," said Jack.

"What?"

"Your eyes, Callie. Look." Jack pointed at the mirror on the dressing table.

I did look. My eyes shone from inside with a silvery gray, like the flash of lightning on a storm cloud. It was fairy light, and it had weight, like a weapon. It could strike. Behind me, I saw Jack swallow. He was scared of the light in my eyes. He was scared of me.

The anger bled away, because I was scared of me too. Slowly the light faded, and my eyes were my eyes again. But we all knew that light was still there waiting underneath.

"It's okay, Callie," breathed Jack, but he wasn't coming any closer to me.

I closed my eyes, but it didn't help. It was too late. I'd changed. My fairy half wasn't ever going back to sleep again.

If I didn't find a way to use it, it was going to come out all on its own, like it almost had just then. I wondered if Shake had known that would happen. I wondered if this was all part of his particular plan.

"Please, Callie," said Ivy softly. "You'll help, won't you?"

She huddled on that frilly bed, a little girl in the middle of something that was way too big for her. I felt bad. At least I'd known how to fend for myself when the Seelies came after me. Ivy'd never had to learn. She'd been sheltered all her life, with whole batches of people to look out for her health and complexion and make sure she turned up to make movies, but here she was alone in this house with a housekeeper who just wanted to keep her job and a mama who couldn't remember what day of the week it was. She was so used to the studio being a safe place that she went out at night with one of the secretaries just because she was told to.

I took a deep breath. "What if I closed the gate under the bridge? That would at least slow them down."

"Do you think you can?" asked Jack.

"I know I can."

"Okay." He scrubbed at his scalp and looked out through the curtains toward the sunrise. "You close whatever's under the Waterloo Bridge, and we get out of here. Then what?"

"We go up to San Simeon and we get my parents," I said

flatly. "And if the Seelies won't give them back, we tear the place down."

In the mirror, I watched Ivy stand up. Her plump dolly face had turned pale, sharp, and angled, and she clenched her fists at her sides.

"I'm coming with you."

15

Comin' for to Carry

"What?" I turned on my heel to stare at Ivy. "No you're not."

"You'll get hurt." Jack laid a gentle hand on Ivy's shoulder. "We'll be back soon, I promise."

Ivy smiled up at him, all warm and tender. I looked away and waited for the bitter feeling to well up in me, the feeling I had no choice but to call jealousy. But I can honestly say it didn't come. I just felt a little sad, and I didn't know why.

"You're not leaving me here alone." To my surprise, Ivy actually stuck her chin out. It didn't look right on her, but the steel in her voice sounded a lot better than the little-girl giggle. "What if they do come for me? What am I going to do?"

Jack and I both knew what kind of monsters the Seelies could send out. Rougarou and his sister were just the start of it. And they weren't even what I was really worried about. What really worried me was how it was going on six o'clock and Tully would be up and about soon. Even if she wasn't working with the Seelies, she would never let Ivy go with us instead of to school and her movie job.

"Besides, you're going to need me," said Ivy. "There's a whole lot of shoots going on today. No one will ask questions if you're with me."

I didn't want somebody else to be responsible for. But I couldn't see another way out. As little as I wanted to admit it, Jack's trick with the clipboard probably wasn't going to be enough cover for us today.

"Okay," I said. "But you have to do exactly what we say, understand?"

"I will." Ivy nodded until her curls bounced. "You'll see. It'll be—"

The clacking of metal on metal cut her off. A split second later, the door flew open.

"Well!" Tully stood on the threshold and planted her hands on her hips. A ring of keys dangled from her fingers. "What is going on here?" She leveled the words at me.

I gaped like a fish, but Ivy stepped between us. "I invited Jack and Callie in," she said firmly. "It was all my idea. So if you want to be mad at someone, you can just be mad at me."

The look on Mrs. Tully's face said there was plenty of mad to go around, and probably enough for second helpings as well. I realized I was holding my breath, waiting to feel the pressure of the magic building around me again, and wondering what I'd do if I did. But nothing came. Instead, I watched Tully shrink reluctantly in on herself. She was remembering what she had told me, how she and I had no real power here, not if Ivy took a dislike to us.

Or maybe she was just biding her time.

"You." Tully turned toward Jack. "You *hooligan.* You get out of here and you wait until you're sent for. Is that understood?"

"Yes, ma'am. Sorry, ma'am." Jack tried his wide-eyed innocent look. I tell you, I'd never before seen it wither as fast as it did under the heat of Tully's glower. The woman had to be Seelie. No human could stand up to Jack's charm.

"I'll just . . . see you downstairs, Callie," Jack muttered as he slipped past her.

"As for *you . . .*" Tully turned the full force of her glower on me. I made myself remember who and what I was, and met her eyes. They were dark and popping out of her head, but I couldn't tell if the light in them was the glare of the sunrise or something else. "You get yourself down into the kitchen where you belong!"

"She stays," announced Ivy.

Unfortunately, this time Tully was not backing down so easily. "Miss Ivy, I am responsible for your well-being while I am keeping house, and this girl is supposed to be in the kitchen making your breakfast."

"And she has absolutely nothing to wear," snapped Ivy. "I mean, *look* at her." Tully did look, all the way down that long nose. I just tried not to squirm or tug at my blouse, which was the same one I'd been wearing the day before. "She'll be down to fix breakfast just as soon as she's decent."

I concentrated on keeping my mouth shut, and remembering Ivy really was trying to help. Tully, meanwhile, looked like she'd just been forced to swallow a spoonful of vinegar.

"Very well," said Tully, but she was in no way surrendering. It was a very good thing I'd already been planning to get out of there, because the last look the housekeeper leveled at me as she closed the door told me I didn't have a job anymore. She'd go straight to Mr. Mayer about it if she had to.

As soon as the door clicked shut, Ivy stuck her tongue out, giggled, and bounced back to me. "There! That fixed her."

"Sure did." I tried to put some feeling into those words but came up more than a little short. "Look, Ivy—"

"Don't be mad," she said. "What I said about the clothes, that was just to get rid of her. Although, I mean, you really don't have anything to wear." She looked me up and down. "Wait here!"

Ivy ran to one of the room's other doors and threw it open. On the other side waited the biggest closet I'd ever seen in my life. Clothes bars ran along both walls, and they were filled from end to end with outfits on padded hangers. You could have stocked Gimbels department store with what she'd crammed in there, even if you didn't count the shoes lined up underneath or the hats in their cubbyholes at the back.

It took me a full minute to find my voice. "Ivy, we really don't have time for this. . . ."

"Yes, we do!" She was already yanking clothes off their hangers. The smell of old roses and new mothballs rose up strong enough to make me cough. "Besides, if we don't dress you up, Tully'll smell a rat." She dumped an armload of clothes on her bed and smiled like she'd never been so happy. "Look. This one brings out the color of your eyes." She held a blue pleated skirt with a matching long sailor blouse in front of me. I looked at myself in the vanity table mirror. It did look good. I wished it didn't. Ivy grinned, tossed it aside, and reached for another outfit. "And this one . . . I never could wear this. My color's not right. I look like a ghost." She held up a burgundy dress trimmed with black ribbons. "You could be like Marlene Dietrich, all mysterious."

I tried to picture myself lounging on a sofa with my hand thrown dramatically over my forehead. That imaginary me looked so ridiculous that I giggled, and Ivy smiled again. It really was pretty. I'd been thinking about big things, I'd been afraid and angry and confused, and I was out of time and probably out of what little luck I'd ever had. It felt funny to be up here looking at something as stupid as clothes, but it felt good too. Like something a normal girl might do, with a normal friend.

"You know, Jack really likes you," Ivy said.

I grimaced. I didn't want to talk about this. I wasn't

completely done with all the bad feelings that had been stewing since we met her.

Ivy, though, wasn't ready to drop the subject. "He does," she insisted. "I can tell."

"You can?" I asked before I could stop myself.

"When you spend your life making pictures, you either learn to tell when people really mean what they say or you get trampled over fast. I've seen it happen." Her voice dropped to a whisper. "Especially to the kids. I wish somebody really liked me," she added, scowling down at the clothes. "But nobody does. It's just the movies."

"But your mama . . . ," I started, and then wished I hadn't, because Ivy's face crumpled up.

"Mama doesn't care about me."

"That's not true. I'm sure it's not."

"It is! She just cares about the pretty clothes and the movies and the interviews and the money. She never loved me!" Ivy busted out bawling.

"It's okay, it's okay," I said quickly. I'd never had anybody cry on me before. I didn't know what to do. I put my arms around her and sat us both down on the bed. I felt ashamed for every mean thought I'd had about her and Jack. She was just a kid in a world that was too big and too strong for her. At the same time, I kept thinking about what Mrs. Tully would have to say if the brightest little star in Hollywood turned up downstairs with swollen eyes and a red nose. I also kept thinking how Ivy might be right. If

Mrs. Brownlow was a Seelie, she probably didn't love her. She really would love the beauty and the lights, and would want to use Ivy to be around them. But I couldn't say that, or anything like it. Not until I was sure. I had to say something, though.

"I used to think my mama didn't love me either."

"You did?" Ivy sniffed. I pulled a lacy little hanky out of the pile of clothes and handed it to her. Ivy blew her nose so hard she honked. Something else I bet *Movie Fan* magazine never saw. But at least the tears slowed down.

I nodded. "Back in Kansas, after the dust storms came. There was no work and no guests for our hotel. We were flat busted and the whole town was half buried in blow dirt, but Mama wouldn't move us. It got so bad I caught the dust pneumonia, and she *still* wouldn't sell out. I thought . . . I thought she was crazy and she didn't love me, but it turned out she was trying to keep me safe. My papa had promised to come back for us, see, and there was some kind of spell or something on the hotel where we lived that was keeping the Seelies from finding me until he did." Grandmother had said the MGM studio was warded against the Unseelies. I guess Papa had warded the old hotel against the Seelies. One day I'd get to thank him for it, I told myself. One day soon.

Anger prickled against my thoughts. But it didn't come from me. I stared at Ivy. She was turning one of her wistful expressions on me. But I wasn't wrong about what I felt. Under that innocent face, she was boiling mad.

"You're so lucky. I don't even have a papa." Ivy's mouth

snapped shut and her eyes went wide. "You can't tell any-body about that. It'd be bad for my image."

"I won't," I said, but I bit my lip as a new question climbed to the top of the pile in my head.

There were all kinds of ways for an unmarried woman to try to make her baby look legitimate. She could move to a new town, tack *Mrs.* onto her name, and pretend she'd been married to a man who had died or was "traveling." Or there was adoption. Everybody back in Slow Run knew why Sandra Keene had been sent away. When her mother turned up two months later with a baby she'd "adopted," we all pretended we didn't think anything of it. Except we all did. Those tricks wouldn't be so easy to pull if you were famous, though, or if the man you were stepping out with was already married.

There were all those pictures on the mantel, and the only man in any of them was Mr. Hearst, and Mr. Hearst was wrapped up with the Seelies somehow. Miss Davies ac-tually looked a lot like Mrs. Brownlow, or like Mrs. Brown-low tried to look. Miss Davies had also gone and given Ivy a whole house to live in. Which was a really big present to give to a little girl who was just a friend. What if the famous Miss Davies had had a baby she couldn't account for, and she'd had to give it away?

Then I thought how Mrs. Brownlow sure didn't act like she was enjoying any of her fame and money and pretty clothes, or even noticing she had them. I thought about how fond of kidnapping people the fairies were.

Before I got any further, Ivy honked into the handkerchief again and wiped her eyes. "We'd better get you dressed. Which outfit do you like best?"

"Gee, Ivy, I can't go climbing around in a nice dress." I'd ruined my silk stockings the last time we'd gone to the Waterloo Bridge.

"Oh, but you don't have to." She rifled through the pile and pulled out a pair of blue jeans and a checked shirt. "Here! I wore this in *Sunrise Farm*. Let's try it on!"

She seemed so cheered up by the idea, that's what we did. The way she fussed over me, you'd've thought I was going to a debutante ball or something. She had to roll the cuffs on the jeans and the sleeves of the shirt just so. She ran back into her closet to get a pair of ankle socks and penny loafers for me to wear. She even unbraided my hair, brushed it out, and tied it back in a red scarf that matched the checks on the shirt.

"There!" Ivy cried triumphantly. "The perfect country girl!"

I knew what country girls looked like, and what I saw in the mirror didn't look anything like one. I looked like a young lady playing a kind of farmland dress-up.

In fact, I looked pretty.

"I can't wait until Jack gets a look at you!" Ivy leaned over my shoulder and gave me a quick hug, and I didn't even mind so much this time. I'd been nine kinds of stupid lately, and right then I couldn't even have said for sure what it had all been about. I also couldn't take my eyes off the grown-up-looking me in the mirror. It was funny—I'd dressed up nice before, but somehow I felt nicer this time. Prettier. Older. Suddenly I couldn't wait for Jack to get a look at me either.

"Oh, and there's one more thing." Ivy ran over to the white princess-style telephone on her bedside table. She dialed, then waited. I heard a voice on the other end.

"Little Red Schoolhouse."

Ivy pinched her nose and lifted her chin. "Good morning, Miss MacDonald," she said in an absolutely pitch-perfect imitation of Tully's voice. "Miss Bright will be absent today. She has a slight fever and will be staying home to rest. Is that understood?"

"Of course, Mrs. Tully. I'll make a note to have Judy bring her homework by."

"Thank you."

Ivy hung up, and she grinned at my surprise. "Not much good being an actress if you can't use it to play hooky every now and then, is there? Now, let's get out of here."

The brightest little star in Hollywood grabbed my hand and pulled me after her.

Of course it wasn't that simple. Or that quick. We had to get through breakfast first. Tully spent the whole meal stationed squarely in the dining room watching Ivy eat her toast and grapefruit. Mrs. Brownlow was nowhere to be seen. Jack was making himself plenty scarce too.

But finally I heard Tully order Ivy off to school. She held

the kitchen door open and kept her glare turned up high while I cleared away the grapefruit dish and the empty toast rack. She stood, arms folded, and watched while I washed the dishes. I clenched my jaw and wondered if I dared a little magic. Just enough to send her running for the toilet or something.

Then the phone rang, and Tully stomped off to answer it. The second she was out of the kitchen, Jack's head popped up over the windowsill. He grinned and jerked his chin sideways. I should have known he and Ivy would have a plan. I ran for the back door without even bothering to wipe the soapsuds off my arms.

When Jack saw me all done up in Ivy's outfit, his eyes flipped open wide. I barely had time to get a decent blush going before Ivy came running up behind us. She must have made that phone call from someplace, but I didn't want to slow things down by asking where. Ivy grinned, grabbed our hands, and all but skipped out the garden gate.

I'll say one thing about having Ivy along: she knew exactly where she was going. It was plain as paint that this was not the first time the brightest little star in Hollywood had gone sneaking around the studio. Lot No. 1 had straight streets, and the streams of cars and trucks and people that made up the studio's private rush hour were filling them up fast. But Ivy ignored the main streets. She led us down alleys, between piles of used scenery and stacks of boards. She ducked through the trucks in the garage and out the back door, which opened onto the street, a route to the outside that Jack admitted in a whisper he hadn't even known existed.

We'd reached the studio gate that opened onto Overland Avenue and the Lot No. 2 side. Ivy had us all crouch behind the garbage cans that had been set out for collection. It stank to high heaven, but she ignored that and looked at her watch. "We have to wait," she whispered.

"For what?" I whispered back.

"Shift change." She nodded toward the guard shack. I could just see a shadow moving in the little white house. "Jeff and Solly will talk racing. That's when we go."

She'd just finished when we saw a blue-uniformed guard coming up Overland, his tin lunch pail in one hand and a big thermos in the other. He strolled up to the guard shack and stood there with his back to us, talking to whoever was sitting in the house. Pretty soon he pulled a paper out of his back pocket and spread it out.

Ivy signaled us with a wave and took off running. She had a turn of speed on her I wouldn't have expected. She darted through the gate and back behind another row of garbage cans on the inside of the fence. Keeping low, she edged out from behind the cans and sneaked behind a tin-roofed shed. I followed with Jack, expecting any second to hear somebody yell "Halt!"

A few more twists and turns and we were in the middle of the warehouse district, with men in caps and shirtsleeves moving whole apartment buildings' worth of furniture in and out of sheds. They didn't even look up as we raced past.

Finally, on a road that ran between the warehouses and a set of old-fashioned small-town houses, Ivy decided we were safe. She ducked into the unfinished back of one of those pretty little houses and made a big show of grinning and fanning her face. Jack made a show of applauding, so Ivy dropped a curtsy.

"How'd you know about all this?" Maybe I shouldn't have been so surprised after her imitation of Tully on the phone, but I was.

She shrugged. "All the studio kids do it. If we didn't, we'd never get any time to ourselves. Now, follow me!"

We did. We ran and ducked and waited and tiptoed. Ivy led us through a city's worth of crowds and confusion in a place where she was easily the most recognized little girl going, and not one person so much as turned their head. We took the long way around, past the small-town railway station and a ramshackle street that was supposed to be China or India or someplace like that. We cut through Italy and Spain and came out in a proper English garden with carefully clipped hedges and blooming roses. I picked up flashes of feeling from the behind-the-scenes workers as we hustled past. They were anxious, tired, strained, focused. Everyone was wishing that this time things would go right. I felt those wishes pushing against me, and I had to push back hard to keep them out. It was tiring and didn't leave much room in my thoughts for planning or wondering, or even for really watching where I was going. So when Jack skidded to a halt behind a gardener's shed, I smacked into him nose-first.

"Oh, no!" gasped Ivy. "Not today!"

I peered around Jack, still rubbing my nose. There was the Waterloo Bridge and the twisty lake in front of us. We only had the lawn and the fake cemetery between us and it. But the cemetery wasn't empty. A woman knelt in front of one small, crooked cross, her head and shoulders bowed.

"What's she doing?" whispered Jack.

I was wondering that too, because even at this distance, I could see the woman was Mrs. Brownlow.

16

Like a Motherless Child

"What do we do?" I shrank farther back behind the shed.

"Nothing," said Ivy through gritted teeth. "Just wait. She'll go away. She never stays long."

Jack said quietly, "She's crying."

She was. Great rivers of tears streaked both her cheeks. She cried like one of the graveyard statues might have—no shaking shoulders, no sobs, just those tears rolling silently down.

Ivy sighed sharply. She looked left and right, then marched out into the movie cemetery.

"Mama!"

Slowly Mrs. Brownlow turned her head and looked up at the girl standing over her. She didn't bother to wipe her wet face. "Ivy?"

"Of course it's Ivy. What are you doing here? For heaven's sake, get up!"

But Mrs. Brownlow's gaze had already drifted back down to the lopsided plaster cross. "It's just so sad. She's dead, you know."

"No one's dead, Mama. This is a movie set!" Ivy got both hands under Mrs. Brownlow's elbows and boosted her to her feet. "Now, go home." Ivy turned her firmly in the direction of Main Street.

"Yes. I want to go home." Mrs. Brownlow swayed and stumbled. She caught herself and fumbled with her pocketbook. But she did not seem the least bit ready to begin walking. Instead, she stepped around in a careful, awkward circle until she faced Ivy again. "Can I please go now?"

I bit my lip. Jack was practically vibrating, he was trying so hard to hold himself still. Our eyes locked, and he nodded as he understood what I meant to do. Maybe I was losing us a chance at the one gate we knew about, or worse, but I was not going to leave Mrs. Brownlow trapped by whatever magic held her. I wouldn't leave Ivy stuck in her confusion and fury either.

"The *bungalow,* Mama," said Ivy impatiently. "You're going back to the bungalow and you're going to stay there."

"Be ready to run," I whispered.

Jack shifted his weight into a sprinter's crouch. I sucked in a deep breath and focused on Mrs. Brownlow. Then I opened my magic and looked again.

It was a good thing I was already hunkered down on the ground, or I would have fallen over. Mrs. Brownlow was enchanted all right, only it wasn't just one bit of magic holding her. It was a thousand. At first, it felt like the puppet strings that held my parents and made them dance. But as I stared with my magic eyes, I saw this was a whole lot different. It was . . . *Sloppy* was the first word that came to me. Little enchantments had been thrown at Olive Brownlow and made to stick until their competing demands wrapped around her like a cocoon. There was still a person in there. I could just barely feel her under all those suffocating layers. What I couldn't feel was how to set Mrs. Brownlow free. If I just started cutting at that huge tangle of magic, I might hurt her.

Jack laid his hand on my shoulder in silent warning. I yanked my magic back in so my regular senses cleared. That was when I heard the crunch of tires on the dirt road. Jack retreated farther behind the shed, pushing me with him, just as the Rolls-Royce pulled up. The back window was half open, and I saw Tully's sour face staring out.

Mrs. Brownlow was patting her curls to make sure they were in place and adjusting her hat. "But I don't want to go to the bungalow," she told her daughter. "I want to go home."

Ivy's temper snapped. "That is home, you silly woman!" she screamed. "What do I have to do—"

"Miss Ivy!" Tully climbed out of the car without waiting for Sumner to get the door. "What on earth . . . ?"

A man clambered out behind Tully. He was short, white, and balding and carried a doctor's bag in his pudgy hand.

Ivy turned, and as soon as she spotted him, all the fury and impatience were gone. In an instant, she became nothing but an anxious little girl holding her mother's hand.

"Oh, thank goodness, Mrs. Tully!" Ivy ran up to the housekeeper and hugged her. "Mama's had a turn. She needs help!"

The doctor stepped forward. He was the kind of man who radiated calm and efficiency. Tully pulled herself out of Ivy's grip and followed along behind him, the thick lenses of her glasses glinting in the sun.

"Now then, Mrs. Brownlow, what's the matter?" The doctor took Mrs. Brownlow's wrist in one hand and pulled out a pocket watch. "Not feeling well today, is it?"

"I'd like to go home now, please," Mrs. Brownlow said politely, like she was ordering a cherry Coke at the soda fountain. The woman was still there under the enchanted tangle that commanded her to stay put, to smile, to forget. That woman really did want to go home to where her daughter was. Even though her daughter was right here. Even though she thought her daughter was dead. It didn't make sense, but it was all in there, and it was slowly dying like it was starved for air.

Tully hovered behind the doctor, ready to jump in if she saw anything she didn't like. She thought she was looking after her interests. Maybe she was, but she was also in the way.

"Wish, Jack," I murmured. "Wish Tully gone."

Jack nodded, and I reached for his wish.

Nothing happened. Nothing at all. It was like some-body'd slapped a blindfold on me. I couldn't feel the wish. I couldn't even find it. In fact, I could barely feel Jack.

"Yes, yes." The doctor tucked his watch away and laid his hand on Mrs. Brownlow's forehead. "We'll take care of that. You come with me now, and I'll take you home."

"What's the matter?" hissed Jack.

"I can't . . . I can't feel." I was smothered and blind, deaf and dumb.

"Thank you." Mrs. Brownlow smiled and followed along, docile as any lost lamb.

I found myself looking at Ivy, who was playing the part of the worried, confused daughter. Then I looked at Tully, frowning like a thundercloud as the doctor gently helped Mrs. Brownlow into the car while Sumner held the door. "You'll watch her, won't you, Mrs. Tully?" Ivy clutched the housekeeper's hand. "I've got my shoot this afternoon—I won't be able to be there. Please say you will."

Mrs. Tully looked sourly down at the young actress. She had only so many options right now, and she knew it. "You should be in school," she said.

"And I'm going. Right now. I just . . . somebody had to stay with Mama." There was absolutely no accusation in the statement, just a pathetic sadness. Mrs. Tully didn't want to buy it, but she had no choice. The doctor leaned out of the Rolls, clearly wanting to get the show on the road. Tully sighed sharply, conceding the battle to Ivy, and got into the car.

The world returned in a rush. I collapsed against the garden shed. Jack shuffled beside me, concerned, questioning. Out at the edge of the cemetery, Ivy stood clasping her hands in front of her and putting everything she had into acting brave as the Rolls pulled away.

I tried to shake Jack off, but he wouldn't be shaken. He helped me stand and waited until my tremors eased. He thought I was weak. I wasn't. I was mad. Burning, boiling, steaming mad.

Ivy was looking around to make sure the coast was clear. Then she gestured for us to join her, quick.

"You shouldn't have seen that," she muttered bitterly as we came up to her side.

"It's okay," I told her. "I've . . . there's some good news."

"There is?" This time Ivy's confusion was genuine. "What?"

"Well, it's sort of good." I hesitated. "Your mother's not sick or anything. She's magicked."

"*What?*"

"Somebody's been magicking her, for a long time now. I tried to help her, but it was too much for me. I'm sorry," I added.

For the first time since I'd met her, Ivy's face went completely blank. "You . . . you tried to magic my mother?"

"Only to see if I could help her. You have to stop being mad at her, Ivy. It's not her fault she's like she is."

Ivy sat down, right on the grass. Slowly she tried on a set of different expressions, like she was trying to figure out which one fit the scene best—wide-eyed shock, scrunched-up worry, or tight, frowning anger.

"We can still find a way to help." Jack sat down beside her. "Once we've got Callie's parents out. Her pop's a real fairy. He'll be able to do something to take the magic off your mother."

"But . . ." Ivy hesitated, and tried on a few more expressions. Bewilderment lifted her eyebrows, concentration lowered them, tears glittered in her eyes.

"It was Tully," I said.

"*Tully!*" Ivy actually giggled. "But she's just a housekeeper!"

"That doesn't mean she can't be half Seelie," I said. "It'd be a great way to keep herself near the movies, and help case the joint for people they'd want to take to their court."

"Tully!" Ivy shook her head again. "I don't believe it. You think *Tully's* a fairy?"

"You've got to believe it, Ivy," said Jack. "No matter what happens next, you've got to get her away from the house. Get Mr. Mayer to fire her if you have to, but get her away from you."

Ivy stuck out her chin. "Okay. That's just what I'll do."

"Go now," I urged her. "It'll be better if you're out of the way."

"No!" cried Ivy immediately. "I'm not going alone.

There might be . . . more of them. I can't." She grabbed Jack's hand. "Please don't make me."

Jack shot a glance at me. He'd seen how fast Ivy could try on expressions and emotions just like I had. I think he was impressed in an almost professional way, as a fellow people-charmer. I also think he wanted to believe she wasn't acting when she looked at him, but he'd been around too much to swallow that easily. At least I hoped he had, because what he did was pat her hand in a big-brotherly kind of way.

"We won't make you do anything, Ivy, but we've got to be quick, and you have to stay out of sight."

"I will. Just like I said."

"Okay, then." Jack flashed one of his best smiles. "Callie? What do we do now?"

I didn't really know, but I faced the dark span of the Waterloo Bridge anyway. I was starting to hate this place. I wanted to be gone from here. My brain was full, tired, and confused. I shoved my wishes and wanting down so I could ease my magic back open.

The world around us shifted focus. The clamor of the wishes and work filled the spaces between normal sights and sounds. It was spiced with the complex, curious feel of the place in front of us, which had been built so fast, and built to be so many things. Wishes and feelings had been crystallized here, and new ones made. All that work, all that new thinking and new hoping blended together like orchestra music. I wanted to stop and savor it all, but I couldn't.

We had no time for me to get dizzy, distracted, and stupid on other people's feelings. I pushed forward. I had to find the gate.

After a while, I felt something that might have been what Uncle Shake called a thin place, but I couldn't quite make sense of it. It was like there was something in between me and it. I thought I could reach through if I strained, but I'd have to open up further, and I was already taking a risk. Tully might return, or she might send one of her friends. Slowly I pulled myself back. It wasn't easy. My magic didn't like being shut off once it started to warm up.

"I need to get closer."

"Okay. Let's go, Ivy." Jack took her hand and nodded to me. Ivy sighed and blinked up at him. I tried not to see. I also tried not to get mad. She'd just been told that her mother was magicked and that she was in real danger, and she was still *acting*. When was she going to cut it out and take this seriously?

We slipped across the road and onto the curve of the bridge. I shivered. Last time we'd been here, the Seelies had almost caught us. I wondered where Mr. Robeson was now, and why he hadn't called. Another sliver of anger stabbed into me. So much for all his stuff about wanting to help.

I could feel the gate more clearly from here. In fact, it was right underneath us. It was small and had raggedy edges, and it squirmed as I tried to get my magic around it. I kept reaching, but my grip kept slipping. I frowned. Maybe the squirm was the ward Grandmother had talked about. Maybe it was the Seelie equivalent of a NO TRESPASSING sign.

For a minute I wished Shake was here so I could ask him what to do. But that probably wasn't a good idea.

"Ivy, you keep a lookout." I took a deep breath. "I'm going under the bridge."

"In that water?" Ivy pulled a face that couldn't have been good for her famously delicate complexion. "Yuck!"

I agreed with her, but I wasn't going to waste any breath on it.

"You'll be okay up here on your own?" Jack asked Ivy.

"Of course, silly." She slapped his arm. "You saw. I can get anybody to do anything out here."

"Okay, then. Let's go, Callie."

We hurried down the far side of the bridge. I kept sneaking side glances at Jack, because he kept sneaking side glances back up at Ivy.

"What're you looking at?" he whispered as we turned toward the water's edge.

" 'You'll be okay up here on your own?' " I singsonged back at him. "She's a big faker, Jack!"

"Oh, lay off," he grumbled. "She's not like you. The act's all she's got."

"I'm not so sure about that. She was awfully good at working the system here."

"Yeah, and if you had to get around Tully all the time, you would be too."

I shook my head. It didn't add up, but there wasn't time to argue about it now. I had to get myself into that black lake.

Yuck.

I didn't bother pulling my borrowed penny loafers off. I just sat at the edge of the lake, gritted my teeth, and slid down into the water. It only came up to my waist, which was good, because I didn't know the first thing about swimming. It was warm and oily, and my feet raised the stink of tar and garbage as I shuffled forward. There was a layer of slime on the bottom that I just plain didn't want to think about, but it did make me really, really glad I'd kept my shoes on.

Jack, as usual, didn't hesitate. He just double-checked to make sure nobody was around and then sloshed forward as though he did this every day. Together we plowed toward the bridge.

The underside of the Waterloo Bridge was a bunch of metal beams and bracing draped with weed, birds' nests, and spiderwebs that glistened in the fuzzy sunbeams that slanted through the arches. The stink had been trapped under here long enough to grow big and strong. I was pretty sure something scuttled away from us. It squeaked too.

"See anything?" hissed Ivy from overhead, where she was dry and not in the middle of the world's most unbelievably bad smell.

"Well? Are we close enough?" Jack's whisper bounced

back from about six different directions. I swallowed, and as carefully as I could, I opened up my magic one more time.

It was different here. The squirmy uncertainty was behind us. I felt like I'd opened a window: warmth and the clean scents of sunshine and rain spilled through the far side of the gate. I could feel its jagged edges as clearly as if I rested my palms against them. If I leaned forward in just the right way, I'd be able to see through it to what was beyond.

What would I see this time? All at once I wanted to get closer, open up further. I squashed that feeling. My magic liked to be let out to play a little too much sometimes, and when it was, my good sense took a powder.

"Find it?" Jack's voice sounded a long way off. I was already halfway out of the human world. I felt myself teetering. One more step with my magic open like this and I'd be all the way gone.

I grabbed Jack's hand to keep me steady, and I stretched out the way I would stretch out one finger, easing forward, trying to trace all those jagged, rippling edges so I could bundle them together and squeeze them shut.

"What's going on?" Ivy stage-whispered from overhead. I tried to ignore her and keep focused on the gate. "Have you found it? What do you see?"

"Ivy, no—" Jack croaked.

But he was too late. She was screaming. "Ahhhh!"

Splash!

I got a gout of water in the face, and it tasted as bad as it smelled. I slammed back into the human world, and the whole place was churning, with Ivy screaming and Jack saying, "Hold on, hold on!"

I knuckled filthy water out of my eyes. When I could see anything again, what I saw was Ivy, looking about as miserable as a drowned cat, all scrunched up against Jack, and he had his arms around her.

"It's okay, it's okay," Jack told her. "You're safe. I got you."

"What're you doing?" I demanded in a loud whisper.

"I just wanted to see!" she wailed, and tried to push her dripping curls out of her eyes and shake the water off her hands. For a second I thought she was going to be sick. "I leaned over too far. I'm sorry!"

"It's okay," said Jack again, and he glared at me. "It was an *accident.*"

"An accident that's going to have the whole studio breathing down our necks, you little screwball faker!"

"Callie!" exclaimed Jack.

"What?"

"Don't be mad," whimpered Ivy. "Jack, please, tell her I'm sorry."

"Of course you're sorry. And you're sorry too, aren't you, Callie?"

No, I wasn't. Not one little bit. She kept messing things up, and I couldn't get rid of her. She was worse than a bad penny. Plus she was a total faker and couldn't even help her mother when she needed it.

"Jack, get her out of here," I ordered, adding, "She might get hurt." If he was going to keep being sweet and stupid on her after everything we'd seen, maybe I could get it to work for us.

"She's right," Jack said to Ivy.

"No! Don't leave me alone! I won't be frightened if you're with me."

Oh, *brother.* Jack wasn't going to buy that line, was he? But the way he was looking at her, I was afraid he might.

"We'd better hurry," Jack said.

He meant that *I'd* better hurry. Well, who needed either of them?

I swung away from Jack. I couldn't concentrate if I looked at the little faker shivering against him and him standing there with his arms around her. I let out a long, slow breath, then opened up inside and edged forward. The water seemed thicker here as it slid across my skin and around my ankles. The smell was thicker too. All kinds of bad things had been stewing under here for a long time.

The gate was just ahead of me. I could feel it waiting like an open well in the dark. I inched forward. Something brushed against me: a stray scent of lemon, a thread of music, a soft voice. I felt Jack's worry and Ivy's worry, and that made things easier. I could pull that out and tuck it into my magic to make me stronger. I found the edges of the gate. I plucked them up one by one, gathering them together, drawing them closed. Something squeaked and scrambled. Ivy screamed. Jack shoved against me hard, and I stumbled—straight into the gate. He grabbed my hand and I spun around, but I couldn't catch my balance, and we were both falling into the water, through the water, and then past it into the gate.

The last thing I saw before it closed around us was Ivy Bright, looking down on us, gold light gleaming in her baby-blue eyes.

I owed Tully an apology.

17

That Bright World to Which I Go

Betwixt and between rushed around us too fast for me to find anything to grab hold of. I screamed, and Jack screamed with me. There was no direction, nothing to hang on to, no way to stop. We tumbled through a blaze of color until I couldn't tell whether we were falling down or rising up. Then it didn't matter which way we were going, because we plunged into cold water.

I gasped. Water filled my lungs. I choked and coughed, fighting for air and getting nothing but more water. My hands flailed and my feet kicked through a wash of blue and bubbles. My lungs were on fire and frozen solid at the same time, and everything was fading down into the dark. I had to breathe but I couldn't breathe, and I couldn't breathe and I couldn't breathe. . . .

I was rising. Somebody hauled me out of the water across a ledge that grated against all my ribs. I flopped sideways, my body cold and heavy as death. It didn't matter. I couldn't breathe.

Somebody whacked me on the back, hard, then did it again. My stomach heaved and I vomited water and pain. I coughed, and my lungs heaved in the other direction, sucking down air. That hurt like blazes too. I threw up more water and coughed and retched, and hurt, and breathed.

After a while, my eyes started working enough to see Jack crouched beside me, soaked to the skin and panting.

"Thanks," I croaked.

"Anytime," he answered with an easy grin that lasted just long enough for him to take a look around us. "Where the heck are we?"

That was a really good question. I managed to push myself up into a sitting position so I could see better, and only coughed a little doing it. We sure weren't under that bridge anymore. We weren't betwixt and between, nor were we in fairyland. The blue walls surrounding us were decorated with sparkling gold tiles that turned the whole room into a gigantic jewel box. Lights shaped like old-style streetlamps lined both sides of an enormous swimming pool. Arched windows overlooked misted hilltops under a cloudless sky.

We weren't alone either. People lounged on deck chairs between marble statues of old Roman soldiers and naked women. There was a little tiled stage topped by a shining black piano. A black man in black tie sat on the bench, creating a stream of slow jazz to blend with the lazy talk that echoed off the tiled walls and painted ceiling.

". . . and did you see that thing Margaret was wearing? Betty, I swear . . ."

". . . no, no, no, old sport, if you want to get a really good shot, you . . ."

". . . well, of course I turned him down! That desperate I am not. . . ."

Men in waiter uniforms and women decked out as maids carried trays of martinis and champagne. The servants moved between the loungers, passing out glasses, picking up empties, and dumping out ashtrays. About half the people on the deck were smoking, and the clouds wreathed their heads like the mist on the hills outside. More people swam in the pool. They called to each other, tossing a volleyball around and laughing and just having a plain old good time.

Nobody looked at us. Two kids in soaking wet street clothes had appeared in the middle of this huge, gorgeous indoor swimming pool, and not one of the people so much as glanced at us. A door opened in the side wall and a new woman walked in. She had a cloud of dark hair and wore a white silk robe. Every head turned and all the people called out to greet her, but none of them looked at us. Jack got himself to his feet and marched up to that dark-haired woman as she shed her robe to show off her scarlet bathing suit. He waved his hand in front of her eyes. She brushed it aside, as if a fly had buzzed in front of her, and walked over to start chatting about the suit to her lady friends, where she got it and how much it cost.

"We're not here," he said. "Wherever this is, we're not all the way here."

"This cannot be good." I scrambled to my feet.

A jazz note faltered. I whipped my head around to look at the piano player, just in time to see him drop his gaze back to the keys.

They keep me playing by the pool during the day. . . .

But right then another door opened, sending a fresh shaft of golden light spilling across the floor. I spun around. The pretty people at the pool party didn't look up.

Uh-oh. "Jack . . ."

"My goodness," said a man. "What have we here?"

He was blond, tall, bronzed, and as perfectly shaped as the marble statues standing sentry by the windows. He wore yellow swim trunks and a white shirt that stretched the word LIFEGUARD tight across his chest. He even had a whistle around his neck. If it wasn't for the rabbit, he would have looked like he belonged there.

But there was that rabbit. The lifeguard carried a fluffy white bunny in the crook of one overmuscled arm and petted its floppy ears as he walked toward us. And still not one of the swimmers looked up. They couldn't see him either, but he could sure see us. The piano player missed another note. I felt the wrongness of it under my skin. I felt something else too. Fear.

"I . . . um . . ." I glanced desperately at Jack.

"We're guests of Miss Davies," Jack said immediately. I nodded in rapid agreement, and tried not to be too obvious about edging closer to him.

The lifeguard ruffled his bunny's ears. "But you weren't supposed to be here until tomorrow."

I about swallowed my tongue. Jack, of course, took it in stride. "We came up a day early. Didn't Miss Davies tell you?"

The lifeguard was rounding the edge of the pool and coming up on our side now. "No. I had no orders about early arrival."

"Really? That's strange." Jack frowned at me, his face all done up in confusion. "You called, didn't you?" I nodded fast, widening my eyes in my best Ivy Bright imitation. "You'd better go ask Miss Davies," Jack said to the lifeguard. "We can wait here until you get back."

"I could do that, I guess. But . . ." He squinted at me. "Can you even swim?"

"Um . . ."

"What's that got to do with anything?" asked Jack.

"Oh, nothing really." The lifeguard smiled, and for a moment I understood what it was to be dazzled. "In fact, it makes things easier."

The lifeguard tossed the rabbit at Jack and himself at me. His shoulder hit my chest. I flew backward and together we sank down into that cold, clear water.

"No!" Jack screamed.

Panic filled me, and I clutched at the nearest solid thing, which was the lifeguard. I climbed him like a tree, trying to get my head above water. I had time to haul in one huge breath and hear Jack shouting and swearing. He was dodging between the deck chairs with their pretty, blind occupants. That rabbit had gotten a whole lot bigger. It didn't look like a rabbit anymore either. Now it looked like a gigantic white stallion, with red eyes and all its big horse teeth bared.

"Catch!" Jack shouted at me, and he was wishing. Wishing hard. Wishing I could swim. I grabbed that wish, flipped it around, dragged it inside me, and made it come true.

"Uh-oh," murmured the lifeguard.

All my fear of water vanished. I sucked in a big breath and dove down deep. My arms and legs pushed through the water as though it wasn't even there, until I crouched on the bottom of that pool. The lifeguard's legs kicked overhead. I grinned and jumped.

I shot up off the bottom in a geyser of foam and bubbles, coming up behind the lifeguard and wrapping my arms around his neck. "Hey! No fair!" he shouted.

Jack was weaving between the statues. That white horse darted after him. It would have looked as silly as the rabbit if it hadn't been for the hooves the size of soup plates, the huge snapping teeth, and the fire in its way-too-smart eyes. It somehow managed to flow between the laughing people on the deck chairs, who gossiped and sipped their drinks and ignored the horse and us.

The lifeguard grabbed my arm where I had it looped across his shoulder, and rolled us both over. I kicked at his back, but I couldn't land a good one. He rolled again and again, trying to hold me under or shake me off. My lungs started to burn, and desperation sank in. I got my face right up to the lifeguard's shoulder and bit down hard.

He screamed. I kicked off against his back, shot free, and collided with another swimmer. She brushed me back and looked around in confusion. A different pair of hands grabbed hold of me, and I was out of the water, on the deck, and staring straight at the piano player.

This time nobody'd covered him with makeup. I could see his real face. My father was lean and tall, with mahogany skin and his hair cut close to his scalp. He had a strong jaw and high cheekbones, a full mouth, and deep eyes the color of smoke and storms. Those eyes set off memory sparks way in the back of my mind.

"Is it you?" he whispered. "Is it?"

That voice reached into me, and I knew him. I knew him like I knew the feel of my heart hammering against my ribs or the light from the Unseelie country.

"Papa," I breathed.

But the lifeguard had climbed onto the blue deck and was staring at us both. "Uh-oh," he said again.

Jack hollered. He tried to duck behind the last of the

Roman soldiers, but his foot skidded on the wet tiles and he fell hard. The horse reared and laughed, a high screaming sound, then brought its flashing hooves down toward Jack. I grabbed hold of all my magic and *shoved*.

The horse screamed again and fell sideways. While it struggled to get back on its feet, Jack launched himself into a run in the other direction. He shoved a waiter into a deck chair, spilling a tray of drinks. Now the pretty people were on their feet crying out and calling the waiter all sorts of rude names. The horse lunged after Jack, snorting.

"Oh, no you don't!"

I whirled around just in time to see the lifeguard's fist coming down. But a brown hand caught it, twisted, and yanked. I felt magic too, twisting just as hard, and the lifeguard went sprawling.

"Go!" my father shouted. "Get out of here!"

I charged across the deck, right at that white horse. Jack tried to run toward me, but the horse plunged forward, got hold of his shoulder in its yellow teeth, and hauled him off his feet.

"No!" I shoved at it again with everything I had. The horse dropped Jack onto the deck, turned around, and opened its mouth. My magic drove straight in and got stuck.

It was like punching tar. I yanked and backpedaled, but it was too late. The monster was sucking me in, dragging me down. Jack was hollering. The lifeguard was laughing, and so was the horse. I think I was screaming, but I couldn't tell because I was being swallowed whole.

Callie!

There was a rope around my middle. I grabbed hold of it.

Now!

And I knew what to do. I aimed straight for the center of the dark and pitched a wish through it. The dark shattered, and I was back on the pool deck again. The horse was gone. All the swimmers were back to talking lazily and laughing all around us. The monster was in rabbit shape again, looking flat, wet, harmless, and just about dead on the pool deck. For a second I felt a flash of hatred so strong it made me stagger backward.

"Go! Go!" Papa hollered. "I'll hold her. Go!"

"But . . . no!" Something shoved at me, making me turn and look.

The lifeguard was missing. So was Jack. The guard was at the bottom of the pool, and he had Jack down there with him. He had his mouth right up against Jack's, and Jack wasn't moving.

I dove in, straight down. I grabbed hold of both the guard's ears and twisted hard. He howled and shook me off, but he'd let go of Jack, and Jack was floating up. He wasn't moving. One bubble lifted slowly out of his mouth. He was drowning, maybe drowned. I grabbed the collar of Jack's shirt and dragged him down toward the gate. I kicked and struggled and held on to Jack's collar like grim death. I dove again, this time into the whirlwind of colors, into the place where it didn't matter if you could breathe or not, because it was no place and I was nothing in it, just motion. Just falling.

But I wasn't the only one. Someone was screaming behind me. I felt the magic, scrabbling, squeezing, trying to yank us back.

Darkness rushed up, but this time I was ready for it. I held my breath, squeezed my eyes shut, and knotted my fingers tighter around Jack's collar. We burst into the oily, black water under the Waterloo Bridge. I kicked until we broke the surface. The water stank and stung as it dripped into my eyes. Jack wasn't moving. If it hadn't been for the bridge supports, I would have fallen into the slime. Jack floated on the water, his eyes shut. I sobbed as I kicked, half swimming and half floundering, to tow him onto the bank. The skin all around his mouth was torn and bloody. And he wasn't moving.

"Jack!" I grabbed his shoulders. "Jack! Wake up!"

Jack's eyes opened. His skin was white as a sheet. He was cold. He wasn't breathing. Footsteps sounded on the bridge. I felt Ivy coming up on us before I saw her.

I didn't bother with magic. I just stood up between her and Jack. "Get out of here," I said, making sure each word was clean and clear. "Get out of here, or I will kill you."

Ivy stopped and backed away. Her face was blank and smooth as her sparkling blue eyes looked into mine. I felt her pushing at me, looking for a soft spot, but I had none left. So she bunched her fists, scrunched up her face, and screamed.

It was better than magic. All at once people were shouting and running toward us. Hands pulled me away from Ivy, and from Jack, and I was shouting something and Jack still wasn't moving. Somebody was saying something about an ambulance. A bunch of men had crowded around Jack and were hoisting him off the ground. A woman was running up with a blanket, but they were all carrying Jack farther away from me.

"Jack! No!" I tried to lunge forward, but somebody held me.

"Calm down, Callie. Calm down," said a deep, rumbling voice.

It was Mr. Robeson.

18

Jacob's Ladder

"Mr. Robeson!" I grabbed his big hand. "It was *them*! Jack's hurt. I've got to get to him!"

As soon as my words sank in, Mr. Robeson started elbowing his way through the milling people. Ivy was crying in the middle of a crowd, everybody around her babbling and issuing nine kinds of orders. She had the nerve to meet my eyes, and I hoped she had her magic open so she could feel the hate and the promise I pushed at her. She'd pay for getting Jack hurt and for whatever was happening to my father right now back in San Simeon. She'd pay with everything she had plus interest, and she was really lucky I had to stay with Jack or the payback would have started then and there.

A whole crew's worth of people surrounded Jack. Mr. Robeson plowed straight through them. The ambulance pulled up, lights flashing. Two white-coated white men leapt out, while a third passed a stretcher out to them.

Jack didn't even twitch as they laid him down on the stretcher, covered him with a blanket, and strapped him in.

"Wait!" I ran past Mr. Robeson.

"Sorry." The nearest attendant, a beefy white guy with tired eyes, pushed me back. "Nobody allowed in but family."

"But he's my friend, he—"

"Rules are rules, sister."

I gaped at him. Mr. Robeson came up behind me, anger smoldering slowly. I took hold of that anger and his hand at the same time and looked the ambulance man right in the eye.

"I'm his sister, and this is his father. You're glad we're here because he's hurt bad."

The attendant's eyes blurred, and he nodded. "Get in— we have to hurry."

"Callie," said Mr. Robeson, and the warning was plain. He had an idea what I'd just done, and he did not like it.

"Please, please, don't," I begged before he could get any further. "I've got to concentrate."

Because it wasn't just the one attendant. I had to keep the wish up for every new person who saw us. So I had to wish at all the ambulance attendants, at the driver, and then at the nurses and orderlies who met us with a gurney at the hospital's emergency entrance. They wheeled Jack into a stark white examination room. I had to wish at the doctor there, who asked us all kinds of questions about Jack: his age, his weight, and whether he'd always had that red ring around his mouth. I was worn out by the time the doctor told us in no uncertain terms that it didn't matter who we were, we had to wait in the hallway.

Mr. Robeson took my hand. His was warm and strong and real. He was sorry. Not angry or suspicious or planning. Just sorry. We sat like that for a long time. He didn't try to talk. He just let me get on with whatever was happening inside me, and I was grateful. Hospitals are full of wishes. People wanted to live. They wanted to die. They wanted to be born. They wanted to be better. Most of all, they wanted to be somewhere else. All those wishes buffeted my head and bruised what little concentration I had left. I felt the tears trickling down my face from trying so hard and being so afraid. I couldn't stop seeing Jack's face all paper white. I couldn't remember if I'd seen him breathe since I'd pulled him away from that other place.

I lost track of time. It might have been minutes or hours until the doctor came out of Jack's room.

"Mr. Holland?"

"Yes?" Mr. Robeson stood up. "What can you tell us, Doctor? How's the boy?"

"I'm afraid he's in serious condition. His pulse is very irregular, and we've had to use oxygen."

"I'd like to see him."

"I can only give you a few minutes. He must not be disturbed."

Mr. Robeson nodded, and the doctor opened the door. Kids weren't allowed in hospital rooms. Nobody really wanted to see me going through that door, so I made sure they didn't.

They'd taken Jack's shirt off and put him in one of those hospital gowns. He was white as the sheets they had pulled over him. His eyes were shut. I couldn't see the red ring around his mouth now because of the black rubber oxygen mask.

I walked over to the bed like I was wading in molasses. Mr. Robeson stayed by the door, in case someone tried to open it. I lifted up Jack's hand. It was stone cold. I reached with my magic, the same way I'd reached for the gate. I tried to feel Jack. But Jack wasn't there. There was a body. It was alive, kind of. But there was nobody inside. They'd bled him away.

"Jack." I stopped, then started again. This time, I whispered his real name. "Jacob. Come back. You said you wouldn't leave me alone. You *promised*."

Nothing happened. I couldn't even feel a stirring of Jack. Fear rose in me, one huge, horrible lump. I swung around to Mr. Robeson.

"You've got to help me." I choked the words out. "Mr. Robeson, you've got to."

"What do you need?"

I thought fast, trying to squeeze all I knew about magic and this man into some kind of idea. I needed to drag Jack back from wherever he'd been taken. I needed all the power I could muster, but I was so hollowed out from everything that had happened that I was sure to fall over any second now. But I couldn't, because if I did, Jack would die. I needed wishes; I needed feeling, human feeling that I could take in and turn around.

"Sing," I begged. "I can . . . I can use the music to pull him back."

I could tell he didn't understand, but it didn't matter. Mr. Robeson drew himself up ramrod straight and soldier proud. He looked down at the pair of us, weighing something in his own mind. Then he gave one solemn nod, took a long breath, and began to sing.

"We are climbing Jacob's ladder . . ."

His voice was deeper than any I'd ever heard. I could have sworn it made the floor and the walls vibrate. The music of the spiritual poured straight into me. It pried the lid off my magic and let it all come rushing out. I barely had time to catch it up and shape it into a wish. I laid both my hands on Jack's arm and closed my eyes. I stepped sideways, turned in place, rounded a corner, and stepped down.

"Every round goes higher and higher . . ."

I couldn't see anything here. All I knew was the feeling of being pulled, drowned, swallowed. It was like when the ghost horse had turned on me, but worse this time. Stronger. Deeper. Pure ice cold slid into my veins and wound around my magic. It tried to pull me under, freeze me solid, but I held on to Mr. Robeson's singing for dear life. For both our dear lives.

"Brothers, brothers, we are climbing . . ."

Blind, I groped farther into the cold. I was cold as death. Frozen to death. I strained to open my senses, but the cold was too thick. I was crying, I was terrified. I grabbed hold of that music, wrapped it around all my memories of Jack, and pushed it out in front of me.

Jack! I'm here! I'm here!

I stretched, I strained. I waited. There was no time, and there was all the time in the world, and I was dying from stretching out and having to wait.

Then I heard it. The faintest breath of a whisper.

Callie?

I threw myself forward, paying Mr. Robeson's music out behind me like a lifeline—and I slammed straight into a wall. I screamed and reeled. Somebody snickered.

Well, well, drawled my uncle's voice. *Well, little niece, what's this?*

For a moment I couldn't understand what was happening. It seeped in slowly. *Oh, no. Oh, no, not now, not now.*

Of course my uncle Lorcan had heard me. He was in my head, and I was in my head hollering for all I was worth because I wanted Jack to be able to find me, and that was how these things worked. You opened yourself up so one person could get a good look at you, and everybody and his uncle could get a good look at you. Or everybody and your uncle.

Get out of the way! I screamed.

I can't, he answered. *Believe me, I'd like to, but I just can't. Poor boy. It's real cold back there.*

I knew exactly what he was doing, and I hated him in that moment as hard as I hated Ivy Bright. But he blocked the path solidly. I couldn't even feel the edge of him, let alone Jack behind him.

What do you want?

Pull back your sleep, niece. Let me go. I won't interfere any further with you rescuing Mr. Holland.

He knew I'd do it too. He knew I'd do anything he asked, because he was between me and Jack and I didn't have the strength left to shift him. I moved to shape one more word, to ask him to promise. . . .

Promise. My uncle had already made a promise about Jack. Relief rushed through me. *No,* I said to Uncle Lorcan. *You have to get out of my way! You're hurting Jack. You promised no action of yours would hurt him. You can't break that promise.*

I charged forward, straight at him. My uncle's presence tore like paper and I heard him scream, but I was through and on the other side.

Nicely played, niece of mine. He'd pull himself together back there and wait for his next chance, but I couldn't worry about that now.

Jack! I called. *Jack!*

"*Sisters, sisters, we are climbing . . . ,*" sang Mr. Robeson, way back in the human world.

I felt it again, the faint whisper brushing against the edge of my mind.

I'm cold, Callie.

I plunged forward, calling his name. I didn't care who heard. I'd fight the whole Seelie court if I had to. They were not taking Jack away from me.

I can't see, Callie, Jack was saying. He was closer now. He was battered and frozen and he was scared like I'd never known him to be before, but it was Jack all the same.

I know. I tried to keep my thoughts calm and strong. *But we're getting out of here.*

How?

Take my hand.

I reached. I reached with everything I had. It was as easy as wishing, as hard as believing. But I had held Jack's hand before, and he'd held mine. I knew what it felt like to have him standing beside me, and he knew me. We both wished we were in the same place, and so we were. I took hold of him in that darkness and that cold, and I pulled.

Jack was heavy. He was so skinny; how could he be so heavy? But he was. I only had one hand for him, because I had to hang on to Paul's song with the other.

"We are climbing Jacob's ladder . . ."

Rung by rung, we were climbing, groping our way up out of the cold, back to the real world, back to the land of the living. Me and Jack both.

And then, all at once, we were there. Jack slipped back into his own skin, easy as breathing, and opened his eyes for one sweet second, smiling at me from under his oxygen mask. I wilted and would have fallen if Mr. Robeson hadn't caught me.

"Will the boy be all right now?" he asked.

I nodded. My tongue felt thick and cottony. I wanted to lie down and sleep for a year.

"We'd better get out of here now, Callie. That doctor might take an exception to our appearance when he comes in."

I nodded and let him lead me out of there. I had just enough strength to glance back to see how Jack's chest rose and fell under the bedsheet.

19

The Trouble I've Seen

I really don't remember much after that. I think there was a cab ride, and I do remember some hot soup. I was shivering. The world kept fading in and out. I wanted to sleep, but I was afraid, because Shake was in there somewhere, waiting for me.

But in the end, my mind just sort of slipped away, and it stayed good and gone for a long time.

When I woke up again, I was in a plain bed in a plain room. *Hotel,* my mind said. *Dunbar,* it went on. I sat up. *Jack.*

I threw back the covers. I was in a clean nightdress and clean socks. I didn't stop to think about it. I ran to the door. On the other side was a tidy sitting room all done in shades of beige, brown, and gold. A slim, light brown lady I didn't know sat on the sofa.

"Who're you? What's going on? Where's my clothes?"

"Ada Freeman," she answered calmly. "Mr. Robeson thought it would be better if you had someone to sit with you, and your clothes are being washed. I'll go tell Mr. Robeson you're awake."

She left me there with my thoughts spinning and my heart hammering, and came back in a minute with Paul Robeson right behind her.

"Thank you, Ada." He touched her arm and gave her a big smile. "Maybe you could see if her clothes are ready?"

"Sure thing, Mr. Robeson."

She left us alone, and I shifted my weight, suddenly feeling strange about being there in a nightdress. He sat down in one of the chairs. "Ada's friends with one of the hospital orderlies," he told me. "He says Jack is sleeping peacefully and was awake enough this morning to drink some water and eat some Jell-O."

"He'd hate that," I breathed. My relief was so big I didn't have words for it. I had to talk about little things instead. "He hates Jell-O."

"That just proves he's got taste," Mr. Robeson said. "Now, as soon as Ada comes back with your clothes, you come meet me down in the dining room and we'll talk, all right?"

I agreed, and he left. I realized he was being careful about appearances, for his sake and mine. That felt strange too. I mean, I had been careful about my appearance my whole life, but this was different. A whole other world of different, in fact.

I was glad not to have too much time to think about that, because it was a lot more than I was ready to deal with, especially now. Ada came back with my clothes all cleaned and pressed. I really didn't want to wear anything I'd borrowed from Ivy. I knew now why she'd distracted me with playing dress-up and girlfriends. She'd been fooling me, the same way she fooled everybody else. But it was take the clothes or go naked, so I dressed. Somebody'd put the penny loafers under the radiator to dry, and they were stiff as boards when I shoved my feet into them. Somehow knowing that I'd gone and ruined her shoes made me feel better. It didn't make sense, but there it was.

Ada walked me down to the Dunbar's restaurant. Mr. Robeson was sitting at a table in the corner, and he stood when we approached. A waiter hurried up to pull out my chair and pour me some water. I ordered a stack of pancakes with syrup, whipped cream, and butter. I could have eaten a horse if they'd had it on the menu. Especially white horse.

"Now, Callie." Mr. Robeson leaned forward and planted his elbows on the table. "How about you tell me what's been happening since the last time I found you by that bridge?"

I glanced around. The room was maybe half full of people, eating and talking and paying absolutely no attention to us. So, softly, one slow word at a time, I told him. I had to stop when the waiter brought my pancakes and Mr. Robeson's fried eggs, ham, toast, and coffee. We ate, and I kept talking until I ran out of words. Mr. Robeson didn't interrupt me or question me until I got around to repeating the prophecy.

"Interesting," he said, pouring himself more coffee from the pot the waiter had left on the table. "What's the third world?"

"Huh?" I mumbled around a mouthful of pancake.

" 'She,' meaning you, is described as being the daughter of three worlds." Mr. Robeson tore his toast in two and soaked half in egg yolk. "Two are obvious—the fairy world and the human world. But what's the third?"

I opened my mouth. I closed it again.

"I don't know." I hadn't even thought about it. "I don't know," I said again.

"Well, we'll look at that later. Go on."

I went on. I told him about leaving Kansas and coming to Los Angeles, sneaking into MGM, finding myself in San Simeon and almost not getting out. That was when he interrupted again.

"You're sure it was your father? It was Daniel LeRoux?"

I nodded. "But . . . but it didn't make any sense," I whispered to my plate. "Why would they leave him, I don't know, unguarded, able to help like that? They controlled him so tight that other time . . . why leave him free at all?"

Paul considered this for a moment. "It's no fun to lord it over someone who can't feel your power," he said at last. "Perhaps they let him out on occasion so he will feel the times of close confinement more cruelly."

Now, that sounded just like the Seelies. "Besides," I added slowly, "who'd be dumb enough to sneak right into the castle to try to rescue him, right? They'd only get themselves caught, so there wasn't any danger."

"Exactly." Paul took another sip of coffee, and then gestured with his cup for me to keep going.

When I finally finished, my head felt clear. The food helped, but having somebody who knew the whole long horrible story was even better. I felt like I could breathe again.

"Why are you helping me?" I asked. "How come . . . how come you believe all this?"

Mr. Robeson sighed and set his coffee cup down. It clicked against the thick china saucer.

"It was some fifteen years ago now, I guess," he said. "I was living in New York City, up in Harlem. That was a great time. The town was full of music, poetry, and artists. Everything was wide open. We were trying to create a new world with words and music, new thoughts, new chances. Some of us were doing it for the race; some of us were doing it because we were young and wild and it was the biggest party in New York City, and that made it the biggest party in the world."

"And my father was there?"

Mr. Robeson nodded. "I don't even recall exactly where I met him first. He'd come to parties and just hang around. I figured him for some kid in from the sticks. I do remember the first time he sat down at the piano."

"He was that good?"

Mr. Robeson chuckled. "He was that bad. Got laughed off the bench, which made him mad as a scalded cat. But he came back the next night and sat down again. I was surprised, and so was everybody else. That time he was better, and the third night he was better yet. I never heard anybody pick it up so quick. He could hear a tune once and play it back to you note for note. Pretty soon he was playing all over town: rent parties, juke joints, anyplace they had a piano and wouldn't throw him out too fast. We did a few house parties together. I'd never met anybody so in love with the nightlife. I tried to tell him maybe he should slow down, it'd swallow him up if he kept at it, but he just laughed at me.

" 'Not me, Paul,' he said. 'I'm home at last.'

"That was when things started going good for me. I was acting, I was making money from my singing, I had my wife and son, and the concerts were getting good notices. Then one night we were in a black-and-tan . . . you know what that is?"

"A nightclub?" I guessed.

He nodded again. "Anyway, this white pair, dressed to the nines, comes up, and they want me to come sing at their party. They named the fee, and it was high. Higher than I'd ever heard anyone get for one night's work. Of course I said yes. We set the time, and I turned around, and Daniel was there.

" 'Don't do it, Paul,' he told me. 'Those two are bad news. You've got to trust me on this.'

"I remember what it felt like to have him say that to me. I wanted to do just what he said, as much as I'd ever wanted anything in my life. But I needed the money. I had a wife and son to support, and it was tough times. In the end, that was what won out. So I laughed him off. He shook his head at me and turned and walked away. He only looked back once. I remembered thinking I'd seen the last of him, but at the time I didn't know why."

I left the remains of my pancakes cooling on my plate. I didn't want to miss one word of this. I could see my father standing beside Paul Robeson, his smoke-and-starlight eyes shining as he tried to persuade the other man to stay away from the party. I could feel his disappointment when he failed.

"What happened then?" I breathed.

"I found another piano player, had my suit pressed, and went to the party. It was in a penthouse on the Upper West Side. Beautiful, expensive place, full of beautiful, expensive white people. There was champagne and food, and I danced with all the girls and nobody batted an eye. We did two sets, and everybody loved it. I felt like I'd found paradise."

I knew just what he'd felt like. He'd felt like he'd come home.

"I lost track of time in all that glitter. Next thing I remember clearly was the hostess coming up to me and saying, 'Oh, you must come out to the country with us, Paul. Stay for the summer. You must. Say yes, Paul, do. Promise you'll come stay with us.'

"I was all set to say yes. Why wouldn't I? It was like I couldn't remember anything outside that room full of beautiful people.

"But then Daniel had hold of me. I don't know how he got there. I never saw him come in. 'One more song, Paul,' he was saying. 'Let's give 'em just one more. Come on.' He pulled me over to the piano, and he sat down and started to play. 'Scandalize My Name,' it was. I started singing.

"And it was like a magic trick. Like someone yanked away the tablecloth and I saw what was underneath. That glittering party I'd been standing in the middle of was a room full of monsters and nightmares. You know what I'm talking about, don't you?"

Oh, yes. I'd been in the middle of that room too.

"Well, of course I started to holler, and of course they knew it was your father who'd pulled the scales off my eyes. They charged up—one big lynch mob of nightmares. But he was on his feet, and . . . I don't know exactly what he did then, but those monsters were suddenly all falling down and banging into each other like Keystone Kops, and me and him were out the window and running for our lives.

"We holed up in a speakeasy cellar, down with the barrels of booze. He told me everything then, about the Seelies and the Unseelies, about how they would take musicians to their country and never let them go again. . . . I shouldn't have believed it, but I did. He warned me they might make another try, told me some things to help me protect myself." Mr. Robeson reached into his pocket and pulled out a big, old-fashioned black iron key. He twirled it once in his fingers and tucked it away again.

"He left town after that, and I never saw him again. But he saved me that night, Callie. I don't know why, but he did, and I've always been grateful. I promised Daniel if I could ever help him, I would. I just never knew I'd be doing it by helping out his daughter."

I didn't say anything. I sat there thinking about that promise and how it had pulled us all together, years afterward. It was the promise that had brought him to me and Jack in time. It had to be. It was strange, and it made me feel very small, just when I was learning how strong I was.

"What are you going to do now?" Mr. Robeson asked.

I didn't answer right away. I just sat there staring at the breakfast dishes. The longer I stared and the longer I thought, the madder I got. I was sick and tired of the Seelies and their games. I was tired of them thieving off me. They'd taken my papa and my mama, and they'd almost had Jack as well. They'd robbed me of the only pathetic little bit of a life I had, and they'd kept me scared and lonely and twisted around until I didn't even know what I was anymore. I was done with that. Starting right now, I was taking back what belonged to me.

A shadow fell across our table. I looked up, ready to tell the waiter he could clear my dishes. But it wasn't the waiter. It was Ivy Bright.

20

Do You Call That a Sister?

"What're *you* doing here?" I was on my feet, and I didn't remember moving.

"Hello, Callie." She blinked those baby blues at me and had the nerve to show a few tears shimmering around the edges. "I . . . I think we need to talk. Is there somewhere we can go?"

I'd been mad in my life before, plenty of times. But this was different. Everything seemed to change. I felt my magic swarming in every nerve. Everything around me took on a sharp, silver sort of edge. Everything was hard except Ivy. She was all soft and fragile. I could crush her. I could crumple her up and throw her out like the trash she was. And I could make sure nobody saw me do it too, even though the whole dining room was whispering and staring because the brightest little star in Hollywood had just walked into the Dunbar Hotel.

"Sure thing, Ivy." I smiled so she could see all my teeth, then I took hold of her arm, hard. I'd noticed a door to a private dining room when we came in, and I pulled her inside. Mr. Robeson came too, and shut the door behind us. The private dining room was snug and luxurious, with its own fireplace and two armchairs in addition to the table laid for six by the curtained window.

As soon as Mr. Robeson shut that door, I grabbed the collar of Ivy's pink coat and spun her around so she slammed face-first against the wall. She squeaked and cried, and I didn't care. I didn't care at all.

"You pushed us in there!" I shouted. "You meant for us to get killed!" *You meant for Jack to get killed.*

"No, it wasn't like that!" Ivy wailed.

I couldn't stand it. I couldn't stand that girlie voice and that pretty face and those stupid, fake, movie-star tears she used to get her way. I raised my hand.

"That's enough, Callie," said Mr. Robeson. "Let her go."

"No!" I shouted back. "She tried to kill us! She's helping them!" I was going to shut her up for good, make sure she never fooled or hurt anybody again.

"And she's got something to say. You need to hear her out."

"She's just putting the whammy on you!" I snapped back. I pushed Ivy's face against the wall again, and she whimpered. "She's Seelie! She does it to everybody!"

"Not to me, Callie." He was right behind me, and I felt

the calm radiating off him, and just a little disappointment. "You know better. Let her go."

One finger at a time, my hand uncurled from Ivy's collar, and I backed off. My mouth was wet. I wiped it on my sleeve. My eyes were hot too, and not just from tears. They were shining again, and I knew it, and I didn't care.

Ivy eased away from the wall.

"Thank you," she whispered. "It's Mr. Robeson, isn't it?"

"It is." He gave a little bow, like he was onstage. "And you're Miss Bright, who had best speak her piece and go."

"I know, I know. Oh, this is such a mess. I . . ." Another tear trickled down her cheek.

"Stop it!" I shouted again. "You're nothing but a phony, and it won't work this time!"

I glanced at Mr. Robeson. He didn't move. He was just watching, taking it all in, turning it over in his mind. I'd never seen anyone so controlled and careful. He wasn't going to make a move until he absolutely had to. I realized he was trusting me not to do anything stupid. That sat heavy on my shoulders.

"Who are you, really?" he asked Ivy.

Ivy licked her lips. She looked from one of us to the other like she was looking for a way out, and not finding one. She sighed so hard her shoulders slumped. Her face changed too. The baby doll fell away and I found myself seeing as much of the real girl as I ever had. I'd been right.

She was a bit older than me, maybe even Jack's age. She looked tired, hurt, and more than a little angry.

"I'm like her." Ivy nodded at me.

"You're half-blood?" I should have known it. I should have felt it the second we got near her. But I hadn't, because she'd been magicking me. Just like she'd been doing to Jack. She'd been keeping us both blind with her glamour, the movie kind and the fairy kind.

"Not just half-blood." She lifted up her nose. "My father is the Seelie king."

"So you're . . . you're a princess? Like me?"

"Yes. Sort of. Mostly."

I folded my arms. "What do you mean, *mostly?*"

"Look, it doesn't matter. I've been sent with a message, Callie." She pulled a piece of paper out of her pink purse and handed it to me.

"No!" Mr. Robeson jumped forward, but he was too late. The paper touched my fingers and stuck tight. I backed away, shaking my hand, but it was no good. Magic crawled straight up my arm, sinking in deep. Mr. Robeson grabbed at the paper and pulled so hard I whimpered, but the paper didn't tear or come off my hand.

"What is this?" he demanded.

"It's a summons," said Ivy softly. "From the Seelie king. I'm sorry, Callie, I *had* to."

I stared at my fingers. The paper was thin and light, more like silk than stationery. It had fallen open, so I could see it was written over in red and gold. The print glowed and smelled of cinnamon and chili peppers.

For her crimes against the Shining Court, I read, *against His Majesty and his subjects and blood kindred, Callie LeRoux, scion of the Midnight Throne, is called to answer before three days of mortal time have passed. If she fails to answer the charges, the hostages against her behavior will be declared forfeit, according to the law.*

There was no signature, just a drawing of a pearl and gold mask surrounded by beams of light. It blazed bright for a moment, searing my eyes and my fingers. The paper vanished then, but it wasn't gone. It was under my skin now, and it was still burning.

Mr. Robeson grabbed my hand and turned it over, looking for burn marks. Of course there weren't any. The fire was all inside me.

Ivy backed away, twisting her fingers together. "This is because I went through the gate," I said, and staggered. Mr. Robeson sat me in the nearest chair. "That's the crime this is talking about."

"You broke in without permission," Ivy said. "You attacked one of the Seelie court."

"Because *you* pushed us in!" I rubbed at my hands, at my arms. The summons was sinking deeper. It was right under my skin now, but it was looking for a way to get deeper, down to my blood, down to my heart. As it moved, it left behind a hot, crawling itch. Mr. Robeson was watching me closely. I shook my head and he eased away, sitting down and laying both hands on the table. But his eyes never left us.

"I'm sorry," Ivy whispered, and maybe she even was. "I didn't mean for Jack to get hurt."

That much was true. I could tell. She liked Jack. She wanted him to look at her the way he looked at me. Which left me with the cold realization that she wouldn't mind so much if I got hurt. Or killed.

"This was all your idea from the start," I said.

"Not right from the start. We really were just trying to bring Mr. Robeson to court. His Majesty had a bounty out, and whoever could bring him in . . . I'm sorry, Mr. Robeson!"

"So you laid a trap for me, with the famous Ivy Bright as the bait?" He'd gone stone still, and I think it was a good thing Ivy could look so small and helpless, because if there was anybody angrier than me in that moment, it was Mr. Robeson. "Waiting for me to stroll in?"

"Except Callie and Jack showed up first," said Ivy. "When we realized who she was . . . plans kind of changed."

"You mean you decided to go after me instead?" I scratched at my arms, trying to lessen the itch. I knew it wouldn't do any good, but I couldn't help it.

"You really think I want it this way?" Ivy sank into one of the armchairs by the fireplace. "They ordered me to trap you. They said if I brought you to them that . . . that . . ."

"That what?" I snapped.

Ivy twisted one of her curls around a finger. I snorted at

the little-girl gesture, and she yanked her hand away. "They said I'd get to be a real princess," she said softly. "They said I'd get to go live with them and be part of the court forever."

My jaw flapped open. "That's *it?*"

"You don't understand what it's like to be left out," she said to her hands. "To not even have your blood family want to know you."

"What do you mean, I don't understand? Because of your people, I spent my life stuck in the middle of the Dust Bowl. We starved out there while you were here making movies and being rich and famous, and now you're whining about how you had it tough?"

"You had someone who loved you, Callie," she answered. "Really loved *you.* You weren't born just to . . ." She stopped, and started again. "The only reason I was even born is because the king thought *I'd* be the Prophecy Girl. When it didn't turn out, he left me with Mrs. Brownlow. Oh, sure, I got the movies because he couldn't have one of his daughters being just a nobody, but that's it. No matter what I do, no matter how hard I try, it doesn't matter. For a while, it was going to be okay because . . ."

"Because why?" I was having trouble sitting still. Perspiration was running down my forehead now, and it was making the itch worse.

"Because the Unseelie prince was going to marry me. But even he didn't want me."

"Wait. Stop." I held up both hands. "You don't . . . you can't . . ." I couldn't say it. It couldn't possibly be true. "You

are not trying to tell me *you're* the one my papa was supposed to marry."

But Ivy nodded solemnly. My stomach plunged and
twisted like an Olympic champion diver. I had to swallow
hard to keep from being sick right then and there. "You're
a kid!"

"So? It doesn't matter anyway. He didn't even want me.
He'd rather have some skinny mortal woman from nowhere
and nothing."

"That'd be my mama," I reminded her, making sure she
heard every word.

Ivy blanched. "I'm sorry. I didn't mean it."

"Yes, you did. And you've given me your message." I
was scratching my arm harder. The itch had worked its way
down to my veins, and it was creeping up to my shoulder.
"You'd better get out of here. Now."

But Ivy didn't get. She leaned forward and took a deep
breath. "Callie, I can't help being what I am any more than
you can. But we can both get out of this. I can free your
parents, and you can all leave, no strings. I'll swear to it."

It was those last words that stopped me from letting out
another holler at her. "How?" I asked.

"You give me the gate power."

"What?"

"You can do it. We can make the wish between us. You
don't want it anyway, and your folks don't want it. You give
it to me, and there won't be any reason to keep any of you
around. You can just walk away."

"And make you the Prophecy Girl?"

"What do you care? It doesn't matter to you. Your people care about you. You're not just one of a hundred. But if I had the gate power, it'd all be different. Please, Callie. I'll promise you anything. *Anything.*"

Ivy's wish didn't just bump against my mind; it banged on the door, crying to be let in. She needed this like she needed breath and blood. She'd give me anything I asked for as long as she got the gate power at the end of it. Then she'd be the special one. Everybody would want her up there in the Seelie palace. She'd never be left alone again.

Which was kind of funny, because being left alone was all I wanted. To be left alone to be a family with my parents, and to have a chance at making the Midnight Club real. That's what Ivy Bright offered to me, right here. If I wished the gate power away to her, there'd be no reason left for the Seelies to be after me.

"And when you have this power, what will you do with it?" asked Mr. Robeson quietly.

Ivy frowned. "I . . . I don't know. That'll be for the king to decide."

"I see." The tone in Mr. Robeson's voice made it plain he saw a whole lot more than she wanted him to. "Like he decided how you should live and with whom, and how he's been running his games around you ever since?"

"No, not like that," said Ivy quickly. "It's just . . . it's an important power, that's all. Because whoever has it can sneak into anyplace. It's not safe."

Where she stays, where she stands, there shall the gates be closed. But I felt Ivy holding something back. It fluttered around behind her words.

"So you don't really know what will happen if Callie gives up her power to you?" asked Mr. Robeson.

"Does it matter?" She said this to me. "You don't want it, and I do. Please, Callie."

Mr. Robeson cocked his head toward me. I saw the question and the answer in his expression, and I agreed with him. "It does matter," I said.

Ivy blinked. *"What?"*

"What you'd do with the gate power does matter. It matters what the Seelie king would do with it."

Ivy leaned forward. "I won't let it be used to hurt you, Callie, or your family. We can make that part of the promise."

I was getting hotter. The itch had reached my shoulder and was creeping across my back. Mr. Robeson eyed me uneasily. A drop of sweat fell into my eyes and I wiped at it, but it stung, and now my eye began to itch.

"I . . . I have to think about it," I made myself say.

"There's no time, Callie. You've been summoned. You have to go to the court or the summons'll burn you alive, and once you get up there it'll be too late to make the wish."

"Why?" asked Mr. Robeson. "Doesn't the king know you're making this offer?"

"What difference does that make?" grumbled Ivy.

"It means things might not turn out as rosy as you paint

them. Callie and her family have made enemies. I happen to know that the Seelies do not let their enemies go quietly." *Or at all.* I could hear those extra words, even though he didn't say them out loud.

"I think you'd better go now, Ivy," I told her. "You've said what you came to say. I'll think about it."

"No!" The word pulled her to her feet. "No! You've got to listen, Callie. You've got to." She grabbed my hand, and I gasped and yanked it away. Just her touch sent the itch flaring bright and hard up my arm. "This is our only chance!"

"Or what?" I cradled my hand against my chest. I was not going to be able to stand this much longer. I could barely sit still as it was. "What's got you so scared?"

She went white, and I knew I'd hit it.

"They've threatened you," said Mr. Robeson. "They're angry with you, and you're in danger."

"You don't understand!" she shouted at him. "You're just a . . . a *human*. And *you!*" She turned on me. "You're nothing! Your mother's a weakling and your father's a traitor and a runaway! You're a pathetic little bad luck girl and you don't *deserve* to be special!" Her eyes glowed white-hot as the sun, and her spell slammed against me.

I'd never had anybody throw magic straight at me before. I'd seen disguises. I'd fought off monsters. This was different. This grabbed hold of all of me and twisted hard, shoving me down, shrinking me, burning me into a new shape, and that shape was as small and pathetic and weak as she said I was. It hurt. It hurt worse than dust pneumonia.

It hurt worse than seeing Jack lying still and cold on the ground.

I sprawled on the floor, and Mr. Robeson lunged for me.

"You stay out of this, spook!" Ivy's hate lashed out and caught him in the chest. Mr. Robeson staggered back. She shouldn't have done that. He was angry and more than a little bit frightened. I snatched the feelings up and threw them back in a spell of my own. Ivy flinched, and I was able to scramble to my feet. I felt her taking aim at me again. She was strong, but she was a spoiled brat. She'd never actually had to fight for her life. I had.

I grabbed a plate off the breakfast table and threw it hard at her head. Ivy screamed and ducked, but not fast enough. The plate glanced off her brow and snapped her head back, and she fell into a chair.

Mr. Robeson was on his feet again. I grabbed his hand. "Wish!" I ordered. "Wish her dead!"

"No, Callie," he said.

"What?" I reached anyway. He had to feel something, something I could use. But he was walled off. I didn't know people could shut down like that. I could have broken through into his mind, I could have glamoured him into feeling what I needed, but even as far gone as I was, I knew that was a door there was no going back through.

"Go ahead!" Ivy tried to stand up, and dropped back down again. "I'm not afraid of you, Callie LeRoux! You or your pet n—"

"Go home, Miss Bright," said Mr. Robeson. "Tell your

people they'll get their answer. You don't really want to pick a fight you can't win, do you?"

But she did, she really did. Except she was also about to be sick, and when she did stand up, her knees wobbled.

"You'll get yours," she hissed at me. "And so will I. Think about *that,* Callie LeRoux."

She sashayed out and shut the door. I turned to Mr. Robeson. For a moment the fury in me burned so bright, it damped down the itch and the sweat.

"Why wouldn't you help me? I could have finished her!"

"I am not going to help you kill another little girl in cold blood," he said flatly.

"She's a liar and a sneak and she's helping *them*!"

"It's not about who they are," he told me with that same implacable, unbreakable calm that had kept his anger from my magic. "It is never about who they are. It's about who you are. You are not a murderer."

"You don't know what I am."

That just earned me a smile. "You've moved heaven and earth to help people and to free the father you never met. You about killed yourself to save a friend. You are a good person, Callie," he said. "Like your father and, I believe, your mother. Your father would not want you to commit a murder to free him."

"She would have killed me," I said.

Mr. Robeson didn't move an inch. "That's on her."

Tears joined the perspiration running down my face. He

still didn't move. The strange thing was, where the tears fell, the itching disappeared. "How do you do it?" I wiped the back of my hand across my cheeks. "How do you stay so calm?"

"You learn control, Callie," he said grimly. "They'll push you and push you until you take your swing. You swing hard and stupid because you're angry, and then they've got you. They're bigger and stronger than you'll ever be. The only way we win is if we stay smart. To do that, we have to keep control of ourselves, and we have to hang together." He smiled at me. "That's the part their kind never learns."

I wanted to listen to him. What he was saying was important, but there was too much else going on in my brain for it to sink in properly—including the fact that Ivy was out on the streets and Jack was all alone back in the hospital. I had to get to him. I rubbed my arms. Then I had to find out what this summons really meant. I knew who to ask. The problem was, I was going to have to wake him up.

21

Where Are You Goin' Now?

Jack was sitting in a wheelchair in his hospital room when we got there. He was way too pale, and even skinnier than usual. If anything, the ring around his mouth looked worse than when we'd brought him in, because it was all peeling and scabby. When I looked at him, the relief was as strong as any magic spell Ivy and all her friends and relations could have hit me with.

Jack smiled up at me, and I thought I'd keel over on the spot. "Hi, Callie."

"Hi."

He held out his hand, and I took it. Where his skin touched mine, the itch doubled, but for that moment it didn't matter. It was Jack's hand, and he was smiling, and after that, everything had to be okay.

* * *

Mr. Robeson talked seriously with the doctor about how Jack needed to go home and rest. He signed the name Jonathan Holland to a bunch of papers, and we wheeled Jack out of there, even though he insisted he could walk for himself. He was steady enough getting into the cab we had waiting, but he was breathing too hard by the time it pulled away from the curb.

The cab took us back to the Dunbar, and Mr. Robeson let us into his tidy hotel room. He called down for some lunch. I wasn't hungry. My stomach was full of itching. I could barely even sit down, but I made myself do it. I didn't want Jack to see how bad things had gotten.

That worked for all of ten seconds. "What's happened, Callie?" Jack asked.

I told him about Ivy and the summons, and what had happened afterward. Most of it, anyway. I felt Mr. Robeson settling onto the sofa and looking at me, but he didn't say anything when I didn't go into detail about how ready I'd been to kill Ivy Bright.

"It was a setup, wasn't it?" Jack asked quietly. "From the beginning. She was just using me. Us."

"She's a Seelie. She magicked us both. It wasn't your fault."

He didn't believe that, and I didn't know how to get him to. He'd just have to work it out for himself. I tried to tamp down the leftover anger, because I could feel how Jack was wishing that Ivy'd liked him because he was strong and brave and handsome and just Jack. It wasn't much of a wish and he was already trying to shove it away, but it was there. I needed to find other stuff to concentrate on, or something important inside me would break in two.

"I'm going with you," said Jack. "To the Seelies."

"No." I wiped at the sweat on my forehead. Mr. Robeson had loaned me a handkerchief. It was fine linen, but it grated like sandpaper across my skin. Even the sunlight hurt where it touched me. "Not this time."

"You got no right to say where I go, Callie."

"They almost killed you!" And he was still weak. Plus I didn't trust Ivy to leave him alone if she got next to him again. She'd turn those baby blues on him, and Jack would go all hero over her, like he did for anybody who needed help.

"You think they're gonna lay off after they're done with whatever it is they got planned for you?" Jack said all slow and quiet.

How was I going to answer him? They would come after him and they wouldn't stop, no matter what happened to me. They'd do it because I cared about him and I was bad luck. And just maybe because he was Jack and even they knew he was special.

"It's not safe," I tried.

"It never has been."

He was right about that. And there was something else: as much as I wanted to protect him and keep him away from Ivy, I needed him. I needed his wishing to help work my magic, but it was more than that. I needed him because he was brave and he was Jack and he was the only person in the whole world I could trust absolutely. I glanced at Mr. Robeson. Well, maybe not the only person.

"So," said Jack, "what do we do?"

I hesitated. I did have a plan. Ivy didn't know it, but she'd showed me what to do. The first part was going to be tricky, though. Like making a deal with the devil is tricky.

I decided I could put off talking about that—for now, anyway—and turned to Mr. Robeson instead. "I need to ask you a favor."

He gave a half smile, because we both knew I should have said "another favor." "What can I do?"

"I need you to go get Mrs. Brownlow."

He frowned. "Mrs. Brownlow?"

"She's been set up as Ivy Bright's mother. I don't know what really happened. Maybe she really is Ivy's mother. Maybe . . . maybe they did that thing Jack says fairies sometimes do, when they take a human baby and leave a fairy one behind."

"A changeling?" filled in Jack.

"That's it. She wants to go home, except Ivy's got her all magicked up." That was why the enchantments were so sloppy. Ivy'd never been taught how to do her magic properly, any more than I had. I remembered all the times I'd wanted to make my mama do what I said. If I'd known about my magic . . . would Mama have ended up like Mrs. Brownlow? I shivered. "Somebody's got to get her out of there, and find her people if she's got any. And it's got to be before Ivy gets back, or she'll just magic her under again. I don't know what's going to happen to me, but you've got a promise on them that they can't touch you. . . ." *And I've got to get you out of the way of whatever's coming next.*

The words trailed off, and Mr. Robeson looked at me for a long time. I think he guessed what I was really doing, but he just nodded gravely. "I'll do what I can."

"Thank you, Mr. Robeson."

He nodded again, and I felt something new, or maybe it was something old. It was like a ribbon unraveling in the air between us. It was the promise, the one he'd made to my papa. He'd paid. He was free and could go his own way now without worrying about being pulled back to us.

It was good for him, and I knew it, but I couldn't quite manage to be really glad.

I may not have been hungry, but Jack sure was. When the waiter brought in the plates of sandwiches and bottles of Coca-Cola, he ate enough for ten. I nibbled on a ham and cheese and tried not to scratch too much. There were red streaks on my arms from my fingernails. Soon I'd be drawing blood, and it still wouldn't be enough. After lunch, Mr. Robeson had the doorman hail another cab, and paid the man twenty dollars to take us wherever we wanted to go. Jack looked surprised when I gave the driver the address of Mrs. Constantine's house.

"I've got to fix Shake before I do anything else," I said. Which was true, as far as it went. I didn't look at Jack when I said it, though. I stared out the window and watched the city streets.

This was not the kind of detail Jack was likely to miss. "What's going on, Callie? What are you planning?"

I didn't answer. The itch dug its claws a little deeper. I felt Jack waiting.

"If he promises to help, and promises to leave us alone afterward, I'm going to give him what he wants," I said finally. "I'll abdicate. He'll be heir to the Midnight Throne."

Jack was absolutely silent for a long time after that. I glanced from the window to the driver. He was ignoring us. Probably he'd heard stranger things coming out of the back of his cab. This was Los Angeles, after all.

"Callie," said Jack softly. "Callie, you gotta listen to me. There're people out there who've just been too bad for too long to turn around. They get hooked on it, like dope or booze. Shake's like that, Callie. He's not going to play square for you or anybody else."

"I know." I clenched my fists and rubbed my knuckles over my raw arms. "But he's also the only one who doesn't care about the gate prophecy, and he's the only one who believes I just want to find my parents and get out of this. He wants the throne, and he wants revenge on his parents, that's all. If I swear off it, he'll let us go."

"You're going to turn him on your grandparents?" breathed Jack.

"They did that themselves," I answered. "I'm just getting me and my folks out from between them."

Even Jack had no answer for that.

When the cab left us in front of Mrs. Constantine's, I started right for the porch steps, but Jack pulled me off to the side. I winced when he touched me, but I let him steer me behind the hydrangeas, where we couldn't be seen.

"I wish they were gone," Jack said. "Mrs. Constantine and everybody. Just in case."

It was a good idea. Ivy was still out there somewhere, and there was no telling what she'd try next, or who she'd been talking to. I took up Jack's wish and sort of spread it out. Nothing too pushy, just getting a kind of feeling out there. Then Mrs. Constantine decided it was time she did her marketing, and Mr. and Mrs. Jones decided it was too nice a day to be sitting inside. And Miss Whitman decided she wanted to go to the library after all. We watched them from behind the bushes while they walked out the door. Mrs. Constantine came last and locked the door carefully behind her.

You too, Jack. I spread that wish just a little further. *You go too.*

I felt him waver and look at the door. But only for a couple of heartbeats.

"Not a chance, Callie. You are not getting rid of me that easy."

I shrugged. "It was worth a try."

We found the spare key under the flowerpot on the back porch. The house was too warm, despite the breeze coming in from the open windows. The foyer smelled like polish and dust and the remains of lunch. The stairs complained under our shoes as we climbed up to my old room. It hadn't been let out yet. It hadn't been locked either, and its window hadn't been opened. It was stifling in there. A trapped fly buzzed against the glass, searching angrily for an exit.

"Nothing to it." Jack's smile was forced, but I let it go.

"Be quiet a second. I've got to concentrate."

It was getting easier to open my magic just a little, and it was no trouble at all to feel the gate I'd created last time I was in this room. It was so clear, I was surprised Jack couldn't spot it. I eased it open, but I didn't step through. I just reached in and found that warm, dreamy, sleepy feeling I'd wrapped Lorcan up in. I took hold of the end of it and pulled.

It took less than a heartbeat. Lorcan was awake and betwixt and between, and then he wasn't. He was in front of me, both eyes wide open and his broken teeth bared. He lashed out, grabbing the front of my checked shirt and hauling me in close enough to breathe his hot and sour breath all over my face. For one panicked second I thought he was going to bite my throat.

"Let her go, old man!" Jack swung the room's rickety chair high over his head. "Let her go now, or I'll bust your head!"

"Ah." Shake's voice was terribly tight. "The young Mr. Holland. Callie, I see you've been busy while I was enjoying my little nap." But he did let go, and stepped back. "Just a little misunderstanding among family. Nothing at all to worry about." The lid closed down over his milk-white eye, winking at me. I felt a promise swirling around him, but I couldn't tell what it was.

"I need your help." I rubbed my neck. The itching redoubled around my throat and on my cheeks where his breath had touched me.

"Do you?" He raised his eyebrows and smoothed his shirt down. "Well, I find I'm a little busy right now, Callie. People to see, places to go. You understand, I'm sure." He smiled, all polite, and walked out of the room, heading to his own.

"You said you wanted to help me." I followed him, and Jack followed me. He left the chair, though.

"I did." Shake picked up his battered hat off the dresser and settled it on his head. "Before. Now things have changed."

What things? I bit my lip. I did not like this. Something had changed with Shake, and it was something important. Was it possible he hadn't been as sound asleep as he was letting on? That he'd done something or seen somebody that had changed his ideas about what was going on?

"I've got a summons from the Seelie king," I said out loud.

"I'd be surprised if you didn't, considering you broke

into his castle with the intent of stealing his property. In fact, I'm surprised it's just a summons."

I almost asked how he knew that, but then I remembered I'd slept since I got back. Of course he knew what I'd done. He'd seen it in my head.

"Had you been willing to trust me for two seconds, I could have explained. There are laws, Callie, and when you break them, you pay. It's an eye for an eye with us, Callie." He touched his scar. "You went into their territory without an invitation. You, or your stand-in, has to pay the forfeit. Or else."

"Or else what?"

"War." He drew the word out long and slow, but not as if he was afraid. He liked the way it rolled off his tongue. "War between the courts, in which you will be the first casualty, because that summons will kill you if you don't offer a life in answer for what you've done." He smiled at me, ice cold and far too happy. "You can feel it already, can't you?"

I could. The itch had gone down beneath my blood now. It was gnawing at my fairy magic.

Shake faced the mirror again, straightening his lapels and adjusting the angle of his broken hat. "Of course, since you won't let them keep either your mama or your papa, it's going to be war anyway, because your grandparents will not let the Seelies have your special power for themselves." He nodded at his reflection as if satisfied. "The only thing for a smart fellow to do is get out of the way and wait for it all to blow over."

And wait for it all to blow over. The words echoed around my aching head. He meant to let the Seelies and the Unseelies fight it out over me and what I'd done, so he could be the last man standing. I gaped at him. I'd made a mistake. A big one. Another one.

Shake tipped his hat at me. "Good-bye, Callie. Mr. Holland."

"No, wait. You said you wanted to see me on the Midnight Throne."

"That was before. Now I don't need your help, which is just as well for me, because you're going to be killed."

"But you don't know that for sure," said Jack. He was leaning against the wall, arms folded and eyes narrowed. "We could pull out of this," he went on. "We've done it before. Callie's still got her power and that prophecy. She could make a deal with the king and queen." Jack waited until Shake had turned all the way toward him. "Or she could make a deal with you."

Shake hesitated. He'd thought he was facing just a couple of scared human kids, but now he wasn't so sure. "What kind of deal?"

I hesitated. If I did this now, I did it for good. "My father, he abdicated, right? That left me as heir to the throne."

"Yes."

"Okay. Here's the deal. You help me find my parents and bring them out safe from wherever they're at, and I'll abdicate as heir of the Midnight Throne."

Shake's smile drew out long, slow, and dangerous, like a

snake coming out of its hole. His good eye sparkled bright in the dim light of that bare room, and I shivered. I felt him turning the idea over in his mind, felt the stumps and scars of the magic they'd cut out of him trying to stretch toward the idea.

"Almost, little niece. Almost. If you'd made this offer earlier, it might have worked. But I'm afraid it's too late for that."

"What do you mean? It's what you want. I can feel it."

"Oh, yes. It's what I want, but why should I bind myself to you with a promise when I can rally my friends and just wait you out? Once you're dead, I'm the heir, free and clear. And if by some stroke of your bad luck you live . . ." He leaned close. "I should thank you, Callie. You gave me a chance to watch you up close and see all the weaknesses your mother bred into you. You're no match for me, little niece, and you never will be." He pinched my cheek, but snatched his hand back before Jack could swing at him. "I'll be waiting for you as well, young Mr. Holland."

He stepped backward, into the gate I'd left open. And he was gone.

22

Climbin' Up the Mountain

I collapsed onto the bed. Jack was cussing and pounding his fist into his palm, pacing around the little space between the door and the dresser. I couldn't move. Perspiration poured down my face. With each drop, the itch settled deeper. It liked being inside me and intended to make itself at home, from the soles of my feet straight through to the crown of my head. It twitched and circled like a dog finding a comfy spot to lie down. I was bleeding through my skin from my scratching. I was bleeding through my spirit from the relentless, deepening itch, and it was only going to get worse.

"I can't stand it, Jack," I whispered. "I have to go."

Jack stopped in mid-cuss and drew himself up. He took in a deep breath and let it out.

"Then we go," he said. "You can take us there, right?"

I could, easily. That was not going to be the problem. "I

don't know what'll happen, Jack. I have no idea what they can do to us."

"So what else is new?" He pulled his old newsboy cap out of his back pocket, slapped it against his leg a couple of times to knock out the creases, and settled it on his head. "Make sure it's through the front door, though. I'm sick and tired of sneaking around."

And that was that. I got to my feet and walked us back into my old room. There I gripped Jack's hand and took my own deep breath. Together we stepped sideways, turned in place, rounded a corner, and stepped down.

Daylight blossomed around us, but no warmth. A cool wind blew slow but steady, carrying off the sun's heat. Jack and I staggered and caught each other. We'd come to rest in front of a white stone wall, set with lampposts and miniature towers and planted all around with roses. A pair of high, arched gates had been set in its center. They reminded me of the ones in front of MGM, except these were gold instead of iron, and they were shut tight. On the other side, the hill had been planted thick with flowers and trees, and set with marble stairs and gravel paths. We weren't quite at the peak. There was still a long slope up, and it was topped by somebody's fantasy of a Spanish castle. It had a pair of bell towers, arched windows like you'd see in a cathedral, and more frills and trimmings on its white walls than Ivy's bedroom had ruffles. Behind us, a white road wound from the gates down the hill, but we couldn't see very far, because a fog was rising off the mountainside, blotting out all the world below.

The wind blew again, curdling that pure white fog and bringing it closer.

"Well, there you are!" called a voice from the other side of the gates.

The trim, smiling woman from the picture on Ivy's mantel trotted down one of the marble staircases. She wore a red-and-white striped top and a long red skirt that wrapped around her hips and tied at the waist. A floppy white hat covered her blond hair, and white sandals decorated her dainty feet. She looked cool, poised, and sophisticated as she sashayed down that path toward the golden gates. There must have been a switch on the other side, because when she laid her hand on the white wall, the gates swung slowly open.

I steeled myself and walked forward. Jack came up right behind me until we both stood under the archway.

"I'm—" I started.

"Callie LeRoux." The woman took both my hands and gave me a peck on the cheek before I could stop her. "Of course you are. And this must be Jack Holland. Marion Davies." Jack shook her hand, but he was looking sideways at me as he did. "Ivy said you'd gotten our invitation. Please, do come in." She swept her hand back.

"Thank you."

The second I stepped into that garden, the itching stopped. I just about fell over. The burn and the bleeding vanished and my skin was my own again. Miss Davies smiled brightly, and another gust of cool wind curled around our ankles.

"Where's Ivy?" asked Jack.

"She's with Mr. Hearst and the others," said Miss Davies. "Come along. Everybody's just *dying* to meet you both." She flashed us a final bright smile and trotted back up the stairs, as though gravity didn't matter to her. Jack and I had no choice but to follow.

If anybody'd tried to tell me about the garden she led us into, I wouldn't have believed them. I didn't even know so many kinds of flowers existed in the world, let alone that somebody could think to plant them on a mountainside, or create all the different grottoes and alcoves and arbors to hold them.

"This is real, right?" whispered Jack. "This isn't the fairy country?"

I nodded. This was real. And it wasn't just a space of flowers and twisting paths. It seemed like under every bush there was a different statue. There were Greek gods, lambs and fawns, and old Romans. But mostly there were women. Naked women carved in marble. The lampposts were shaped like golden women, also naked. Women's faces decorated the walls around the beds of greenery. Tiny women lifted up their hands to hold up benches where people could make themselves comfortable.

Somebody had bought and built every square inch of this, all these statues and gold-trimmed marble buildings and acres of gardens. They'd created a paradise, walled it round, and locked it behind golden gates, way up here in the hills, where they never heard about the Depression or the Dust Bowl or anything else bad in the world. Where they didn't have to care about anything they didn't want to.

"Something's going on, though," I whispered back. It brushed at me like the cool wind and curdled like the fog. The feeling didn't seem to be coming from any one direction. It was all around, and the inside of my mind—still rubbed raw from the summons—prickled and shifted, trying to get away from it.

Jack nodded and set his sights right between Miss Davies's shoulder blades. He lengthened his stride so he could get right up next to her, but he also shoved his hands in his pockets, making himself look nonchalant.

"So," he said, looking up at the gardens rising around us, "this is all Mr. Hearst's property, right?"

"Of course, dear," she said. "But he frequently allows his *special* friends the use of the house and grounds."

"I'll bet he's met all kinds of people," Jack went on in his best gosh-wow voice. "Presidents, maybe kings, even."

"Oh, everyone who's anyone comes to San Simeon. Kings, even." She said it with a big wink. "Many of them come to regard this as their second home."

It made plenty of sense. This place was beyond beautiful. It was perfect. It would attract the Seelies the way jam did yellow jackets. Only they weren't sneaking any more than we were. They'd moved right in.

Miss Davies kept on talking to Jack about the size of the grounds, all the trees and plants carted in specially for the gardens, and how Mr. Hearst had searched the world for the most beautiful art and antiques to bring back and lock up here—not that she put it that way, of course. But the farther in I went, the more sour I felt. I didn't like this place. It was so elaborate, so perfect and lush, it didn't feel like there was any room for me here. I wasn't pretty enough. I wasn't famous enough or rich enough. Any one of these marble statues was worth twenty times as much as me.

It hit me Miss Davies was doing this on purpose. She was leading Jack and me up these garden paths with the idea of making us feel small and poor. My temper started to smolder, and for the first time since we'd come through the front gate, I felt warm.

Just for spite, I kicked at the pedestal of the next naked statue we passed.

Help me, sobbed a lady's voice.

I jerked back and whirled around.

I want to go home, she pleaded.

My magic opened. I couldn't help it. Now I heard all the voices. They were everywhere, crowding in on me, clamoring for attention. Dozens of whispers. Hundreds.

I didn't mean it. I didn't mean it.

I just wanted . . .

I wanted . . .

I just wished . . . Please . . .

Help me. Somebody help me.

I slammed myself shut. Jack was staring at me. Miss Davies was smiling brightly, patiently.

"They're people." I turned in a tight circle, staring at the beautiful garden with its grottoes and arbors and statues. Hundreds and hundreds of statues, faces, mosaics, and murals tucked cunningly among the vines and trees. "They're all people."

Miss Davies shrugged. "They made bargains they couldn't follow through on. It was their own fault." She waved dismissively at the garden.

My hands began to shake. Jack's face flushed scarlet as the reality sank in. They were people, people who'd wished and wanted. They'd wanted fame and luxury and beauty, and they'd gotten it, imprisoned in these gardens. But why? I turned around again. What was it all *for*? I didn't dare open my magic again to try to find out. The voices and their sorrow would drown me.

"What kind of bargain did you make?" I croaked at the pretty, smiling woman who led us through this beautiful prison.

"You wouldn't understand, dear." She shook her head and tucked one curl back behind her ear. "You're still young. But one day you'll get tired of being poor and dirty. You'll remember that every woman can be a queen if she really wants to, and you'll make your own bargain." She looked up at the statue reclining beside us, and the sneer on her lips was the nastiest thing I'd seen yet. But it was gone with the next breath, and she turned up that path like nothing was wrong. I didn't move.

"Where's my mother?"

Miss Davies sighed. "She's with Mr. Hearst, as is your father. I told you, Callie. *Everyone* is waiting for you."

There were more staircases after that, and more beautiful arbors and flowerbeds, but I couldn't tell one from another anymore. Miss Davies hurried us along. Jack had come back to my side, his face still flushed. I could feel him turning plans over in his head, wondering which he could make work. But he couldn't settle on anything any more than I could. The scale of the wrong done here, the number of prisoners trapped by twisted promises and betrayed wishes—it was too huge for either of us to wrap our brains around.

At last we reached the top of the hill and crossed into the shadow of the Spanish-style castle with its pure white walls, its towers, and its terra-cotta roofs. I thought we'd be going inside, but Miss Davies took us in the other direction, toward a kind of broad hollow. The view would have been breathtaking if it hadn't been blotted out by the fog that churned and crawled beyond the terrace. The hollow itself was an expanse of pure white marble decorated by yet more sculptures.

A pool of turquoise water spread in the center of the marble deck. If Roman emperors had had swimming pools, this was what they would've looked like. It was even bigger than the pool where we'd almost gotten killed by the life-guard. Marble columns and temples surrounded it, and a waterfall poured down into it. A crowd of men and women were milling around the deck, and they all turned toward us as we approached. But we didn't see a single face. The whole crowd was dressed for a masquerade, with blank-eyed masks made of feathers and sequins and dangling beads. They looked like birds. They looked like demons and in-sects and angels. A pair in the corner wore glittering emer-ald crocodile masks. I didn't even need to open my magic to know we weren't seeing the human guests this time. These were all fairies, come to court to watch my punishment.

When we reached the deck, the crowd parted to make an aisle for us and Miss Davies. She walked through the fairy crowd calm, smiling and nodding as she passed—like the perfect party hostess. I found myself wondering if she could really understand what she was seeing, or the kind of place she was in. Except she knew about the prisoners. She understood, all right. She just didn't care.

Curving staircases rose on either side of the waterfall, leading to a raised terrace. On a wide marble bench sat Mr. Hearst.

I recognized him from Ivy's photo, and from the night-mare my uncle had showed me. In real life, he was big and bluff and perfectly at ease. He had pockmarks on his face, a fleshy neck, and a potbelly under his spotless white trousers and white shirt. Which meant he had to be human. No Seelie would look like that.

So where was the Seelie king?

Ivy Bright stood beside Mr. Hearst and grinned. She looked perfect, of course, dressed in a pink version of Miss Davies's outfit. As we walked across the pool deck down below her, she giggled.

My parents were there too, as Miss Davies had promised. They'd been posed on the far side of the marble bench from Ivy, done up as Rags and Patches once again. My father was down on one knee holding out both hands. My mother was leaning over, ready to slap his face. Enchantment anchored them so tightly they couldn't even draw breath.

Miss Davies skipped up the stairs, as if she hadn't just walked through about a half mile of garden. She leaned down and kissed Mr. Hearst and patted Ivy on the head. Ivy beamed like she was seeing an angel, and Miss Davies took her seat on the bench. None of them even looked at my parents.

It was the last straw.

Jack's anger burned under his skin, and he wished with all his might there was something he could do. I took hold of the wish and the anger behind it and aimed my magic toward my parents.

Nothing happened. My parents stayed where they were. I tried again and again, and still nothing. I didn't feel blinded or smothered this time. It was simply that my wish had no more effect on the world around me than a normal girl's would have.

I'd spent months wishing I had no magic, that I wasn't a half-breed fairy, that I could just be normal. Now my magic was out of my reach, and all I wanted was to have it back so I could touch my parents and let them know I'd finally gotten here. That I was going to get them free.

Mr. Hearst looked down on my confusion and laughed. The rest of the masked court laughed with him. The noise filled that artificial swimming-pool hollow to the brim, and the echoes bounced back and forth so many times it sounded like the mountain itself was joining in the fun.

"Oh, no," boomed Mr. Hearst. "Not here, Miss LeRoux. You have no power here." His voice rang against the marble and the curve of the hill at his back. It wrapped around me and over me, and it was crawling with power.

Hearing it, I understood where the Seelie king was. He was inside Mr. Hearst, the way the human beings were inside the garden statues.

Mr. Hearst not only let the Seelies move into his house and grounds whenever they wanted; he'd let their king move right into his body. Revulsion clenched my stomach. Why would anybody do that? Of course I knew the answer. The man had wished to be king of the world, and his wish had been granted—provided, of course, that he let himself and his house serve the king of that other world whenever it was required.

Mr. Hearst, or the Seelie king inside him, raised one

hand. Power stirred. It rose from the gardens all around us, and the sky overhead faded to black. At the same moment, the lamps around the pool and lining the paths lit themselves. The masked and glittering crowd applauded politely. The bells in the castle towers began to ring, long and sonorous, tolling midnight.

"Calliope deMinuit," thundered the Seelie king, "you are called to answer for your crime of violating territorial boundaries of the Seelie kingdom. What have you to say regarding your actions?"

I clenched my fists and took one step forward. "I—"

The crowd laughed. The noise tumbled down like bricks. It vibrated through the deck under our feet like the beginning of an earthquake. There was no way in the world—in any world—one voice could have been heard over all that.

Eventually the king raised his hand and the laughter died away. My ears were ringing. I wasn't sure I was going to be able to hear myself.

"Well?" demanded the king. "I ask again. What have you to say regarding your actions?"

"I—"

This time they booed. And for good measure, they hissed and whistled. It was a riot of noise that rose and fell and sounded like you'd think a whole convention of ghosts and teakettles would sound. It was as bad as laughter could ever be. Jack whirled around to face the crowd. I saw his mouth moving. I knew he was yelling, "Shut up! Shut up!"

But as close as I was to him, I couldn't hear a thing. There was only the hissing and the booing from the Seelies.

The king raised his hand again, and the court fell silent. "I ask a third time, Calliope deMinuit. What have you to say regarding your actions?"

I took one more step forward. I felt them getting ready to drown me out again. Ivy was standing beside the throne grinning. I looked at her and clenched my teeth. I made myself think. I thought about everything I'd seen and done since coming to California. I thought about my parents and Ivy Bright, and I thought about Mr. Robeson, who was the only person I'd ever met who'd walked away from all of us free and clear. And I knew what I had to do.

"I'll make a bet with you."

This time the fairy court stayed silent.

23

Take That Away from Me

Silence can be more terrible than any sound. But I was ready for this one, and I had no intention of standing still for it. I started up those marble stairs. I heard Jack's footsteps behind me, but I didn't look back. I kept my gaze on my parents, forced into their clown costumes and their clown poses for this masquerade. I wasn't even sure if they could see me. Their eyes were just as frozen as their bodies.

I reached the top of the staircase, and the king and I were finally on the same level. He smiled, and I felt how he appreciated my daring and my drama. He was a connoisseur of such things, and he liked to see them well played. I didn't flinch. I didn't look away. His eyes were human eyes, blue and piercing, but the king stirred underneath. The king could give you anything and everything. All you had to do was be brave enough to wish.

"Oh, no," I said. "You're not fooling me with that one.

I've got no wish for you. We're taking this round back. Me against you. If I win, my parents, Jack, and I all walk out of here safe and sound. No strings, no side deals. Nothing."

"And if you lose?" he drawled. I could tell what he was thinking. I was funny. I was entertaining, even better than my parents. He should have brought me here before.

"I stay with you," I said.

"No, Callie!" hissed Jack.

I ignored him. " 'See her now, daughter of three worlds. See her now, three roads to choose. Where she goes, where she stays, where she stands, there shall the gates be closed.' That's what this has always been about. You never wanted my parents, and you sure don't want Jack." I'd apologize to Jack later for pointing that out. "You want me, so I'm going to give you your chance."

The king leaned back and ran one stout finger over Mr. Hearst's mustache. He was intrigued, and more than a tiny bit amused. I was an audacious little thing. I wondered if he could tell how badly I wanted to smack that face he wore like a carnival mask. Probably. I was just so funny that way.

I opened my mouth, planning to let him in on a few of Jack's more entertaining cuss words, but Ivy Bright spoke up first.

"Let me do it," she said. "Let me fight her."

"Be quiet, Ivy," snapped Miss Davies. "This has nothing to do with you."

Ivy clearly did not agree. She faced the king. I'd seen the baby-doll Ivy and the wounded and confused little girl, and

I'd even seen the savvy actress, but this was something new. This Ivy was tall, proud, and fearless—and, I realized as a tremor of nerves flickered through me, more than a little bit dangerous.

"I claim my rights, Your Majesty," she said. "She's insulted me and raised her hand against me!"

"Ivy," breathed Jack, "you don't have to do this."

The look she turned on him then should have been pure poison, and it was, mostly, but there was something else too: regret. Jack saw it, and his hand moved, like he was going to reach out. But at the last moment he curled his fingers in.

Whatever the king thought of all this, he was keeping it to himself. He just leaned over to Miss Davies and whispered into her ear. I looked at her as hard as I could manage. She had no fairy light in her. There was nothing under that skin but a human heart and a human brain. She'd been telling the truth. She'd made a bargain to become queen of this hill and its castle, whether it was playing hostess for Mr. Hearst or for the Seelie king. I would have bet my last dime that her bargain included giving birth to a half-Seelie daughter who might just grow up to fulfill a prophecy. These were Ivy's parents, right in front of me, and I knew it and Ivy knew it. The one thing she wanted most in the world was to come live with them forever. And I had no doubt they knew that too.

I really wished I had the time to crawl away somewhere and be sick.

The king straightened up and inclined his head toward

Ivy. "Your petition is denied," he said to his daughter. "You are not strong enough to take this challenge."

Ivy gaped at him. "I am! I'm every bit as strong as she is! Stronger! I can prove it!"

"Ivy," said Jack urgently. "Ivy, come on. This isn't a game anymore."

She didn't look at him. "I have the right," she said through gritted teeth. "Please, Your Majesty, let me prove myself."

The Seelie king smiled down at Miss Davies. She looked adoringly and approvingly up at him, barely glancing at her daughter.

"Very well," said the king. "You shall have your wish, Ivy Bright. You will be our champion for this challenge."

I wasn't the only one who knew there was way more going on here than I could see. "Don't do this," Jack muttered. "You don't know what rules they're playing by."

I didn't even bother to answer. It was already too late to back out. I could feel it in my Unseelie blood and my human bones.

"Make us proud, Ivy," said Miss Davies. "We are counting on you for the victory."

Ivy beamed—a real smile, not an acting smile. It was the smile of someone who had just been handed the chance of a lifetime. She swung around, and the Seelie light flashed gold in her eyes.

"What shall be the contest?" asked the Seelie king. "As challenged, Ivy Bright, the choice is yours."

Ivy raised her arm and pointed one finger right at Jack. "Him."

Jack stiffened.

"Wait!" I shouted.

The world went black.

Reality swam slowly to the surface. I wasn't on the hill any-more. Hot and blinding lights shone in my face. Voices shouted orders from every direction. I was in a chair and someone was slathering stuff on my face and yanking at my hair. I glimpsed Jack sitting beside Ivy Bright on a folding chair, reading a set of pages.

This is a movie set, I realized. *We're making a movie.*

The world went black again.

"Rolling!" shouted a voice.

"Playback!" shouted a second.

"And . . . action!" shouted a third.

The lights came up slowly. I raised my head, looked out across the room, and smiled.

It was the Midnight Club, exactly as I'd pictured it—a big room with curved walls, fancy chandeliers, and bunches of round tables with white cloths. The band, big and brassy, filled the stage at my back. Papa was sitting at his piano to the right, sketching time. Waiters streamed out of the kitchen carrying Mama's food to the patrons. The whole place was filled with the scents of warm spices, tobacco, and ladies' perfume. Jack was there too, at the best table in the house, right at the foot of the stage. He was in evening dress with his hair slicked back. He was smiling up at me in the way I liked best.

Cameras whirred beyond the solid wall of blinding lights. Filming had begun, and I knew my part perfectly. I stood at a microphone. I had on a gorgeous, heavy gown of beaded silver, with a matching band on my forehead. I wrapped one hand around the microphone stand and waited for Papa to signal my intro. Two long, loving bars of slow blues rolled through that room—the movie set, my dream of a nightclub—and I began to sing.

"Love, oh love, oh careless love. You fly to my head like wine."

Jack's grin widened. This was his favorite song, and mine too. Everything was perfect. I finally had everything I'd ever wanted, and everybody I'd ever wanted was here with me. I held this audience in the palm of my hand. My voice was low and smoky, just as it should be, caressing the lyrics, turning them sad and just a tiny bit seductive. *I've won,* I thought. *I've won.*

"Love, oh love," I crooned. *"Oh careless love . . ."*

All at once, I wasn't singing alone. Another voice, higher than mine, sweeter, took up the lyrics, strong and true.

"You've ruined the life of many a poor girl. And you nearly wrecked this life of mine."

The doors at the back of the club, the back of the set, opened, and she stepped in. The room fell silent, and everybody turned to see her.

"All my happiness has left. You filled my heart with these weary blues. . . ."

She was beautiful. A white cloak with a fur collar fell from her shoulders. Snow sparkled in her golden curls. There was nothing seductive in the way she sang. For her, it was all sorrow. My throat closed down around my own song. Backstory filled in. We'd been friends as children, but she'd gotten a part in the movies and gone on to stardom, while I'd been stuck singing in nightclubs and dying of jealousy. But worse than that, I knew Jack loved her. He always had. He always would. He was here tonight only because I'd tricked him.

I was the dark-haired, dark-skinned bad girl in this movie, and Ivy was the good girl, the golden girl.

"I trusted you, now it's too late . . . ," she sang.

Jack was on his feet, walking toward Ivy. She smiled up at him, and tears swam in her perfect, innocent eyes.

"I love you, Jack Holland," she whispered. "Don't leave me alone." She lifted her hand, palm out. Jack swallowed and gazed down at her. He lifted his palm too, and pressed it to hers.

Anger filled me, anger and, yes, jealousy. I had every right to be jealous. This was my dream. *Mine.* She was a little thief. She'd already tried to steal everything else from me. She wasn't going to steal Jack Holland or the Midnight Club.

I had a gun in my hand. I didn't know where it'd come from and it didn't matter. It felt good and solid as I curled my fingers around it. It swung around, or I swung it around, to point straight at Ivy Bright. All I had to do was pull the trigger and she was gone. Dead. Everybody called me the Bad Luck Girl? I'd show them just how right they were. Somebody was going to die tonight.

No, said a voice way in the back of my head. *No, this isn't what you want to happen.*

Except it didn't matter what I wanted to happen. This was a movie. There was only one way it could go. When I pointed my gun at Ivy, Jack would get between us. He'd try to save her and I'd kill him, and I'd be arrested and dragged away, leaving Ivy weeping over his body and everybody feeling sorry for her. Loving her. That was the script. I'd read it. I'd seen it a dozen times.

But movies aren't real, protested the voice in the back of my head. My own voice. *This isn't real. It's just a dream.*

The problem was, this script was built around a core of my dream. I was tied to it the way I'd been tied to Lorcan. I couldn't get loose, because I was holding on to this.

And because I really did hate Ivy. I hated her and I wanted her gone. I wanted her dead. I remembered every single time she'd laughed with Jack. I remembered how he'd tried to save her and she'd nearly gotten him killed, and how it had taken everything I had to bring him back. She was doing it again. He was on her side. She was making him do this. She'd never let him go. He was mine, but he wouldn't know that as long as she was alive.

Papa stopped playing. The band was shouting, and

so were the patrons. Mama burst out of the kitchen and pressed both hands to her mouth to cover her shriek of terror. People were running and screaming and turning over the tables, trying to get away from me.

I hooked my finger around the gun's cold trigger and pulled it back.

"Jack," I whispered. "Jack. Look at me. Please."

But what I shouted was, "Out of the way, Jack!"

He turned and put himself right between my gun and Ivy, just like the script said he should. He spoke his line.

"No, Callie." That was the line. That was all he was supposed to say. But Jack's jaw shook, and he kept going. "This isn't you. This isn't who you are."

"Then who am I?" I couldn't see him clearly. All I could see was Ivy Bright standing there, beautiful, pure, perfect, and out to steal everything I'd ever had. I couldn't let her do it. I couldn't. I had to kill her. That was the way the movie went.

Jack didn't answer. He was supposed to. I'd messed up his cue but he could still get us on track. He'd toed his mark. I knew what his line was supposed to be, but he kept his mouth shut. We'd left the script. He didn't shake his head the way he was supposed to. He didn't reach for the gun the way he was supposed to. He just looked at me.

They'd dressed him up in a grown man's clothes. They'd given him a part in this movie that was nothing like his own life. But they couldn't change his eyes. I knew those eyes. I remembered them, and I remembered Jack. I remembered how I'd first seen him in the cell of a small-town jail. I remembered walking with him through the dust storms, and running through rail yards, and him teaching me how to hop a freight, and lying our way across the California line.

These were not wishes, not dreams or shiny movie feelings where you knew how it was going to go. These were the memories of what we'd really been through. This was our friendship that came pouring back to me.

Ivy must have felt it too. She raised her chin and stepped out from behind Jack.

"I'm not afraid of you anymore, Callie," she said. "You cannot win, no matter what you do to me."

I felt her magic. She took hold of my arm and my head. She was forcing me back into the movie, back into her world, where she had the power. She was the good girl, the golden girl. The one who would always be there at the finish. I was the bad girl. I had to lose. That was how these things went.

But it was more than that. Ivy had a real world beyond this living movie, just like I did, and in that other world she was desperate. She had to win. Victory would buy her the love of her father—what love there was, anyway. She'd thought she could get the gate powers from me, but that had failed. The only thing left for her was to win this twisted challenge. That was the only way they'd ever love her.

Her magic tightened around my body and my mind, forcing me back down into the script. My finger tensed around the trigger. One tiny little movement and she'd be dead.

But I had my real memories back now. I thought about all the times I'd hated her, and the other times I'd wished I could be her. Ivy Bright was a liar, a thief, and a pathetic girl. She'd tricked us and betrayed us, all to try to earn love from someone who was incapable of giving it.

Then I thought about what Mr. Robeson had said. *It's not about who they are. It is never about who they are. It's about who* you *are, and who you want to be.*

I was the Prophecy Girl and the Bad Luck Girl, but before that I'd been the dust girl, and before that I'd been just plain Callie LeRoux. And it was Callie LeRoux I wanted to stay.

This was my cue. I had my line, right on the tip of my tongue. I was supposed to say, "Get out of here, Ivy Bright!"

But I didn't. Instead, I said, "Ivy . . . come with us."

"Wh-what?" Ivy drew back a step, confused.

I strained with all my might, and slowly, painfully, my finger slid off the gun's trigger. "We'll bust out of here, one way or another. You can come with us."

She glanced at Jack. He turned his back on me. I couldn't lower the gun, but he could take both Ivy's hands. "Do it, Ivy. Come with us."

Jealousy tried to surface and shift my finger back. I fought it, harder than I'd ever fought any monster.

"I can't promise you power or movies or anything, but I know you could stay with us," I said. "My parents would understand."

A sob caught in Ivy's throat. "You don't want me around any more than anybody else. You think I'm after Jack."

"That's gonna be what it's gonna be." I was proud of myself for getting those words out at all, considering. The iron bar that seemed to be holding my arm in place gave way, just a little, and I was able to lower the gun, just a little. "But you don't have to stay here and be a stooge for some-body who kicked you out when you didn't measure up. You can come with us and just . . . be Ivy."

"But Ivy's nobody," she whispered.

"She could be somebody if she had a chance," said Jack. "But she'll never get that chance if she stays here."

The gun lowered another tick. The room was beginning to blur around us. The movie was fading to black. We were getting past the story, back to real life.

"You said you wanted a real friend, Ivy. This is what real friends do. We can help each other get out of here, all of us."

She swallowed. "But what about . . . what about . . ." She wrapped her hand around Jack's. My arm quivered. We were back in the lamplight at the top of the marble stairs. The Midnight Club and the movie lights were all gone. But those masked fairies were back; so was the Seelie king. They all watched, and listened to the question Ivy asked, and we all knew what she really meant. There was nothing I could do. I still held the gun, though. I could still lose this. I gritted my teeth, drew up every bit of self and strength I had, and pointed that gun I'd been given—the one I was supposed to try to kill my rival with—toward the floor.

The Seelie king and Miss Davies sat grim-faced. Beyond them, I saw my parents. They were moving—slowly and stiffly, but they were moving. Straightening up, lowering their arms, blinking at the world around them, at the Seelie king and his consort. At me.

I'd won. I'd won. It had already happened. Jack had already decided. The contest was over, and the spell was already broken. I knew it.

But what Ivy Bright knew was that she'd failed.

"I'm sorry, Ivy," Jack was saying to her. "I really am. But that doesn't mean—"

Ivy screamed. She hurled herself past him right at me, her fingers hooked, ready to claw my eyes out. Somebody else screamed, and hands grabbed me from behind. Ivy was right against my face, and I jerked my hands up to shove her away.

The gun went off. Its thunderclap echoed off walls and hills. The kick knocked me back, and Mama's arms enveloped me, pulling me away.

In front of me, Ivy's blue eyes went wide, and she fell back. But she had no one behind her, just the flight of stairs. She fell, rolling down the expanse of white marble, leaving a trail of scarlet behind.

"No!" Jack dove after her.

I stared at the gun. I stared at the Seelie king and Miss Davies, neither of whom had moved. I stared at my parents, whose freedom I had just won.

I tossed the gun away and ran down the stairs.

The masquerade crowd was still there. They all drew back. Not like the patrons in the nightclub scene trying to save themselves, but like people trying not to get their hems dirty. Jack crouched beside Ivy. She was bent in all kinds of wrong directions, but none of that was as bad as the big red stain in the middle of her chest.

I dropped to my knees and grabbed her face in both hands. I had my magic back. I could feel it, and I shoved it out toward her like a lifeline. "Come back, Ivy. Come back!"

Slowly she turned her face in my hands. Slowly her eyes blinked at me.

"That's it, Ivy. You can do it. Come back."

Her mouth struggled for a minute, and finally she croaked, "What for? You won."

And just like that, Ivy Bright died.

24

Your Castles Come Tumblin' Down

I stood up. I couldn't feel my hands. My head was spinning and the world was going gray at the edges. Bony arms wrapped around me and turned me away from Ivy's broken body.

Mama. She looked thin. The tattered ballerina outfit was truly pathetic on her, and she still had gray Kansas dust on her arms. I hugged her hard, and she hugged me back. I smelled that dust and felt her hot tears on my forehead.

"Callie." My mama rocked me back and forth. "It's okay, Callie. It's okay."

It wasn't. I'd killed a girl who was just like me. She'd just wanted her parents and to be part of a family.

But at the same time, I was in Mama's arms for the first time in forever.

"Margaret?"

Mama and I lifted our faces. Papa was standing there, staring, a prince of the fairy world who could not believe what he saw.

"Daniel?" Mama reached out her hand. "Oh my God—Daniel."

Their fingers touched, then knotted around each other.

A shadow fell over us all. The Seelie king had gotten to his feet. There was a smile on his face like nothing I'd ever seen. It was ten times worse than Lorcan's. A thousand times.

"You killed her," he said, climbing ponderously down the steps. "You killed my daughter."

Papa pulled my mother and me back, getting between us and the king. Jack stood slowly, his face soaked with tears.

"This is your fault!" Ivy's blood stained Jack's shirt and hands. "You did it on purpose!"

"I did nothing." The king was down on the deck now, with his court closing in at his back. Beads and sequins sparkled in the lamplight, but their eyes remained blank, black holes. Miss Davies hadn't moved. Her daughter was dead down here with us, and she stayed up there patting her curls back into place.

"The terms of the contest have been met." Papa drew himself up. I felt a shiver of magic. The clown outfit and makeup were gone. He was neatly dressed in a dark suit with gloves and a hat. He looked serious and dignified. He looked like a prince. He'd fixed up Mama too. She was clean and dressed for church, all sober and respectable. "You cannot interfere."

"Oh, no," replied the king. "She was killed after the contest was won. That makes it murder, Donchail deMinuit. Murder by your daughter's hand. Murder done against the Shining Court by the Midnight Throne!" He spread his arms, and the whole Seelie court inhaled. "It is war!" he boomed. "By the laws and the power of starlight and shadow, I claim the blood right!"

Mama yanked me and Jack backward. I didn't resist. The world was spinning again. It had been a setup from the very beginning. Everything, from Ivy being stashed at MGM to them egging her into believing they'd love her if she rubbed me out. She'd been used as a sacrifice. She'd been used to start the war.

I'm sorry, Ivy. I was crying. *I'm sorry!*

Jack was lunging for the king, but my father shoved him back. Papa swung his arms up and his magic lashed out. It hit the Seelie king in the chest, right where my bullet had hit Ivy. Except he only hit Mr. Hearst. The Seelie king was gone—I felt him leap into the air, leaving the human skin he'd borrowed to crumple to the marble floor. Finally Miss Davies noticed that something might be wrong. She screeched and ran down the stairs.

Papa wasn't waiting. He was herding all of us away from the fallen human and the crowding fairies. "Run! Run!"

Jack and Mama were stumbling, trying to obey. The crowd of fairies surged behind us, laughing and howling.

What were they waiting for? They could have been all over us in a half second. Jack was sprinting up the nearest stairs, leading us into the maze of gardens, heading for the gilded gates. I followed as fast as I could. And suddenly I knew what the fairies were waiting for: the Seelie king. He wasn't gone. I could feel him in the air around us, laughing.

The ground shook with a noise like thunder. I staggered and bumped against Jack and Mama. Behind us, the masked court laughed and joined hands, dancing in delight at the coming of war. The thunder spread out from the pool and up to the top of the hill. It crawled up the walls of the Spanish castle. The castle shuddered once, twice. I thought it was falling, but it wasn't. It was unfolding.

The crenellations and filigrees worked together like tiny bones. The foyer stretched out, becoming a neck. The windows opened to turn into eyes, and the double doors twisted sideways, changing to a set of jaws. The two bell towers were horns on a monstrous head, and the sprawling wings of the castle spread and lifted into the air. This was where the king had gone. He'd slipped into the castle the way he'd slipped into Mr. Hearst, and now it wasn't a castle at all. It was a dragon, ivory white and terra-cotta red, glittering with great glass scales. It raised its wings and arched its neck.

The dragon of glass and stone tore itself free of the foundations with a mighty splintering noise. I stared, unable to move. It was too big. Nothing could be that big and still be alive. It blocked out sun and sky. When it opened its great jaws, the world spun and the ground slammed into me and a weight knocked all the breath out of me. Fire blazed overhead, sizzling the air and filling the world with the scent of ash and blood.

Jack... But it wasn't Jack climbing off me. It was Mama.

"Run, Callie!" she shouted. "Daniel! Wish it gone, Daniel! I wish it gone!"

The dragon laughed, and the contempt was worse than the fire, because it got down inside you and paralyzed your heart. My father grabbed up Mama's wish and the love and tossed it at the king. The dragon's flame poured down, and Papa stood in the middle, like a stone in a river. It flooded around him, making the air sizzle and hiss. The wish flew forward, an arrow, a sword, and the flame winked out. The dragon flickered, like a skip in a film.

But it wasn't enough. My father staggered, and the Seelies laughed. The dragon reared back. It swooped down, its mouth open, its hunger raging beyond the limits of imagination. It would swallow us whole.

Next thing I knew, Jack was beside me. "The gate, Callie!" he bawled in my ear. "The pool gate!" And I knew what he meant. Of course. Of course.

I grabbed my father's coat and my mother's hand. "Run!" I screamed to whoever was listening. "Run!"

"Where?" cried Mama. "There's nowhere!"

"Yes, there is!" There had to be. I plunged into the crowd of masked fairies, ducking, twisting, shoving. They laughed like it was a great joke, though the world was dark from the dragon's shadow. They parted, but not for me. For the monster behind us. We were already dead. They were just here to watch the finish of that particular show.

My papa had my hand. I felt him throw his magic over us for a shield. Jack wanted to live, Mama wanted to live, and heaven knew I did. He was a full-blooded fairy. They could not change his nature; they had not taken his power. He took our wanting and granted it. His magic sheltered us as I ran up to the hilltop, straight under that dragon. There wasn't enough air. Ash clogged my throat. I heard Jack and Mama choking behind me. Papa fell back, catching them up, one in each hand, hauling them along with him, trusting me to lead us.

The king hadn't expected us to run toward him, and he had to twist now, awkwardly, because the dragon's body was so big. Infuriated, he roared, and the fire leapt up to fill the air with smoke and the smell of hot stone and green wood burning.

A massive hole stretched out where the dragon had ripped itself free. We stumbled up to the very edge. It was like looking into a dollhouse smashed by some spoiled child. There was a wine cellar filled with broken bottles, a movie theater half covered in crushed marble. The second swimming pool, the blue-and-gold one, lay broken beneath the fallen stones, its waters swirling away down the holes and cracks.

But the gate was still there. I'd never closed it. If we could get to it, I could get us through.

"Papa!" I coughed. "Papa, we need to be down there! In the pool."

"Hold on!" He snatched me up under his arm and grabbed Mama with the other. I grabbed hold of Jack. I felt Papa steel himself and start running, carrying us all with him, right over the edge of that cliff.

We were falling, we were screaming, and then, impossibly, we slowed and settled in a tiny cleared space among the ruin.

Unfortunately, the dragon, the Seelie king, had finally caught on. It roared again, and magic shivered through the smoke and fire. Around us, fallen statues of old Romans and naked women moved. They lifted their white arms and raised their weapons.

Anger poured through me. There was a burst of golden light and heat. Papa had aimed another bolt at the dragon, but he was faltering. I stretched, trying to grab up some wish, any wish. I was surrounded by frozen wishes, stored up like treasure, and I couldn't touch any of them. They belonged to the Seelie king, who was laughing in his dragon shape and raising one great taloned foot to flatten us all.

Except they didn't really belong to him. He'd stolen them and locked them away up here. All those wishes, all those people. One of them must want to get away. Somebody, something out there wanted to be free. I knew what that felt like, and I reached through the chaos and the fear. And I found it. A tiny wish, a little crack in the roiling wall of power. I touched that wish, and I granted it.

The ground shook again, and the statue froze and fell, the soul inside it gone. The dragon screamed.

That was mine! The king's fury rolled through my brain. *Mine!*

It wasn't much in terms of defiance, but it was enough, because there was another wish out there, and another after that. Freedom, escape. They did not want to fight, and they did not want to burn, any more than we did. They wanted to be gone. I could grant those wishes easily, because I understood them. I knew what it was to need to run, to break free, and I gave them that. One by one the statues toppled, cold marble shattering against the ruined tiles.

The dragon bellowed again, and its magic pulled back from us. The king was snatching at the wishes, at the people as they flew free. I shouted wordlessly and dove forward, straight down into the pool. I heard Jack shouting at my parents to follow me. I had to trust they'd do it, because I needed everything I had left to focus on the gate in front of me. I felt somebody crowding close. I grabbed the hand and kicked into the roiling waters. I twisted, pressed down, and leaned sideways, hauling the heavy weight of my family into betwixt and between. They were shouting and struggling in the chaos. They were too heavy, and I couldn't make them hold still. My hand was slipping. There was something else too, and it hated me, and it jammed itself into the gate.

We burst up into the black and oily studio lake, choking and coughing. Mama and Papa and Jack splashed and coughed and fought to find their feet.

"We did it!" shouted Jack.

"Not yet!" cried Papa.

The lake exploded. The world spun all over again, a rush of noise and blazing light and pain. I skidded and rolled across the ground and should have broken my neck, but something caught me and slowed me down.

The Waterloo Bridge was gone. Where it had been, the dragon's head reared up. It struggled and roared, its flame shooting up toward the sky.

"Callie!" shouted Papa.

I staggered to my feet. Jack was helping Mama stand, and they stared at the dragon coming through the gate, coming for us all.

"This way!" Jack hauled Mama sideways, getting her out of the way. Good. Maybe they could live. The dragon shook its head free of the pathetic ruins of the Waterloo Bridge, and its neck shoved through the gate, raising that head high into the air. I could feel the dragon straining against the gate, distorting and tearing the passageway, making room for its clawed legs, for its spreading skeletal wings.

I reached for the gate edges, but I couldn't find them. The dragon was in the way. I couldn't get my magic around it. It was too big. It was too strong. Its struggles shifted the edges of the gate, snatching them away from me. I hurt in every bone of my body, and I couldn't breathe because of the smoke and ash. Jack and Mama had run away, and I was alone with the dragon.

Except I wasn't. Papa was there. His strong musician's

hands clamped around my shoulders, and his magic surged into me. But not just magic. Love. My father's love and pride poured into my blood, extinguishing the pain and fear and lending me strength, enough to face a dragon. Enough to see Jack and Mama ducking into that fake farmhouse.

Jack had a plan. Of course he did. Jack always had a plan, and I knew what this one was. In front of us, the dragon had worked one skeletal wing loose to stretch up and over the sky. It bellowed in triumph. Air and ground shook. People shouted and screamed, and lights and alarms flashed.

"Hey!" My voice sounded pitifully hoarse and small. "Hey, ugly!"

The dragon swiveled its glittering neck. The contempt in its eyes pinned me in place. It saw that I was small, and that I was not moving. I was not moving a single inch.

"Yeah, you!" I shouted. Papa was trying not to be afraid. Jack and Mama were running out of the farmhouse, carrying something awkwardly between them. "I can't believe you were dumb enough to follow me! You oughta be president of the Complete Dope Society, you big, ugly—"

The dragon opened its jaws and swooped down. It smelled of hot stone and rotten eggs, and the ground shook.

Jack and Mama were in front of us.

"Now!" shouted Jack.

They swung the barrel they were carrying between them, heaving it straight into the dragon's maw. Its jaws snapped shut, exploding the keg. The nails, each one a pointed shard of black iron, flew every which way, including into the monster's skin and straight down its fire-breathing throat.

The dragon bellowed, a sound of raw pain. Flame spewed in all directions. I was burning. Fear and rage and a thousand wishes all battered my brain. I reached, I reached, I reached, and I had it. The gate was torn open, wide enough to hold a dragon, but it was a gate, and it was my power. I could close it. I would close it, if it was the last thing I ever did.

Stone ground against stone and snapped. The dragon screamed, and the gate snapped shut.

And it was gone. There was nothing left but a pile of rubble jutting out of the steaming black lake, the crackle of settling dust, and the four of us.

Oh, there were people running around, shouting and screaming and demanding to know what was going on, but they weren't important. What was important was that my mother, my father, Jack, and I were all still standing.

"Mama?" I whispered.

She opened her arms and I fell into them, and then Papa had his arms around both of us. It was a long time before I could loosen their hold and open up toward Jack. Slowly, almost shyly, Jack came forward, completing the embrace. We stayed like that, arms around each other, holding on for dear life. We didn't know what would happen next. The Seelie king was still on his hill, but the odds were good he wouldn't stay there long. He'd declared his war. If my grandparents didn't know what had happened yet, they would soon. And behind them, Shake, grinning his broken-toothed grin, was waiting and watching for his chance.

It didn't matter. These people I called my parents were mostly strangers to me, but that didn't matter either. We were alive, and none of us was alone anymore.

For now, that was enough.

Author's Note

I love old movies. I always have. Give me a black-and-white film from Hollywood's golden age, silent or with sound, and I'm a happy camper, especially if I have a bowl of popcorn to go with it. I recognize a lot of these films (maybe most of them) have not aged well, and the social attitudes depicted can range from antediluvian to infuriating to horrifying. But there is joy there, and food for thought, and yes, there's magic.

When I started thinking about how the glamour of fairy would translate into the United States during the Great Depression, I knew the story would have to turn toward Hollywood. Hollywood was where glamour was created and defined for the majority of the country, and that glamour was as tempting and as treacherous as any spell of legend when it worked on people, inside the movies and out.

There are more historical figures in this book than in *Dust Girl,* and more than there will be in the upcoming *Bad Luck Girl.* Paul Robeson was a real man, and he really was, among other things, an all-American football player (and in the College Football Hall of Fame), lawyer, singer, actor, and political and civil rights activist. William Randolph Hearst was the most powerful and wealthy media tycoon of his day, and he used that power to try to shape the world as he wanted it to be. He also had a long relationship with both MGM Studios, run largely by Louis B. Mayer and Irving Thalberg, and the actress Marion Davies. His massive mansion called San Simeon still stands and is open to the public.

I've included a playlist of the songs that are quoted in the book and were running through my head as I wrote. The music in *Golden Girl* is a combination of traditional spirituals and the songs of George and Ira Gershwin. You might notice many of the Gershwin songs were written after the story takes place. But as they are some of my all-time favorites, I decided to pull out my artistic license and let love override a bit of historical accuracy.

Because we're on the MGM back lot for so much of the story, I've also included a watch list of some classic movies and musicals that were in my mind as Jack and Callie made their way through the story.

A historical book always owes a lot to existing writing and research. I'd like to particularly acknowledge Donald Bogle for *Bright Boulevards, Bold Dreams: The Story of Black Hollywood,* and Steven Bingen, Stephen X. Sylvester, and Michael Troyan for *MGM: Hollywood's Greatest Backlot.*

Playlist: The Spirituals

I chose these songs not only because they fit the story well, but also because most of them were recorded by Paul Robeson. Many are available from the Smithsonian Folkways label and can (hurray!) be found online.

"Joshua Fit the Battle of Jericho," traditional spiritual
"Nobody Knows the Trouble I've Seen," traditional spiritual
"Poor Wayfaring Stranger," traditional spiritual
"Scandalize My Name," traditional spiritual
"Sometimes I Feel Like a Motherless Child," traditional spiritual
"Steal Away to Jesus," Wallis Willis, circa 1862
"Swing Low, Sweet Chariot," Wallis Willis, circa 1862
"Wade in the Water," traditional spiritual
"We Are Climbing Jacob's Ladder," traditional spiritual

Playlist: The Gershwins

Gershwin songs form the backbone of some of my all-time favorite movies and musicals, so they were playing in my mind and on the headphones as I wrote. I also have suspicions about a connection between the Gershwin brothers and the Seelies, but that's another story.

"I Loves You, Porgy," 1935, from *Porgy and Bess,* George Gershwin, Ira Gershwin, and DuBose Heyward

"Let's Call the Whole Thing Off," 1937, words by Ira Gershwin, music by George Gershwin

"Nice Work If You Can Get It," 1937, words by Ira Gershwin, music by George Gershwin

"Shall We Dance," 1937, words by Ira Gershwin, music by George Gershwin

"Someone to Watch Over Me," 1926, words by Ira Gershwin, music by George Gershwin

"They Can't Take That Away from Me," 1937, words by Ira Gershwin, music by George Gershwin

Watch List

Here's another case where some of the works cited were released a little later, or a lot later, than the events in the story. But these are films that shaped my love of old movies, and it was my love of old movies that led me to this world and this story.

1929, *The Broadway Melody,* Charles King, Anita Page, Bessie Love. The first of the great MGM musicals, produced by Irving Thalberg.

1935, *A Night at the Opera,* The Marx Brothers. I love the Marx Brothers and this is probably their best movie, although that title could also go to *Duck Soup.*

1936, *Captain January,* Shirley Temple. Just because she comes up several times in the book. I'm not a huge fan of Shirley Temple movies (although the woman had a fascinating life), but this one is charming, especially her dance number with Buddy Ebsen.

1936, *Show Boat,* Irene Dunne, Allan Jones. This musical has been filmed a couple of times. This is the one with Paul Robeson singing "Ol' Man River."

1937, *Shall We Dance?,* Fred Astaire, Ginger Rogers.

Possibly the best of the Astaire/Rogers musicals, with a full Gershwin soundtrack.

1940, *Broadway Melody of 1940,* Fred Astaire, Eleanor Powell. Because I simply love this movie and not enough people remember what a fabulous dancer Eleanor Powell was.

1941, *Citizen Kane,* Orson Welles. Welles's critique of William Randolph Hearst. Widely considered the greatest Hollywood movie ever made. I don't know about that, but it is great.

1943, *Stormy Weather,* Bill "Bojangles" Robinson, Lena Horne. This one I do know about. This is one of the greatest, most talented casts in the history of movies. The number with the Nicholas Brothers and Cab Calloway might be the best musical performance ever.

About the Author

Sarah Zettel is an award-winning science fiction and fantasy author. She has written more than twenty novels and many short stories over the past eighteen years, in addition to practicing tai chi, learning the fiddle, marrying a rocket scientist, and raising a rapidly growing son. The American Fairy Trilogy is her first series for teens. Visit her at sarahzettel.com.